THE HAPSBURG VARIATION

THE HAPSBURG VARIATION

A COLD WAR THRILLER

Bill Rapp

Seattle, WA

Coffeetown Press
PO Box 70515
Seattle, WA 98127

For more information go to: www.coffeetownpress.com
www.billrappsbooks.com

Cover design by Sabrina Sun

ISBN: 978-1-60381-643-4 (Trade Paper)
ISBN: 978-1-60381-644-1 (eBook)

Library of Congress Control Number: 2017945204

Printed in the United States of America

For Didi

Also by the author

Cold War Thriller Series

Tears of Innocence

Suburban Detective Series

Angel in Black

A Pale Rain

Burning Altars

Berlin Breakdown

Acknowledgments

My first thanks go to my editors at Coffeetown Press, Jennifer McCord and Catherine Treadgold, who were instrumental in keeping the story on track, filling in gaps, and correcting my numerous mistakes. This would certainly be a less enjoyable story without their assistance. I would also like to thank my many friends and colleagues who, over the years, spent time with me in Vienna, enjoying all that that wonderful city has to offer, not least its remarkable history and role in European culture. This book arises in no small part from the many discussions we had on those subjects and the many hours we spent there. And, of course, my family deserves the most gratitude for putting up with me as I wrote this book, particularly my wife, to whom the book is dedicated.

Chapter One

IT SEEMED TO Karl Baier as though he could never escape history, certainly not while working for the CIA. Not that he minded. He enjoyed slicing through the bureaucratic maze that came with any large organization, especially government ones. He had joined the Agency eight years ago at its inception in 1947 and found that studying the past helped. Especially working as the deputy chief of station in Vienna. Every once in a while, though, Karl wondered if he had at least one foot on the wrong side of history—if he was straddling that indistinct line that separates us from the past. Would he lose himself behind the curve of time by falling too deeply into the personalities and traditions of the past? How fully did he comprehend history's effect on the present—enough to allow him to have a positive impact on current events?

This time it started with a call in the middle of the night. Three o'clock, to be exact. Or almost. It might have been more like two forty-five or two fifty. He was disoriented at first, blinking his eyes to clear away the haze and confusion. Karl Baier studied the clock for several seconds before groping through the darkness that draped his bedroom like a shroud to pull the receiver closer to his ear.

"Hello?" He shifted his weight, raising himself on one elbow. The bedsprings groaned and something tumbled off the night table. Baier hoped it was a book. "Yes? What is it?"

"Sir, there's been a call for you from the local police. A body or something."

"A body?" The first thought that came to Baier was that this had to be a duty call, someone from his office he would have to identify; then he'd need to set in motion the painful process of informing the family and returning the remains. Struggling to recognize the voice, Baier paused to rub the sleep from his eyes and shift the receiver to his left ear.

"You mean a dead one?" Baier sent a silent prayer to no one in particular that it was a case well short of death. "Please tell me it's just some drunk kid in a uniform who's run afoul of the Russians or the locals again, someone we have to haul out of jail." Baier took a deep breath and glanced at the clock to confirm just how early it was. *Please don't let it be one of ours.* "Are you sure you need to be calling me and not the Army or the Embassy?"

The voice on the other end of the line was apologetic. Baier recognized it now as Adams, a first-tour officer who had the bad luck to pull night and weekend duty for the week. "It's a corpse, sir. And they specifically asked for you. Otherwise I would have pushed this whole thing off on the military."

Baier shoved back the covers and slid his legs off the mattress until his feet reached the floor. He stood, cradling the phone between his shoulder and cheek while he slipped on his watch. "So, why didn't you call the MPs first off? And just who are 'they'?"

"It was the Austrians, sir. The Interior Ministry Police. It's not just the local cops. It sounded pretty serious. Otherwise, I wouldn't have—"

"No, that's all right. I understand. It's just a bit of a shock getting a call at this hour." He paused to glance out his bedroom window, not really sure what he expected to see beyond the impenetrable darkness. "American? It's not one of ours, is it?"

"No, sir, not one of ours. I don't think he's been identified yet. At least, no one mentioned it." Baier could hear the rustle of paper at the other end of the line. "It sounds like he's Austrian, an older gent. He was dressed as a civilian for the most part, except for his jacket."

"Where is this body then?"

"Down by the river, sir. Some drunk apparently saw it from the sidewalk walking home."

"What do you mean 'for the most part'?"

"Well, that's what's kind of odd, and it may be why they wanted you there. His jacket was actually an old Wehrmacht coat."

"Wait a minute." Baier stifled a yawn and ruffled his thick brown hair that felt like a patch of alfalfa after a draught. The early morning disorientation was beginning to wear off. "Did you say a Wehrmacht coat? Did this guy not realize the war's been over for ten years now? Did he just get out of a Soviet POW camp?" Even after the big release of 1948, there were still numerous German and Austrian prisoners of war languishing in the Soviet Union, probably because the work projects they had been assigned to were not yet finished.

"The locals said they'd know more by the time you got there and that they'd bring you up to speed at that point."

"So where do I need to go? What part of the river are we talking about?"

"Well, the good news is that you're nearby. It's right in the center of town—almost, anyway. At the end of Rotenturm Street."

"*Strasse*. That's what the Austrians call a street. So it's Rotenturmstrasse."

"Whatever you say, sir." A pause. "Sorry, sir."

Baier smiled, in spite of the hour. "That's all right. I don't mean to be picky. I'm just tired." And the day hadn't even begun.

"I think you can see the spire of the Stephensdom from what they said."

At least he had gotten the proper name for the cathedral. "I should hope so, son," Baier replied. "It's a pretty tall steeple. But thanks anyway."

WHEN KARL BAIER arrived, he found the local police, along with two officers from the Interior Ministry, much as he had expected. This was, after all, their turf. The Austrians had been running their country for several years now, despite the continued presence of the four victorious powers who had divided Austria and Vienna into four zones of occupation, much as they had in Germany and Berlin. The difference was that the Austrian occupation was about to come to an end. May of 1955 was less than a month away. These same four powers had finally agreed to a peace treaty and a permanent state of neutrality for the independent nation of Austria. It had been dubbed the *Staatsvertrag*, or State Treaty, which would restore Austria to its full sovereignty and independence. Most important in the eyes of the locals, it would send all four Allied powers home. Baier was surprised that they would make such an effort to pull the Allies into what appeared to be a local killing with the occupation coming to an end in just a few weeks.

He was equally surprised to see representatives of the other three powers waiting for him on the riverbank. The French officer, a man Baier recognized as a member of their military intelligence, was in uniform and slouched in a sign of indifference to the entire affair, his lean, shaven face distorted by an obvious frown. It was as though he could not figure out why he had dressed so formally for such an insignificant affair. Still, the uniform did give his squat figure—perhaps the result of too much pâté and foie gras—a more official aspect.

Baier had not seen the Soviet before, but identified him from his uniform as a lower ranking officer from the regular Soviet military, infantry most probably. The brawny man stood nearly erect, sucking in his shallow cheeks and glancing continually from side to side, as though wary of being lured into some sort of a trap.

Only Baier's British colleague, a civilian like himself, wandered over to shake Baier's hand and commiserate for the early morning conference on the slick banks of the Danube. The man appeared to have taken the time to shower and shave. His dark, wet hair was combed straight back, and his raincoat was wrapped and belted tightly around his thin frame. Baier guessed his height to be just about six feet, since the Brit's forehead was just below his own.

Baier swept his hand over his own semi-combed hair and pulled his raincoat tighter around his chest and waist to ward off the damp, cool air. His thin nose was running, and his light hazel eyes were misting slightly under the soft morning breeze. For most of April, the Viennese weather hadn't quite left winter behind and made that final transition to spring. The frequent rain had left the riverbank where they stood slippery and moist, and the weather kept Baier longing for some of that fabled Viennese coffee. His right foot skated across the mud when he tried to move. Glancing toward the opposite bank, he cursed his luck that had left the corpse lying on the muddy side of the river still under repair and construction. Why couldn't the dead guy have been left on the paved and tree-lined path along the other bank?

"I insisted that we wait until your arrival before proceeding further," his British colleague whispered. "I definitely wanted to have someone from your side, as it were, here to help in case the French or bloody Soviets tried anything inappropriate."

"Like what?" Baier had met Henry Turnbridge once before and found him to be a likeable colleague from MI6. As likeable as possible, that is, with suspicion of a 'third man' in MI6 still lingering in the long, torturous wake of the Maclean and Burgess defections. Baier had sought to maintain a certain distance from his British colleagues, which seemed to suit Turnbridge just fine. Maybe he had his own doubts about his service. Or maybe he didn't care for the pressure Washington kept putting on his superiors in London to pursue a more thorough house-cleaning of suspected Soviet agents buried within their service.

"Should we expect something like that from those guys just now?" Baier swung his gaze from the riverbank to the row of office buildings and apartment blocks that rimmed the road above. It was a panorama typical of Vienna today: four- and five-story buildings either reconstructed from the long granite blocks and classical designs of years past or the austere lines of metal and glass favored by modern European architects in their hurry to reconstruct a devastated central Europe. "What's this all about, anyway?"

Turnbridge motioned with his head toward the Austrian officials from the Interior Ministry, who were flanked by two more police officers in uniform. "I'll let them do the explaining. Not that I'll expect them to have much to say in any case."

Baier and his British colleague walked over to their Allied brethren, who followed the two Anglo-Saxons over to the Austrians standing next to the corpse. The body of an elderly Austrian—at least Baier assumed he was an Austrian since they were in Vienna—had been rolled over on his back, one arm thrown wide and pointing downriver, the other arm folded across his chest. His front was wet and dirty, as one would expect if he had been lying face down on this patch of riverbank.

"Good evening, gentlemen," one of the Austrians said. "My name is Stefan Huetzing. I work at the Interior Ministry and will be leading the investigation into this murder. I already have your names from your respective commands so that I will know whom I should contact if it becomes necessary."

I apologize for asking you to join me at such an early hour, but given the potential complications of this case, I wanted to be sure you were kept informed of all developments from the outset."

The Austrian was tall, almost reaching Baier's height. Baier figured him for 5'10" or maybe 5'11. His body was shrouded in a deep green *Lodenmantel*, which he left unbuttoned, and the damp morning air had plastered his light-blond hair to his scalp. Baier marveled over the man's excellent command of English. He wasn't sure just how much his French and Soviet colleagues would be able to follow. But in view of the difficulties the American authorities had encountered working with both, he wasn't about to offer any assistance by pushing for a discussion in German. They'd probably have just as much difficulty following a conversation in that language.

"What sort of complications are we talking about, Herr Huetzing?" Baier asked. "How could this possibly affect the Allies, especially at this stage?"

The Austrian nodded. "I appreciate your uncertainties, Herr Baier, and again I sympathize with you for this early morning call." He smiled and spread his arms. "It may come to nothing, but at this stage we want to avoid anything that might upset progress toward the signing of the State Treaty, which you understand remains our priority."

Turnbridge pointed toward the body. "But what could this man have to do with our interests or the State Treaty, for that matter?"

Huetzing nodded again, apparently his way of acknowledging the question. "Hopefully nothing. But there is the matter of his jacket, which suggests an affiliation with the previous regime and its military forces. We also hope to identify him shortly, which should help us determine if there will indeed be complications. His jacket suggests he may have just made his way back here from the Soviet Union, and we naturally want to ensure that his departure and travels were all above board, as you say." The Austrian sighed and glanced up and down the riverbank. "Moreover, until we know the exact circumstances of his death, it is probably best that we all keep an open mind."

Baier and Turnbridge glanced at each other, then Baier studied the French and the Soviet officers. Both wore blank expressions, as though they had understood nothing and cared even less. Baier stepped closer to the body and found a face that appeared to be too old for active military service, although an extended period in Soviet captivity would age any man quickly. Still, Baier guessed his age as no younger than fifty. There were no other clues as to his background. The pants were made of a light-gray wool, and the shoes were of a well-worn black leather that looked as though they might have cost a fair bit when they were new. Of course, Baier had no way of knowing when that was, or if they originally belonged to this individual. The hands were rough and weathered, not surprising in one who'd performed years of hard labor in the USSR. Of course they didn't know if the man had indeed just returned from Soviet captivity or even been a prisoner there at all. Baier sighed, wondering just what they were supposed to know this early on. Or why they should even bother. The loose cotton shirt gave even less indication of the man's history, covered as it was with a large bloodstain over the chest.

"Oh, one other thing, gentlemen," the Austrian Huetzing announced. "This man was not shot here. He appears to have been killed somewhere else, and then whoever committed the crime dumped the body here." He pointed at the ground and circled the area with his index finger. "You see, there is no blood around here, and no sign of a struggle."

"Would you be able to determine that so soon and in this light?" the Frenchman asked. Baier grinned. So, the guy did speak English.

Huetzing nodded again. "Oh, quite." He looked upward. "The sun is already coming out, so we have been able to see well enough. And I think you will find that we are not so primitive in our investigations here. It may not be Paris, but we have done this sort of thing before."

As he approached his house afterward, Baier could have sworn that he had turned off all his lights when he left for his rendezvous at the Danube. But standing in the front walk, he could clearly see a single bulb casting a soft round glow from his kitchen at the back. Admittedly, it had been pretty damn early, and Baier remembered rushing from the house and locking his door in a flurry tempered only by exhaustion. Nevertheless he was pretty sure that he had indeed turned the key in the lock and that the house had been dark, matching the pre-dawn sky that surrounded it. But there it was: a soft shaft of light sliding toward him across the small lawn and along the walkway in front of the house.

He inched through the front door—definitely unlocked at this point—and crept toward the back of the house. A man sat at his kitchen table, a navy-blue overcoat draped over the chair next to him with a hat resting on the tabletop. He faced the front of the house, presumably to greet Baier when he entered, and he had already helped himself to a cup of what appeared to be freshly brewed coffee. Baier was sure as hell he had not made any before he left.

"Would you like some?" the stranger asked in a German that had the soft musical tones of an Austrian dialect. Baier had not placed it just yet. The interloper held his cup aloft and offered it to Baier.

"Thank you, but I'll get my own." Baier moved toward the cabinet next to the sink and pulled a mug from the bottom shelf. "In this sort of situation, it's probably best if I handle hot liquids on my own."

The stranger smiled. "Of course. As I had already drunk from this one, I meant to fetch you a new cup." He placed his own coffee cup back down on the table top. "Since it's your house, please do as you wish."

"That's very generous of you." Baier studied the man, who was easily as tall as himself, but looked to be about twenty pounds heavier despite his thin, angular features. He was wearing a well-tailored dark-gray woolen suit, a white dress shirt, and blue-and-red-striped necktie. It looked as though he had tried—without really wanting to—to hide a set of broad shoulders and a waist that appeared to be growing with his country's postwar prosperity. Baier could not see the man's shoes, hidden as they were underneath the table. He had learned that a good way to judge a man's true standing and situation in postwar Europe was to assess his footwear. "How did you get in?"

"Oh, it wasn't difficult. The lock was not all that challenging, actually." He smiled. "But you needn't worry. I did not break it."

Despite his annoyance, Baier managed to keep his voice even. "I thank you once again. You're quite the considerate visitor." He added a few drops of cream to his coffee, took a sip, and was glad to discover that his visitor made a nice, strong pot of coffee. Then again, he was Austrian. He was almost surprised the guy hadn't boiled any milk to create the foam the locals often liked to use to top off their coffee. "Now, who are you and what do you want?"

The uninvited guest pivoted in his chair to face Baier, who was leaning against the front of the sink. "My name at this point is unimportant—"

"I disagree. After all, you have broken in to my house."

The smile returned. "Actually, the house belongs—or belonged—to a former regime official from the Gestapo—"

"Whom I would love to see return to claim it."

"I agree, that is hardly likely." He held up his hand in a form of supplication or even consent. "And I agree that he would be unlikely to retain it, at least at the outset, since a prison sentence surely awaits him."

"Not necessarily. Not if he's Austrian."

"*Touché*. But we are digressing, Herr Baier. I am really here to discuss this morning's discovery at the riverbank."

Baier strolled to the table and grabbed a chair opposite his visitor. He sat heavily and stared at the man. "And …?"

"Let me get right to the point. I hope you will agree to investigate the man and his murder."

"Why should I? You have a capable police force and the authority to do that yourself. I'm assuming you are an Austrian and a representative of the government. Or is that incorrect? I mean, I still don't know your name."

"Yes, yes, Herr Huetzing is a very capable officer. He works for the criminal investigations office in the Interior Ministry, by the way."

"I know. He told us."

"And he is a man of considerable experience."

"He didn't go that far. But I'll take your word for it."

"Nonetheless, I'm sure you'll agree that there are international ramifications to this murder, coming as it does so close to the signing of the peace settlement and State Treaty. And there are questions about what this man had been up to." He paused to study Baier's face. "That was why I insisted Huetzing contact you." He leaned back and waved at the air around him. "He's the one who decided to bring in the other Allies. He was afraid it might affect his relations with the others if he only brought in the Americans."

Baier leaned back in turn. "So I have you to thank for my lack of sleep this morning." He shook his head and smiled. As he considered the sharp blue eyes and dark blond hair of this stranger, he leaned forward again, stretching his arms across the table and pushing the coffee to the side. "In the first place, ever since your foreign minister and his delegation returned from Moscow about a week ago, the treaty is practically a done deal. The Soviets have removed their objections, and there are no remaining territorial disputes, even with the Yugoslavs."

"Oh, come now. Even you are not that innocent. Your own army nearly fought with the French to get them out of northern Italy, and we all remember the standoff with Tito's

Yugoslav partisans in Carinthia. You know how powerful those emotions remain in this part of the world, and that it would not take much to exploit them."

"But who would want to? It's getting a bit late in the game for anything like that."

"Yes, hopefully." The visitor leaned forward, facing Baier, his arms outstretched to where he was almost touching Baier's hand. "But that's what we need to find out. We must be certain that this goes no further."

"Just who is 'we'? And why me?"

The man let out a mouthful of stale breath, his teeth stained by too much coffee, too many cigarettes, and not enough brushing. " 'We' are the Austrian government. I really can't say any more at the moment." He studied Baier's face, apparently unmoved by the bags under his eyes and the ruffled patch of hair. "And we have chosen you because of your position and the country you represent."

"You want an American investigating this case … or at least the international aspects, as you put it?"

The Austrian nodded vigorously. "Yes, of course. We have found your country to be the most cooperative and helpful throughout the occupation." He shrugged. "The British have been good partners as well, of course, but there is a limit these days to what they can achieve. You Americans, on the other hand …."

It was Baier's turned to smile. "I appreciate the flattery. But why me, exactly?"

The Austrian leaned back in his chair and pondered the half cup of coffee still sitting in his mug. "I am aware that you occupy a deputy's position in the CIA station here. That gives you a certain amount of authority and access. It will also allow us to keep your part of the investigation discreet, as it were." The smile returned. "And your German is almost as good as mine."

Baier was tempted to tell this interloper that his own

German was probably better. After all, the guy was Austrian, whereas Baier's parents had come from Germany. Then again, the Austrians had had enough of the arrogance and condescension their German brethren brought with them when Berlin incorporated Austria into the Third Reich. Baier studied his interloper for a full minute. He broke the silence with two loud sips from his coffee cup. "You understand, of course, that I will confirm nothing you have claimed about my position here. I work as a political advisor to the American commander's office in the Occupation Authority. Period. Nor am I in a position to accept, formally or informally, your request for assistance." He paused. "And my German is pretty damn good. It's my Austrian that needs the work."

The visitor let out a long sigh. Then he stood. "Be that as it may, I would like to assume that you Americans will assist us in the matter, as it is in your interests as well as ours that we conclude this State Treaty next month, and that we establish at least a modicum of stability here in the heart of Europe."

He moved behind his chair, which he pushed back into place against the table. Baier glanced at his shoes. They were polished black leather dress shoes in good shape. Baier guessed that they might even be a new pair.

"There are some in Washington who are not so sure," Baier replied, "or who might see it a bit differently, at least. Bonn, too." The Austrian smiled, as did Baier. "This neutrality thing makes them nervous. They think it leaves your country open to pressure from the Soviets. And that it could set an unfortunate precedent."

The Austrian displayed the first sign of impatience Baier had seen this morning. "Oh, come now, Herr Baier. Your leadership must learn to think of the Europe we shall inhabit a bit more creatively. There is a great deal we can do in Austria if we are free of both camps."

Baier shrugged. "Yes, but will you stay free? And will you stay aligned with the West ultimately?"

"*Ach*, of course," the Austrian exclaimed. "That is our goal. But we will need your help and understanding. That is why we would like to have you involved in this case. You may discuss this with whomever you like in your chain of command … wherever that might be." He seemed to relax and smiled again. As he retrieved his hat and pulled on his overcoat, he said, "There is no need to show me out. I know the way."

"Obviously. How will I contact you if I need to discuss this further?"

The Austrian paused and considered Baier with a gaze as cold and hard as stone. "That will not be necessary."

Baier stood and watched his visitor walk toward the door. By now he had concluded the man was a complete asshole. He had invaded his home, issued orders, and refused to identify himself. "Well, that's convenient, for you anyway. Can you at least give me the man's name? The dead one, I mean. Do you know that much yet?"

The Austrian paused by the front door while he set the hat on his head. His right hand dove into his pants pocket, pushing the folds of his coat back in an aristocratic gesture. "Von Rudenstein. Herr Heinrich Rudolph von Rudenstein. Before the war, his family owned a large estate near the Hungarian border, and they served with distinction for generations in the Hapsburg army. In fact, the lands originally extended over the border into modern Hungary."

Not anymore, Baier thought. "Well, that's a start, anyway." If he had served with distinction, it had been a waste of time in the old Austrian army, defending the Hapsburg's declining Empire in its later years. "How did he do in the more recent war?"

The visitor smiled. "Very well. Some would say even better." His brow furrowed in thought, as though he was carefully considering his next words. His gaze set on Baier like a cloak.

"Oh, one other thing, Herr Baier. You might want to be sure that your wife returns home from visiting her family near Leipzig." The Austrian paused again to study the floor as though weighing his words. "It may be best if she were not in a position that would bring extra pressure to bear upon you while this investigation is underway."

You son of a bitch, Baier thought. "What did you say? Pressure from whom?" Baier's teeth clenched, and his eyes narrowed. "And just how in the hell did you know where she is right now?"

The Austrian never answered. He straightened the brim of his homburg, smiled again, and walked out the door. "*Pfertig Gott*, Herr Baier."

So the bastard's a Tyrolian, Baier said to himself. *We shall see just who investigates whom and how cooperative I'll be.* Baier turned and marched back to the kitchen, where he threw the rest of the coffee into the sink. As he stared at the brown puddle resting under the spigot, Baier thought back to his immediate postwar days in Berlin, the first encounter with his Soviet counterparts, German refugees, returning prisoners-of-war, ex-Nazis, and of course, Sabine, his wife. It had been a time of fear and uncertainty, but also excitement and suspense in the midst of a dangerous and changing world.

Those same emotions had just returned.

Chapter Two

"SABINE? IS THAT you?"

"Of course, Karl. What's wrong? Why are you calling at such an early hour?" Baier did not respond, not right away. "Are you at work already, or still at home?" she pressed.

Baier was amazed at how relieved he was to hear her voice. And how much he missed her. The anxiety and concern were a natural response to her absence, particularly one spent in the Soviet zone in Eastern Germany. She had dealt with the Soviets in the past, and even made a nice living for a while in the ruins of postwar Berlin on the black market and smuggling refugees out of the Soviet-occupied territories. Sabine had proven that she could take care of herself. But there was always a threat—perhaps a lesser one and hidden, but a threat all the same. He was not aware of real or explicit danger at the moment, not based on the brief comments of his Austrian visitor, just a vague sense of unease. This worry and anxiety would now be constant companions until Baier had her back home. For her part, Sabine sounded blissfully unaware of anything out of the ordinary. He could detect no sign of fear, or even concern. Other than perhaps over his calling so early in the morning.

"I'm still at home, Sabine." He stood by the phone on the kitchen wall and glanced at the clock above the stove, surprised to learn that it was only a quarter past seven. He had tried to go back to bed but could not settle in enough to sleep. No surprise there, of course. "But I'm heading to work in a few minutes."

"You sound tired already. Are you all right? Is something wrong?" his wife asked.

"No, Sabine, I'm fine. It was a bit of a rough night, and I didn't sleep well." Baier smiled at the irony of his words. "I just wanted to see how you're doing and when you might be coming home." He thought for a moment, then stretched the cord so he could sit at the kitchen table. "How are your parents doing?"

"Better, I believe. The doctor seems to think they were improving, but it's just so hard to get the proper medications in the Soviet Zone here. We've already used the ones I brought from Vienna."

"The ones we got from the Commissary?" Baier asked. "So soon?"

"*Ach*," Sabine exclaimed, "there weren't that many. And they both needed the pills and the painkillers." Silence stretched out between them. "Karl, is that the real reason you called? We spoke of my parents' health just two days ago. You can't expect that to change much with cancer. Is there something else?"

Baier took a deep breath. "I wanted to make sure no one up there is bothering you. I know how much you hate the Soviets"—her favorite phrase for them was 'those fucking Russians'—"and I wanted to be sure nothing had happened."

"Thank you, Karl, but no, nothing has happened. Should it have? Is there something I should know?"

Baier surprised himself again at how quickly he responded. "No, no, of course not. It's just … it's just that you never know when those bastards will try to provoke something." He did not want to frighten her, especially since he had so little himself to go on. "They can never leave well enough alone."

"Yes, yes, I know, Karl. I know what to expect of them. I am always careful up here around Erfurt and Leipzig, or anywhere in their zone. I've dealt with these bastards before. You should know better."

Baier blew out his breath again. "I do, Sabine. But sitting here alone, my imagination starts to work in overdrive. I need you to come home."

"Karl, dear, I miss you as well. I will come back to Vienna as soon as I can. But my parents need me here a little longer. I never know when I will see them again. And they really rely on what I can bring in from the West, you know."

"Yes, of course. You're a wonderful daughter. I wish they would leave for the Federal Republic, or even Austria. It would be so much easier and much more comfortable for them."

"Karl, we've discussed this before. You know they won't leave their homes, no matter what has happened here. They've been through a lot in their lives. They've become very fatalistic." She sighed. "I promise to come home soon. As soon as possible."

"Okay, dear. I will be waiting. But promise me you'll be careful. If even the slightest thing happens to concern you, if you think someone might be following you—"

"Karl! Now you're scaring me."

"I'm sorry. I didn't mean to. I just want to be sure you're careful. Remember, you're up there in the middle of 'those fucking Russians.' "

"WELL, WELL, MEETING at the Café Demel. It's kind of like a Viennese stereotype, isn't it?"

Baier leaned back against the neat wooden chair and peered out the window toward the Imperial Palace, or Hofburg, down the street. His glance took in the junction between the palace itself and the famous Spanish Court Riding School. After half a minute, he let the frown evaporate and stared at his boss, Ralph Delgreccio. He had not known Delgreccio before this assignment, but Baier had instantly taken a liking to the man, perhaps because of their almost parallel backgrounds. Delgreccio had grown up in Brooklyn, the second of two boys in the family of a grocer who wanted nothing more for his sons than to get them through college and off in pursuit of the American dream. Of course it had to be a Catholic school, but Notre Dame, Baier's alma mater, had been too far away. Even when Delgreccio had settled on St. Bonaventure's in upstate New York, his parents had acted as though he was leaving for China. Not only did the two men have many stories to share from their Catholic school days, but Baier also welcomed another middle-class and especially Catholic ally in the internal Agency battles. The snobbish Ivy League adherents acted as though their work for the government represented a modern form of noblesse oblige and entitlement. As though their country should be *so* lucky to have them. For a Midwestern boy like Baier who grew up in Chicago, finding a kindred spirit—even one from the Eastern seaboard—had been like a gift from Heaven.

"Hey, I like the place," Baier responded. "I like the feel of it, all the history here and in the streets around us. And I like the coffee." Baier breathed in the café's unique aroma, the chocolate, marzipan, the blend of fruits, and of course, the coffee.

"There are others, you know, like the Landtmann, reputedly Freud's favorite hangout."

"Too big and impersonal for my tastes."

"Well, you certainly seem to enjoy the cake and pastries here, although you can find those elsewhere, too," Delgreccio said. "What's that one you're munching on like some happy goat?"

"Their version of the Sacher torte." Baier noticed his boss's smug smile. "Hey, I've been up for a while, so as far as I'm concerned it's afternoon." He glanced at his watch. "Even if it is just past 9:30."

"Well, it can't be the sexy waitresses. Not with those lame black smocks they wear. Reminds me of the nuns in grade school." Delgreccio laughed lightly, amused at his own words. "You're right. I admit that I like the royal feel of the place. I guess it's the location and the fact that they address you in the third person all the time. Makes me feel like I'm important." Delgreccio puckered his lips and said in a toady's voice, "Would the Herr like something else?"

"You *are* important, Ralph, despite that lousy impersonation." Baier studied the palace again. "Just sitting in a place like this and glancing out the window, you can't miss all the history here. That's what makes this café so typically Viennese." Baier surveyed the room. "I mean, Jeez, just look at the woodwork and design framing the walls and windows."

Delgreccio shifted in his chair as he pulled off his jacket and draped it over the extra chair at their small, round wooden table. He studied the wall decorations and draperies, floral patterns and bold black outlines set against a light gold background. "Yeah. So why are we meeting here and not back at the office?"

Baier shifted in turn, pivoting away from the window to lean across the table toward his boss, the local chief of station. "I wanted to talk to you alone." Delgreccio looked around the room at the nearly fully occupied thirty or so tables. "You know what I mean. No one is going to barge in on us here or overhear our conversation."

"Let's hope not. I always considered you a true and cautious professional, Karl."

"Besides, it's close to where I need to go afterward."

"Which is?"

"More on that later." Baier waited to finish his cake. "Look, Ralph," he continued, "I need to talk about what happened this morning and how I'm getting pulled into something that could be either a wild goose chase or a setup."

It was Delgreccio's turn to lean in. "Setup? By who?"

"By whom, Ralph."

"Answer the damn question, Karl."

"By a local in the Austrian government and with whomever he's linked." Delgreccio leaned back again and blew out his breath. "No, hear me out, Ralph. Sure, I doubt this guy is working on his own. I'm not even sure if it's for the Austrians alone, although I can't rule that last part out. The intriguing part is that he knows so damn much."

"About what? And just who do you think he's working for?" Delgreccio rolled his eyes. "I mean, for whom is he working?"

Baier smiled. "Sorry about that, Ralph. For one thing, he knows too damn much about me. And I'm not really sure whom he could be working for. He was cagey about his background. He even refused to give me his name." Delgreccio arched his eyebrows and smiled. "That's why I think I need to follow this up."

Delgreccio signaled the waitress for an individual pot of coffee. "I think you'd better start at the beginning, Karl. I'm lost already. I mean, why would an Austrian set you up? What could possibly be in it for him?" Delgreccio's eyes narrowed as he seemed to stare off into nothingness. "Unless he is working for someone else."

Baier nodded vigorously. "Right, right." He looked up into his boss's eyes. "You may not have heard about this yet, but a body was found down by the Danube in the city center early this morning. Very early."

"And that's why you've been up so long?" Baier nodded. "Why were you pulled in? Sounds like a clear-cut case for the locals."

"Me and reps from the other Allies as well," Baier explained. He recounted the early morning call, the meeting on the riverbank, the discovery of the corpse, and the Austrian desire to keep the Allies informed. "There was some talk of not letting this upset the signing of the State Treaty next month."

"One goddamn corpse is going to do that? Who are they trying to kid? I mean it's what, two weeks or so away? May fifteenth is the signing date, right?"

"Yeah, I believe that's right. But someone is trying to wrap the dead guy in a big cloak of mystery." Baier moved on to his morning visit from the enigmatic Austrian. "Some old aristocrat who may or may not have just returned from a Soviet POW camp."

"One of the lucky ones who earned a stay in the workers' paradise for a full ten years?" Delgreccio asked.

"Maybe. But I haven't been given anything other than a name and a reference to some estate out near the Hungarian border." Baier ran his hands through his hair and realized he had yet to shower this morning. "Jeez, this damn thing has already ruined my day."

Delgreccio grinned. "You have to admit, it does sound like a long shot at best that this murder—if that's what it was—will have any real impact on the State Treaty and Austria, much less Europe's future. You mentioned earlier that it could all be a wild goose chase. Maybe we should just leave it and let the locals settle the whole thing. If it has broader implications, they'll let us know." Delgreccio paused to stir his coffee and savor a spoonful of white foam. "What's the old geezer's name anyway?"

"It's a mouthful, like all these old aristocratic names. Von Rudenstein, Herr Heinrich Rudolph von Rudenstein."

"Mouthful is right." Delgreccio shrugged. "Sounds impressive, though."

Baier shook his head. "Yeah, but who knows what part he may have played in anything. I guess it could still be important, even without upsetting the State Treaty's apple cart. What might be bubbling under the surface? I mean, why the hell go to the trouble of insisting I get involved if there isn't something at work here? If we just walk away, the whole case could go cold. And if someone else is involved, they'll have a helluva head start."

"Who else?"

"Hard to say, Ralph. The Soviets, some revanchists, other East Europeans."

A new pot of coffee arrived. The short, squat waitress in her black frock and white collar set it on the table between the two men in the tiny open space next to Baier's empty cake plate. She picked that up and waddled back to the serving station. Delgreccio poured himself a cup from the new pot. "I have to admit; this stuff does beat the crap out of that swill Cooper brews back in the office." He stirred in a small drop of thick, vanilla-colored cream. "So what do you propose to do? What can you accomplish that the locals can't? And what do we know about this Austrian visitor you had?"

"Well, for starters I can check up on the history of the guy from the riverbank. If there's nothing of interest there, I'll discuss the next steps with you."

"Here at the Demel?"

Baier laughed. "If you'd like. I'll even pay for the pastries."

"I've got news for you: you're paying for these. The coffee, too."

Baier nodded. "Oh, all right, you cheap bastard. But I know next to nothing about the dead man. So I should find out why he's of such importance … or interest, at least. Then we can decide whether it's worth putting more time into it."

"And the Austrian visitor?"

"Let me check on the dead one first. It might point me in the right direction for the live one."

"Why you and you alone?" Delgreccio asked.

"Good question. For now I think the lighter our fingerprints, the better. And no one else has my facility with German." Baier paused, then finished the last of his coffee before pouring himself another half-cup. "Besides, I'm the one the Austrians approached, so I'm involved already."

"True," Delgreccio said. He sipped his coffee, a glow of appreciation spreading across his face. "By the way, how's Sabine doing up there in Saxony, or wherever she is?"

Baier leaned back, exhaled, and shook his head. He glanced at the window and noticed the patchwork of clouds arriving from the east. “Why the hell is everyone so interested in my wife’s travels and welfare all of a sudden?”

Delgreccio frowned and set his coffee cup back on the saucer. “It’s a simple enough question, Karl. Why would that upset you? Who else has been inquiring?”

“That bloody Austrian this morning. He had the gall to suggest it would be a good thing if she returned home soon.”

Delgreccio’s brow furrowed, and his eyes narrowed. “Mr. Mystery Austrian, you mean?” Baier nodded. “That doesn’t sound right. Did he happen to mention how he knew?”

Baier shook his head and toyed with the fork on his plate. “No. He threw that out as he left, and I was too stunned to press him.”

“Shit, Karl, maybe you’d better let me look into this.”

Baier held his hands up. “No, Ralph. This is my gig. At least for now. I promise I will keep you informed of every step I take. I don’t like heading down a dark alley half blind any more than the next guy.” He gulped down the fresh coffee he had poured, grimacing at the slight burning sensation in his tongue and throat, then tossed a small pile of Austrian schillings on the table. “Finish your coffee. I’ve got a date with some research files.”

Delgreccio grabbed his wrist. “I know I don’t need to say this, but I’m going to anyway. I want you to be real careful, Karl. For Sabine’s sake, if not for your own. I’ve suddenly got a bad feeling about this.”

It was an inspiring walk. At least that’s how Baier had always thought of it before. In fact, he often found excuses to go out of his way so he could stroll along the streets circling the historical markers of Vienna’s city center, so many of them monuments to Hapsburg history and the Austrian cultural legacy, and all of it within sight of other pieces of the country’s past imperial grandeur: the opera house, state museums, city hall, parliament, and so many more that evoked Vienna’s past.

And that's just what it was, Baier reminded himself time and again: past. Gone with the smoke and chaos of two lost wars and the breakup of an empire.

Despite the sweet taste and sour mood he carried with him upon leaving the Demel and its array of cakes and pastries, Baier actually heard himself whistling as he strolled down the Kohlmarkt toward Michaelerplatz, which pointed most travelers into the main entrance of the old imperial palace, the Hofburg. Off to his left stood the stables and the riding school, but Baier swung right around another one of Vienna's emblematic cafés, the Griensteidl, and headed up the Herrengasse toward the Ministry of Interior, located just a block up the street in what had been the Modena Palace. The street had once been famous for the elegant buildings that housed the Empire's nobility, living in the opulence one expected and the proximity to the emperor they needed. Now, the new era of twentieth-century capitalism was bringing in expensive art galleries, jewelry shops, fashion houses, and a few government ministries.

It was at the Interior Ministry where he hoped the records of Austria's halfhearted denazification program might provide some explanation of von Rudenstein's history, at least during the years of Nazi rule in Austria and the Second World War. Baier had to admit that he was perplexed by the image of the corpse wearing a Wehrmacht jacket, even if he suspected it might just be a red herring—intentional or not—or even a simple coincidence. Maybe the man had been cold or without another coat or jacket and had simply grabbed the first thing that came to hand. Whatever the case, Baier hoped that some additional information might help explain the man's death and why someone or some people in Vienna were so concerned about it.

At the front desk, a short, attractive blonde woman with blue eyes and round, full cheeks greeted Baier and nodded at his identification card that placed him with the occupation authorities. Rising from her place behind the desk, she led Baier to a cellar room where the denazification files were kept. Then she immediately turned and departed, climbing back up the stairs to her perch at the front. Baier could hardly blame her. The room was damp and poorly lit, and Baier wondered how long the files would survive in such conditions. There appeared to be little maintenance, either in the files or in the room. It reeked of mold and mildew, and it seemed to have been weeks since anyone had bothered to sweep the litter spread across the floor. Given how few visitors the place probably had, it had more than likely been even longer. It figured, since the Austrians had basically been trying to sweep the seven years that followed the Anschluss in 1938 from their collective memory as soon as the Wehrmacht had surrendered. The Austrians preferred not to acknowledge their celebrations at becoming a part of the Reich, their active participation in and support for the war effort, and their enthusiastic complicity in the regime's murderous anti-Semitism; instead, they insisted on describing themselves as "victims." Baier did not expect that he would find a whole lot of material to wade through in the files, since the Austrians had effectively ended their prosecutions of Nazi criminals in 1948, and the country's leadership had been busy courting the ex-Nazi vote ever since.

It did not take long then—roughly half an hour—for Baier to experience the pleasant surprise of finding a file on Herr Heinrich Rudolph von Rudenstein. It was a thin one, no more than twenty pages. The man had not been a Nazi party member before the Anschluss, waiting until the spring of 1939 to join. Formerly an officer in the Austrian army, von Rudenstein had transferred his professional allegiance to the Wehrmacht, like most of his countrymen, and apparently had not encountered much anxiety or guilt in doing so. Baier wondered if the man had signed on with enthusiasm, greeting the great Pan-German revival with joy, or if he had been more of an opportunist, eager to promote his military career. The prospects for that were clearly better under German leadership. And it had certainly not suffered during the war. Von Rudenstein had entered the Wehrmacht a major and departed what was left of it a general officer. Along with serving with distinction in the invasions of Norway and France, he'd fought on the Eastern Front as the Red Army closed in on the Reich at the end of the war in the north Italian campaigns.

What else might have occurred during those years remained a mystery; at least the files gave no indication. Baier noted with some surprise that von Rudenstein had been listed as one of the 'less incriminated' by the Austrians after the war, by far the largest category of ex-Nazis in the Austrian batch of those implicated in the crimes of the regime. Roughly ten percent were serious enough to be designated as "incriminated." There were no specific crimes entered for von Rudenstein, but it still suggested something troubling in the man's background. His case had also been brought before the Austrian's People's Court, one of the twenty to thirty thousand cases—Baier could not remember the exact figure—that actually made it past the prosecutor's office. No verdict had been returned. This was particularly surprising because the case had originally been raised in Vienna, the seat of the People's Court for the Soviet Zone. About a week later, von Rudenstein's dossier had been transferred to Graz, the location of the court for the British Zone, where it was summarily dropped. The file contained no explanation. There was also no reference to imprisonment in a Soviet camp or time spent in the Soviet Union. Of more immediate help, it did confirm the location of his family estate in Burgenland.

"Son of a bitch," Baier muttered. He could have said it louder, since there was no one else in the room. For all the Austrians seemed to care, he could have slipped the file inside his jacket and walked out with it. Instead, he inserted it back into the row on the shelf where he had found it and where the index said it should be. Then he made his way back up the two flights of stairs to the main entrance.

Just before leaving the building, however, Baier noticed a tall figure in a dark-gray suit. It was the man Baier had encountered in his kitchen that morning. He looked slimmer in the daylight. Baier watched his head bob above the crowd in the hallway as he moved in the opposite direction. Baier opened his mouth to shout, but then remembered he had never learned the stranger's name. He cursed under his breath, then simply yelled, "Hey!"

The visitor glanced over, along with nearly everyone else in the corridor, and even a few on the sidewalk outside, perhaps several dozen people in all. When the man saw Baier, he refused to acknowledge the American. Instead, he frowned, shook his head as though to clear his mind of an unwanted intrusion, and quickly dropped down a corridor to his right.

Baier turned to the receptionist. "Did you notice the tall gentleman in the gray suit just now who turned when I shouted?"

The young blonde woman shrugged and gave Baier a pleasant, well-meaning smile that conveyed absolutely nothing. "I'm sorry. I've seen him here on occasion, but I don't know his name. I'm not even sure he works here."

Baier thanked her and left. On the way back to his office, Baier could have sworn that he had company. But each time he stopped to check, the shadow evaporated.

Either his imagination was overactive despite or maybe because of his exhaustion, or the guy, whoever he was, was very, very good.

Chapter Three

HE WAITED UNTIL the second day after the discovery of the corpse before making the two-hour drive to Burgenland, Austria's easternmost province nestled against the Hungarian border. It was known mostly for its wines, especially the Noble Red, a sweeter wine that Baier found hard to swallow if it wasn't paired with dessert or some fruit. Maybe a dry, hard cheese would do. Not the fruit that often accompanied meals in Europe, though. The Blaufraenkisch was another thing. That was a nice light and semi-dry red that went down well with any variety of the schnitzels or pork dishes served all over this country.

It had rained for the better part of the day after Baier's visit to the Interior Ministry, which had sapped his spirit of any desire to make what was admittedly a short drive, certainly by American standards, and quite scenic. Although this part of the country lacked the majesty of the Alps or even the hilly regions to the north of the capital, it did have some long, flowing flatlands with slight rolling hills that marked the beginning of a European plain that swept east into Eurasia. It had been a popular invasion route into the towns and estates of Europe over the centuries, first used by the Ostragoths, the original Germanic settlers in this part of the world, who had eventually agreed to serve as a form of border guard for the Roman Empire. Others, such as the Huns, had followed, and the region ended up as part of the world contested by the Germans, the Hungarians, and the South Slavs. The district remained one of mixed ethnic settlements, with a predominantly German cast that had seen some fighting between the Germans and Hungarians at the end of the First World War until the final peace treaty had awarded the territory to the new Republic of Austria. Now a peaceful wine-growing region greeted Baier as his Jeep navigated the long stretch of highway and narrow village roads.

In addition to vineyards, Baier encountered truckloads of Soviet soldiers and equipment making their way east in the direction of the Austrian border. Baier assumed they were preparing for their withdrawal from the country, seeing as how the State Treaty would require the complete withdrawal of all Allied troops. He doubted, though, that they were leaving already. That kind of generosity would be a very un-Soviet thing to do. Curious, Baier decided to swing behind one of the lorries and follow it to see just what the Soviets were up to. If they traveled all the way to the border, then Baier would stand corrected. If they were beginning their pull out, it would suggest that any concerns over the prospects for the State Treaty expressed by his early morning Austrian visitor were ill-placed. At least as far as Moscow was concerned.

To be sure, Baier was taking a chance. Burgenland had been a part of the Soviet Occupation Zone, and he was really here on a bluff. It wasn't like he had the freedom to travel wherever he damn well pleased in the various occupied territories, and there were numerous stories of GIs who had been detained by the Soviets for straying into their zone. There was a good chance the Soviet authorities would blink if he followed through with his cover story about exploring the wine region with the hope of purchasing a few cases of some nice Blaufraenkisch, given the pending resolution of Austrian independence and neutrality. And under the new leadership in the Kremlin, the Soviets were even in the midst of a charm offensive to remove the sour taste left by Stalin's oppressive reign. Pursuing a military convoy as far as the border was another matter entirely. Still, when an opportunity presented itself, Baier had learned to seize it and then deal with the situation if pressed. Despite the Hollywood version of the life of an intelligence officer, he considered his best weapons to be powers of observation, discretion, and a quick wit.

It didn't take long for his hunch to pay off. The convoy reached the border in about fifteen minutes. That was to be expected, seeing as how Burgenland was not more than a couple dozen miles wide in most parts and a good deal less in others. When Baier pulled off to the side of the road at the top of a long incline, he was shocked by what he saw. The Soviet soldiers disembarked and joined hundreds of their compatriots erecting a tall chain-link fence rimmed in barbed wire and surrounded on both sides by workers stocking explosives and wiring into what appeared to be a huge minefield that ran as far as Baier could see. It almost certainly ran the length of the border. At least Baier assumed this was the border, since he did not have a properly demarcated map with him, just a Michelin road atlas. More surprising to Baier was how far behind the Soviets seemed to be with their construction. With the signing of the State Treaty just weeks away, these guys had a lot of work to do yet.

"Can I help?" Baier's head shot around. He was shocked to hear a human voice, this one speaking German with a heavy Slavic accent. Baier struggled to understand and cursed his own carelessness. He had just failed to apply one of those valuable precepts he preached at junior officers time and again. With his powers of observation focused on the work in the fields below, he had neglected his immediate surroundings.

"And I would like to see some identification," the voice added.

The Soviet captain could not have been more than thirty years old, possibly thirty-five. He had a clean-shaven, tanned face and close-cropped black hair that peeked out from under a smart military cap. The uniform looked clean and pressed; he was clearly not doing any of the digging down below. His hand rested on the butt of a holstered semi-automatic, the ubiquitous Makharov, so Baier was not inclined to ignore or protest the man's sudden presence. "Yes, of course." Baier reached into his inside jacket pocket and pulled out his diplomatic identification. "Here you go." He smiled as he handed over the card.

The officer read Baier's card and immediately switched to English, also heavily accented but easier to follow. "What is the purpose of your visit here?" The Soviet glanced toward the work underway in the field below.

"Oh, it's just a personal outing." Baier jerked his thumb backward in the direction from which he had come. "Just checking out some of Austria's wine country." He did not want to talk too much, which tended to increase the odds of saying the wrong thing.

"I see. But there are no vineyards in this particular stretch of country, as you can see." He gestured at the area below. "I believe they grow wheat in these fields." The captain glanced at the sky and then the inside of Baier's Jeep. "Or at least they did. There will be less room for it in the future."

"Yes, it does look that way." Baier flashed another wide smile in the officer's direction, the better to let his straight, white teeth shine in the innocence of the afternoon sunlight. "I guess I just got a little too curious when I saw your trucks heading this way."

The Soviet let his gaze roam over the interior of Baier's car, then strolled along the side and around the back before returning to the driver's-side window. "This is a restricted area, Mister ..." he glanced down at the identification card, "Baier.

You should get back to your wines." His eyes met Baier's, as a shadow slid from the man's face like the opening of a doorway. "We would not like to have any incidents disrupt the momentous event that awaits this country's future."

"You are absolutely right, Captain." Baier accepted his diplomatic card from the Soviet, smiled, and even gave a halfhearted salute. "I'll just turn my car around here and drive back to the vineyards."

As he cruised down the dirt road, Baier looked in the rearview mirror to see the Soviet officer standing in the middle of the road, dust drifting past his immobile figure. His right hand rested once again on the butt of his Makharov. Baier noticed that he was sweating and wiped the beads of moisture from his brow.

It took Baier another thirty minutes to locate the von Rudenstein estate, largely because he got lost, twice. In the end, the estate turned out to be closer than he thought to the border, not more than a few kilometers from the spot where he had encountered the Soviet officer. Or what presumably had been the von Rudenstein estate. The road leading to the manor house was a thin stretch of dirt covered with gravel—Baier guessed limestone—that ended in a large oval by a front door of thick, brown oak. As far as Baier was concerned, the building was of modest construction, relatively speaking, this being an aristocrat's home. The red brick walls were well-worn, and four large pillars of cement and stucco marked a front porch that was littered with small branches and twigs. Two large windows stood to either side of the front door, and there was another set of four along the second story. The house looked large enough for a small family used to living the life of a Hapsburg noble, but it was certainly nothing luxurious. It also looked empty.

Baier parked his car off to the side of the porch, then strolled around the side to see if anyone was home or even lived there still. There was not much of a yard, as most of the land appeared to be given over to the cultivation of grapes and the working areas that wine-making would require. Kind of like the farms Baier had seen in the fields that lay not far from the city environs of Chicago in middle and western Illinois, although those had grown corn and soybeans, not grapes. Along those lines, there was a barn of sorts at the side of the house that stored several large vats and rows of shelves stacked with cases and bottles. Hoses lay along the floor by the entrance, and a couple dozen cases with full wine bottles stood stacked along the front wall next to the entrance. There were even more cases with empty bottles. But Baier could not see anyone at work, or even taking a break. The place, as best he could tell, was deserted.

"Hello!" he shouted, marching through the barn and out onto the grounds behind it. Nothing. Vines stretched along the rolling fields as far as he could see, and Baier wondered how many of them belonged to the von Rudensteins. Probably all. Or at least they once had.

"What are you doing here?"

Jesus, Baier thought. *I have got to pay more attention to people wandering around out here.* A plump, older gentleman had snuck up behind Baier with all the stealth of an Iroquois brave. Baier turned to study the figure confronting him. The man stood no taller that Baier's chest, but he appeared to weigh about twice as much. Gnarled hands rested on wide hips clad in brown leather pants, weathered even more than the skin on this working man's hands. He wore a dirty white shirt over broad shoulders. His neck was buried in flesh and his face was marked by years of history, years that must have seen many battles and shifts in leadership and government across this land. Thin patches of white hair ran back from his forehead, ruffled periodically by the light breeze from the east.

"I'm looking for someone from the von Rudenstein family," Baier replied. "Would that be you?"

"I am the groundskeeper here. What do you need the family

for?" His eyes stayed locked on Baier's, suspicion simmering there.

"Have you worked here long?" Baier asked.

"Long enough," the man said with a nod. "Why do you ask?"

"I was looking for someone in the family. Have you heard what happened to Herr von Rudenstein?"

The man's eyes narrowed. "Do you mean his death? If so, yes, the son was here just yesterday to inform me."

"Well, I wanted to pass along my condolences and see if there was anything I could do." Baier held out his hand. "And your name is?"

The Austrian's eyes widened as he glared hard at Baier, his face darkening with what looked like anger and resentment. Then he sighed and said, "My name is Carl Joseph Leibner. I grew up on the estate here. My father was the groundskeeper, as was his father. We've been here for some years, obviously." His expression remained hard and suspicious as he glanced at the Jeep and then back at Baier. "Where are you from?" His brow furrowed as though he was trying hard to process what little information he could glean from this stranger wandering about the family estate. "You wouldn't be a Reich German, would you, one of those damn *Saupruess* from up north? Your German sounds a bit like it. Because if you are, there's nothing for you here."

Baier couldn't keep himself from smiling at the reference to Prussian pigs, a common resentment in the southern German countryside toward the 'Prussians,' whom most Austrians and Bavarians considered cold and aloof. On top of that, there had been a good deal of resentment, Sabine had told him, toward the more prosperous northern Germans who had often shown up in the Ostmark, as the Nazis called Austria, with plenty of cash and arrogance. They had also dominated the local Party offices.

"Actually, I'm an American."

The groundskeeper nodded with a grunt. “That would explain the car. How come your German is so good?”

“My parents were both born in Germany, and we spoke it at home.” Baier held up his hand. “But they came from the southwestern part, in Baden. They weren’t crazy about the Prussians either. In fact, my grandfather left for America to avoid serving in Kaiser Wilhelm’s Reichswehr, which he considered a Prussian army.”

Leibner nodded again and looked at the ground and out toward the rows of vines that ran into the distance as though marking the family’s history. “Well, that’s okay then. But do you know how the master died?”

“Yes, I’m afraid so,” Baier said. “He was shot and left by the side of the Danube in the center of Vienna.”

The man hissed as he sucked in his breath. His gaze fell to the ground at his feet. Then he crossed himself and shook his head slowly before looking up again. “That doesn’t sound right. Herr von Rudenstein was a good man. That is probably why the son said so little about it. Do they know who did it?” Baier shrugged, and Leibner shook his head again. “He never harmed anyone, not even the Jews here.” The man looked up at Baier. “You’re not Jewish, are you? If you are, there’s no need for revenge against this house. They never took any property or belongings from those people when they were taken away.”

“No,” Baier waved his hand, “that’s not why I’m here. There are other organizations following up on that sort of thing. Besides, I’m a Catholic. Not a very good one, I’ll admit, but a Catholic all the same.”

The old gentleman grinned and nodded. “Like most of us, probably. Me, I never trusted the damn priests so much, but the master was different, God bless him.” He frowned. “What would you like to know?” He motioned toward the house. “Would you like a coffee?”

Baier shook his head. “No thank you. I can’t stay long. I have to drive back to Vienna, and I’d like to be underway before nightfall. What I'd like to know is if there is any more of his family still around, and what sort of man he was."

"Well, the family fled when the Russians arrived, and they refused to come back as long as the Red Army was here. The son's return yesterday was his first since the family moved to Vienna in 1948. Frau von Rudenstein passed away a few years after the war. That's when the rest of them moved to Vienna."

"Any other surviving children?"

"Besides the son, there's a daughter. She married a doctor and moved to England. London, I believe. The boy is also married and lives in Vienna in an apartment he'll probably inherit from his father now. He may return once the Russians leave for good in a few weeks. At least, I hope so. They haven't kept me up on their plans."

"But you've been keeping the wine business going here?" Baier pointed toward the barn.

"*Ach*, that. Only a couple hundred cases a year. Never more than that even in the best of seasons. It's just to keep things going in case they want to come back. Really only enough for me to get by and maintain what equipment we have left and to tend the vines. It's too hard to find the labor nowadays, what with all the young men killed in the war and the foreign workers gone. Besides, the damn Russians made off with a lot of the equipment, and I've only been able to pull together the basic machinery we need, which breaks down a lot. Maybe it will get better once we're free again."

"Can you tell me anything about Herr von Rudenstein?"

"Like what? What would you like to know? He wasn't a Nazi, I can tell you that much."

"But he fought as an officer in the Wehrmacht."

The old man's arms shot up in the air. "Of course he did. He was a patriot. Besides, what was he supposed to do. Refuse and be shot? What do you Americans expect?"

"You say he was a patriot. But what does that mean? Did he believe in the Greater German Reich?"

The arms waved at Baier this time, and the groundskeeper look aside and spat. "Oh, come now. It wasn't like that. He was a German patriot, sure. You'd have to be with the Croats and Hungarians trying to rob our land from us after the Great War."

"Rob you of your land? You mean they tried to take the vineyards away?"

Impatience showed in the old man's face, and his eyes rolled. "No, not that. Not just ours. After the war, the Hungarians wanted Burgenland to be a part of their new country. I guess they were mad after losing Transylvania and all that. There was plenty of fighting and shooting around here. But this is German land. Has been for centuries. Our Hapsburg Kaiser made sure of that." His eyes narrowed, as he studied Baier's face for a reaction. "As I said, *our* Kaiser, not one of those damn Prussians like the last one, Wilhelm. That's the kind of patriot Herr von Rudenstein was."

"What kind exactly?"

"An Austrian patriot. German, sure, but not for the greater glory of those nuts up north. It was the old Empire he was loyal to. The Hapsburg one."

"But then why did he fight for the Reich with the Wehrmacht? He seems to have done quite well at it."

"Well, what would you expect? Kaiser Franz Josef and his family were gone, along with our Hapsburg Empire. How else could he protect his lands and culture from the Slavs and all the others to the east, the damn Bolsheviks?"

"What happened to him after the war?"

"The Herr was taken prisoner outside Vienna, first by the Soviets, but then somehow he ended up in a British camp. They let him go, and he returned here for a while. But he left in 1948 when the Frau died."

"And you kept up the business, so to speak? Was it hard? Did Herr von Rudenstein help much or give you much in the way of guidance or direction?"

"Yes. Why do you ask? I told you he was a good man." He

eyed Baier with some suspicion. “Isn’t that what you would expect?”

“Frankly, that doesn’t surprise me. But his departure does. Why didn’t he stick around?”

“Well, I guess he must have had other business. I don’t ask those things of the Herr. Besides, he didn’t need to stay here all the time. He glanced back at the ground, then at the house. A breeze whistled past. “I don’t think his heart was really in it anymore. Not after all that happened.”

“Like what?”

The look of impatience returned. “All the history, of course.”

“And why didn’t he need to stay around?”

“Because we had help, valuable help.”

“From whom?”

The old man looked around, as though afraid of being overheard. “The British. They provided some money that Herr von Rudenstein needed to get things going again after the war, and they even brought in some workers now and then.”

“Why would they do that?”

The groundskeeper shrugged. “I don’t know. It’s not for me to ask.”

“What about the Russians? Did they object or interfere?”

He shook his head. “Not that I recall. They may have said something to the Herr, but we never saw much or anything of them around here. And no one interfered with us getting what we had to market. Little as that was, it wouldn’t have done them much good.”

“It always sold well?” Baier pressed. “Nothing was confiscated by the Soviets, aside from some equipment?”

Leibner nodded. “That’s right.”

Baier stepped in close. “So tell me this. How did Herr von Rudenstein greet the Anschluss if he was such an ardent Austrian patriot and loyal son of the Hapsburg Empire?”

Leibner blew out his breath and studied Baier for a long moment before answering. “Herr von Rudenstein was not overjoyed to see the Nazis and the German Eighth Army march in that day. He told me that our world had just collapsed, that the one we had lived in was now gone for good and we needed to make our peace with the new one."

"So he didn't join the cheering crowds?"

The old man stepped back, as though to distance himself from this innocent American stranger. "Heavens no. Herr von Rudenstein wept that day. I heard him crying late into the night."

In the end, Baier purchased a case of wine. Old Mister Leibner insisted on carrying the wine and placing it in the back of Baier's Jeep, and he only took the money when Baier pressed it into the curled fingers of his fist. Before driving all the way back to Vienna, Baier decided to stop at a *Gasthaus* at the edge of the village. It offered a lovely view of the rolling hills set under a sun that sank slowly along the horizon and cast the rows of withered vines in a purple glow. Baier sat back against the padded cushions of the bench alongside the table just inside the door. The waitress was a young woman wearing a faded green dirndl, the south German peasant smock. A deep cleavage was revealed by the plunging neckline of her white linen shirt. She immediately served him cool golden wine contained in the moist green bulb of glass common to the region. For him it represented an invitation to relax and enjoy life. Baier was tempted, mostly by the wine.

"How did you know that's what I wanted?" he asked.

"It wasn't hard to guess. It's what everyone wants." She smiled, and her blue eyes found the Jeep just outside the window, then Baier's face. "You're American?"

Baier nodded. "That's right. Was it the car?"

She shrugged. "Mostly that." She glanced outside, then smiled at Baier again. "Would you also like something to eat?"

Baier smiled back. "Sure. I'll have a Jaegerschnitzel and some pommes frites. Also a green salad, if you have any."

"Of course. I'll be right back."

Baier watched her retreat and knew he would have to try to reach Sabine once more. When he had spoken with her yesterday, she had complained about a visit to her parents' house by the local authorities that had bordered on harassment.

"You were right, Karl. Those fucking Russians are at it again."

"Was it just Russians, Sabine? What did they do?"

"Oh, the usual. Kept looking at my papers and asking about you and your work in Vienna. My father got very irritated, God bless him, but it was not good for his health. My mother fretted and wrung her hands the whole time."

"You need to come home, Sabine. I mean it. And now."

"There was also some East German prick with them. He must know the Russians well. They kept calling him Mishka. I don't like the way he looked at me."

"I'll see what I can find out about him. Do you want me to come up there?"

"Let me see. I'd like to get my parents out of here, too, but that will be hard. They're very ill now, and they don't want to go anywhere."

"Okay. I'll talk this over in the office, and think about what our options are. But don't do anything that will aggravate the situation there, Sabine. We'll play this straight and cooperate with the governing authorities." He paused to swallow the bitterness rising in his throat. "I know it may take longer that way, but in the end, it will probably be easier."

"Whatever you say, Karl. I miss you and love you. You know that."

"Of course I do, Sabine. I love you, too. We'll be together again soon. Don't worry."

Baier had no intention of playing it straight with East Germans and their Soviet overlords, not if he ran into trouble. It looked as though the Soviets were increasing the pressure, for whatever reason, and Baier would have to find out why.

He had tried to sound cooperative and pliant at the end only because he reminded himself they were probably listening in. Those fucking Russians.

Chapter Four

"MISHKA, YOU SAY?" Delgreccio asked.

Baier studied his boss as he sat facing Delgreccio in his office the following morning. The room was spacious enough, certainly larger than his own. The view captured steeples that jutted over rows of apartment houses and office buildings, with varying ages and pedigrees that stretched between centuries and a few years before sliding toward the office window. A gray haze of smoke drifted from rooftops and chimneys as the Viennese strove to banish the morning chill from their homes and workplaces. The office was expansive and well-furnished, the size and the view to be expected, given the reverence CIA station chiefs enjoyed in the field. But Baier did not begrudge his chief the luxury. Delgreccio was a good officer. He had proven himself on several tours in the Middle East, and Baier had heard rumors to the effect that this assignment in the heart of Old Europe was a reward of sorts for some of that work. Delgreccio was also proving himself to be a good friend and a man with sound judgment. Baier occasionally wondered why his boss had never married, but then he came to realize that Delgreccio was one of those officers who had become wedded to their work. The man was not unattractive, although his tendency to stockiness on the short 5'8" frame had not been helped by the heavy Austrian diet. It was almost certainly a matter of not having had the opportunities to meet that right person. Not like Baier, who had fallen into his good fortune in the unlikely world of ruins and deprivation in the heart of postwar Europe.

Delgreccio leaned back in his chair and observed Baier. His face reflected the same studious intelligence Baier hoped to convey, a difficult challenge considering his anxiety and concern over Sabine. "Are you sure that's the name she heard?"

"I think so," Baier replied. "Sabine's not the type to confuse something like that, not given her own history."

"Can you remind me of that 'history,' as you call it?" Delgreccio pushed himself forward until he was leaning halfway over the desk. "That is, if you're comfortable with it. I know you've held back on this, and I figure it's for a good reason."

Baier sighed and glanced from the window to his boss. Delgreccio's round head and receding hairline seemed to invite confidence. He waited patiently for Baier to speak.

"Yeah, you're right, Ralph. It *is* tough, and I'm not sure how much Sabine would want me to share. I know the security people back in Washington had to check her background, so it's not a complete mystery. You do know that we met in Berlin when I arrived there after the war, right?"

Delgreccio nodded. "Yeah, sure. You've said that much."

Baier continued, cautiously, "Well, the circumstances were a bit strange. It turns out I was living in what had been her home before the war—"

"Which we had confiscated? Was she a Nazi or something?"

Baier shook his head. "No, not at all. But her husband was missing on the Eastern Front, and the house was vacant, so we took it. Anyway, we met and obviously became quite close. I won't bore you with all the details, but one thing led to another and we eventually found her husband, who passed away some months later from his wounds. They were pretty bad. He got them in the fighting around Budapest."

"And that's when you were married?"

"That's right. Shortly after."

"And her family. Were they from Berlin?"

Baier shook his head. "No, they were not. And that is the funny part. Originally she told me she came from Franconia, up in northern Bavaria. Only later did she 'fess up that her family was actually from Saxony."

"So, why the mystery?" Delgreccio asked. "Did that ring any alarm bells for you?"

Baier nodded. "Sure. She claimed she didn't want to scare me off by telling me she had family in the Soviet Zone, so she picked a culturally similar place nearby that was in the American Zone." Baier leaned forward with his elbows on the desk so that he was only about a foot away from his boss. "I believed her then, and I still do now. Her reasons, I mean."

"Well, that's good. I trust your judgment, Karl. But you're obviously worried about something now."

"Hell, yeah. First of all, I don't like it that Sabine's up there alone and getting hassled by those fucking Russians, as she calls them."

"Ouch! She must really hate 'em. But I also recall you saying she had learned how to deal with those people, even profit from them."

"Well, she had some problems with them when they took Berlin, like most Germans there."

"Say no more. I can understand her feelings on that score."

"Yeah, thanks. But you can never be sure, especially when they have a home-field advantage, as it were."

"Man, you people from Notre Dame are all alike. Always with the football analogies."

"Well, there is the matter of her parents living in the Soviet Zone. And I also don't like the way this is coming together with the case of our dead Austrian friend. It's all happening now that I've been drawn into this case. And then there's the fact that some Austrian bureaucrat or whatever he is brought the case of Sabine and her family up from the very start."

"Yeah, I remember you mentioning that early on. What are your thoughts?" Delgreccio paused to study the city outside his window. "I mean, it is pretty odd and awfully coincidental."

Baier leaned back and nodded. "I'll say. It's got me wondering just who this guy is and the role he might be playing in this entire affair."

"We don't even have a clear sense of what this 'whole affair,' as you call it, really is yet."

"Absolutely," Baier said. "But to me it suggests that there is something at work here, and that this Austrian has a part in it."

"You haven't been able to run any more down on this early morning visitor of yours, I take it."

"Nope," Baier shook his head, "not yet, but I certainly mean to try."

"Well, buddy, I hate to say this, but it may actually have gotten worse," Delgreccio said.

"How so?" Baier could feel his fists clench. He had also started to sweat under his arms. Delgreccio must have noticed his heightened tension, because he shot a quick glance at Baier's hands then leaned back to give the two of them more space and distance.

"I can't be sure, and I'll ask our guys in Berlin to check, but this 'Mishka' name sounds kind of familiar. And not in a good way."

"What do you mean 'familiar'?" Baier was almost standing. He leaned so far forward he had risen from his seat.

"Familiar in that we've heard the reference before. Someone with that moniker has been involved in a couple of exfiltration cases in the past."

"You mean kidnappings?"

Delgreccio nodded. "Yeah, not to put too fine a point on it."

He paused and stood. "Karl, I think it's time for you to go get your wife and bring her home. And drag the parents along if you have to. If they don't want to come, then you may have to leave 'em there. But give it a good, hard try, okay?" He paused again to give the words time to settle in with his deputy. "These guys are not the kind you fuck around with. We should be ready to move before anything really bad happens up there."

Baier stood up straight and turned for the door. "I'll call her today and tell her I'm on my way." Before leaving, however, Baier turned back to Delgreccio. "One other thing, Ralph. When I was visiting the von Rudenstein estate, I came across a Soviet work detail at the border."

"So? We know they're working to finish things up before the Treaty is signed. They know they'll need to wall off the entire area to keep all those happy proletarians at home."

"But that's just it," Baier said. "They don't appear to be going anywhere fast with it all. It didn't look to me like they'll be done anywhere near the signing date."

"You think they have plans to stay? That maybe they're mixed up in this murder even?"

Baier shrugged. "Hard to say at this point, but it's worth keeping in mind."

In spite of the new uncertainty about Soviet intentions, his chief was right about one thing, Baier thought as he marched into the hallway. Given his and Sabine's joint history in Berlin and their past associations with the 'other side,' it was best not to fuck around. She was certainly experienced, and her time in Berlin and during the war had clearly toughened her. All the same, she was vulnerable on their turf, and he doubted that the new crowd that had shown up—who the hell was this Mishka character, anyway?—would be as easy to manipulate as the jubilant Red Army officers who had rolled into Berlin in the wake of their triumph over the Nazis.

Fortunately, the sunny weather held later in the day. It seemed a bit cool for the end of April, but at least it wasn't raining. Regarding the Central European weather, Baier had learned to count his blessings, regardless of how small. He was sitting on one of the concrete benches in the Belvedere Park that was off to the side of a circular fountain surrounded by manicured shrubbery about waist high. The site provided perfect cover for Baier to look out on the Rennweg and await the approach of his British colleague, whose embassy was located on the other side of the major thoroughfare and around the corner from Juaresgasse. Baier was happy for the blue sky, which was marked only by an occasional cloud of puffy white vapor that barely threw a shadow.

It took fifteen to twenty minutes for his fellow spook Henry Turnbridge to show up at the corner and wander into the Park, a wide smile on his face and his bright blue eyes shining in the late morning sun. In the full light of day, the man was taller and thinner than Baier remembered from their previous meetings, especially the early morning encounter at the banks of the Danube. The other times, he and Turnbridge had been seated at tables, the slab of wood between them. Now Baier had a full night's sleep behind him, but that morning was a jumbled mess in his memory. It was one of the reasons he wanted to touch base with an ally he hoped he could trust. Turnbridge did indeed have the pale skin and peaked nose that had stood out so prominently against the banks of the Danube that morning; Baier remembered that much correctly, at least. Today he was wearing a lightweight blue-plaid suit that seemed to represent an effort to hurry spring along.

"Not that I don't enjoy the chance to pull away from that damn desk, mind you, but why all the mystery of meeting out of doors, Karl?"

Baier stood from his bench, strolled over to Turnbridge, and took his hand. "Thanks for coming, Henry. The weather did actually have something to do with it. You can never take this stuff for granted, as you must know, coming from England and all that." Baier nodded toward the sky.

"All too true." They began to walk along the narrow, graveled pathway that led through the park, away from Turnbridge's embassy office, and toward the city center. "But I suspect you did not call me out here just to enjoy the day's sunshine, pleasant as it is. Just where are we heading?"

Baier shook his head and shrugged. "You suspect right, Henry. We should reach our destination in about fifteen minutes, twenty tops. I was wondering if you'd bothered to follow up at all on our Austrian corpse, over which the locals were so determined to ruin our sleep. Have you learned any more about the man's history or the case itself?"

Turnbridge turned his head in both directions, as though checking for surveillance. "Well, Karl, I do have a name. Heinrich Rudolph von Rudenstein. It seems he was a minor aristocrat from somewhere in the eastern part of the country, Burgenland, I believe." He raised his hands and let them fall. "I'm afraid beyond that, there's not a whole lot I can tell."

"So you haven't done much in the way of research?"

Turnbridge stopped to look at Baier. "Karl, why should I? We have enough on our plate as it is, with the State Treaty thing, which as I'm sure you're aware will require our complete withdrawal from the country. Hasn't that kept you busy?"

"We've got others to take care of that."

"Ah," Turnbridge resumed walking, "lucky you. We're not so well endowed, I'm afraid."

"What about the others, the French and the Soviets, I mean?"

"Well, Karl, I'm afraid you'd have to ask them yourself. They certainly haven't said anything to me. No reason why they should, I suppose."

"Have you spoken to the Austrians, or has anyone tried to contact you from the police? Say, our friend from that early morning social call?"

Turnbridge shook his head. "No. No one. And you?"

Baier smiled. "Well, I have done some research into the man's history during the Third Reich, and I've even visited his ancestral home." Baier glanced out of the corner of his eye at his English colleague. "You're right. It is Burgenland, by the way."

"Brilliant. And what have you learned?"

Baier stopped and pinched Turnbridge's sleeve between his thumb and forefinger to bring the man to a halt as they passed through Schwarzenburgplatz. They paused in the middle of the square in front of the Soviet memorial to the liberation of Vienna. Baier pointed to a statue that stood perhaps twenty feet away, the glorious Red Army soldier atop his enormous column reaching for a sky that always seemed just beyond his grasp. "I sometimes wonder if the locals will allow that monstrosity to remain, given the pain the Soviets caused here during the 'liberation,' as they call it. Especially when you consider all the other monuments in this city that celebrate the Austrians' own history." He pointed off in the distance toward the Burggarten, and beyond that to the Volksgarten. "Not only can you find the expected tributes to the likes of Mozart and Beethoven, but even what we might call the lesser lights like Grillparzer. And right around the corner, we pass by the home of Gustav Mahler. I mean this city is awash in such tributes." Baier paused to consider his observation, as though incomplete. "I have yet to find ones to Brahms or Schubert, though, which is odd, considering that the latter was a native son."

"They must be here somewhere, Karl. Perhaps you haven't looked hard enough."

"Well, it doesn't really matter which of the musical geniuses it is who spent so much of their creative lives in this city. But it does strike me how revitalizing and wonderful it is to think about the gifts that men like these and many others gave to the world, and how this city honors their memories in their central parks and squares."

"What is your point, Karl?"

"My point is that I wonder what it is that brings such great minds to the same environment over a period of time, a pretty long one in this case. Was it the cultural atmosphere, the rich court life, the political turmoil and concentration that comes from being the capital of a great empire? I'm not sure myself. But there was clearly something that brought them here, something more than mere patronage."

Turnbridge furrowed his brow in concentration, as though he had never considered this possibility until today. "I say, Karl, that is interesting. It probably had to do with success building upon success, you know. That happens as well. What has that got to do with anything, much less our Austrian corpse?" He shrugged. "In any case, I'd say it's all well in the past."

Baier raised a finger to make a point. "Ah, but some things stay with us. Perhaps not Vienna as a cultural capital, rich as it has been and as enjoyable as it is to live in today. But take your country, Henry. You've had a rich cultural and political legacy as well. We Americans are certainly familiar with your literature and drama."

"Well, I certainly hope that's not done with."

"Time will tell, Henry. Time will tell." Baier started to pace along the sidewalk and crossed over to Karlsplatz. "But let's walk a little farther and pay a call on the Ministry of Interior. We can take a shortcut through the palace courtyard." He turned to the Englishman. "That is, if you have the time."

Turnbridge indicated the path. "Lead on, Karl. You have my interest now."

Baier and Turnbridge were sitting across from Herr Stefan Huetzing, their acquaintance from two mornings ago, in his narrow windowless office on the third floor of the Interior Ministry building. Huetzing sat stiff and straight in his light-gray suit, and Baier noticed that the Austrian kept his suit jacket on even while sitting at his desk. Maybe he only did that for important visitors. Or maybe the office heating had been turned off weeks ago. It felt that way to Baier at any rate.

Turnbridge appeared to be uninterested in the entire proceeding, letting Baier take the lead as they entered the building, inquired after Huetzing's office and the way there, and marched up the three flights of stairs that did not seem to leave Turnbridge as short of breath. He might be one of those English hikers, or 'hill walkers' as they were known back in Britain. The Englishman's gaze had wandered down every hallway and stairwell they traveled. Was he looking for a friend or simply satisfying his curiosity?

Turnbridge's hands rested on his lap as he sat next to Baier and across from Huetzing.

"Unfortunately, we have not made much progress in our investigation," Huetzing began. "I wish I had more to tell you."

"Can you give us any more on the victim?" Baier asked.

Huetzing coughed into his fist and stared at his desktop for several seconds before looking up at Baier. "The man's name was Heinrich Rudolph von Rudenstein." He glanced over at Turnbridge. "He was a minor aristocrat from the eastern part of Austria and came from a family that had long served the Hapsburg rulers with distinction."

Thanks for the obvious, Baier thought. "How about the time and place of his killing?"

"We met you at what, three o'clock that morning?"

"A little later," Baier replied. "More like four by the time I got there."

Huetzing nodded. "Yes, of course. You were the last to arrive, and your colleague here, Herr Turnbridge, insisted we wait." Turnbridge smiled at that. Baier wasn't sure how good his German was, but Huetzing carried the conversation in pretty passable English, so that was not an issue. "We believe he had been shot to death sometime the night before, possibly around nine or ten o'clock. It was a single shot to the heart from fairly close range. There were scorch marks on the shirt that you may not have seen that morning through the blood and mud."

"So it was an execution of sorts?" Baier asked.

Huetzing nodded. “Yes, that is certainly one possibility. Also that he may have known his killers.”

“But you have no suspects yet?”

“No, none yet.” Huetzing glanced at Turnbridge. “We are still trying to reconstruct his last few days.”

“And what have you found?” Baier asked. Turnbridge sat relaxed in his chair by the door, almost in a slouch. His hands had slid to his pants pockets. Baier hoped he could stay awake.

“We have a record of him returning to Austria from Hungary the day before his death. What he was doing there we do not know, and the Soviet authorities have not been forthcoming. In fact, they have pretty well stonewalled our investigation. At least from that side of our border.”

“What a surprise,” Turnbridge stated. *So he was awake and listening after all*, Baier thought.

“Yes, you might say that,” Huetzing agreed. “But there is not much we can do in that regard. Huetzing held Turnbridge in his sights for a moment longer before turning back to Baier. “He had been out of the country for several weeks. Six to be exact. At least that's what our records show. He had left for Prague in early March. Again, we have no idea as to why he traveled.

“I doubt it had much to do with his wine business,” Baier volunteered.

“You can't be so sure,” Turnbridge broke in. “Maybe he was looking for new markets. Those people would certainly be familiar with Austrian wines.”

Huetzing did not respond. Baier turned to study Turnbridge, who shrugged. “Just making a suggestion—”

“Well, we can rule out robbery as a motive. His wallet and a handful of Austrian Schillings were found in his pockets, undisturbed.” Huetzing shrugged in turn, then stood. “I'm afraid I have nothing more for you gentlemen, and I have another staff meeting to attend now. I will keep both of you informed if anything new comes in.”

Baier and Turnbridge stood. "Just one more question," Baier said. "Have our French or Soviets friends shown any interest in this case?"

Huetzing shook his head and smiled. "No, none at all. I'm not really surprised by that, though."

"And why is that?" Baier said.

"Because the French don't care about one more dead Austrian. They just want to go home and take care of their own problems."

Baier nodded. "Like Algeria. Fair enough. And the Soviets?"

Huetzing chewed his lip for a few seconds, then started to maneuver past his desk and head for the door. "Probably because no one in their command is concerned at the moment. And I hope it stays that way."

Baier leaped up to block Huetzing's departure before the Austrian could reach the door. "Just one more thing, please."

Huetzing frowned as his eyes searched the corridor. "Yes, what is it?"

"Just tell me again why you called us out that morning? There doesn't appear to be much interest in this case. Or progress for that matter."

Huetzing sighed. "I was instructed to do so. I did not think it was advisable or necessary then, and I still do not think it is now."

"By whom?" Baier kept on.

"By our deputy minister."

"Why?"

"He never said." Huetzing began to slide by Baier so he could reach his door. "Now, if you'll excuse me …."

Once outside, Baier turned to his English colleague. "Interesting, wouldn't you say?"

Turnbridge shook his head. "I got very little out of that conversation that I didn't know already. Did you actually learn anything?"

Baier started to stroll back in the direction of Belvedere Park. Turnbridge hurried to come alongside him. "I agree there was little in the way of new facts, although von Rudenstein's travels before his death are intriguing."

"Why is that?"

"Because he was obviously traveling with the concurrence of someone official, one of the occupying powers, maybe the Soviets. Then again, maybe not. It would explain why the Soviets are not pressing for more information here, if the former's the case. Interestingly, I found out that he never did spend any time in a Soviet POW camp after the war. Can you guess why?"

"Not really," Turnbridge answered. "I told you I haven't had the time to look into the matter."

"Well, I'm willing to bet, Henry, that someone in your office is following this affair. Do you recall our discussion a few moments ago about the particular genius of Vienna that seemed to draw so much remarkable musical talent here?"

"Yes, I do. And you were going to tell me if we Britons had any other remarkable talents, as you label them, besides literature and drama." He stopped and returned Baier's gesture of grabbing his sleeve to hold the American up. "Well?"

Baier laughed. "Well, you do have another particular skill. And that's in the work of intelligence. Perhaps it's because you've been at for so long. Although not always successfully, given what happened a few years ago." Turnbridge grimaced. "I mean, your history in that field stretches all the way back to Elizabethan times. And I'm not talking about your current monarch, attractive as she is."

"I see. I thank you for the compliment to our queen, but just what are you getting at?"

"Henry, I'm getting at the point that I keep running across your countrymen's footprints in this case. And your comment back in Huetzing's office confirmed my suspicions."

"And those would be …?"

"Now, I can't say this for certain, but I suspect that you guys have been running von Rudenstein for some time now. And for whatever reason, you do not want to share that information with me, or perhaps any of my colleagues. You guys pulled him out of the Soviets' grasp at the end of the war, and you made sure he did not serve time for any wartime infractions he might have committed. You helped get his vineyard going again, small as that effort may be. I'm guessing it gave him good cover for his travels, wherever those may have led."

Turnbridge bit his lip. His gaze roamed all over the palace courtyard and the Volksgarten, where the Viennese were beginning to stroll in the spring weather once again. In fact, his gaze roamed anywhere but in Baier's direction. When he did finally look at the American, he seemed to be in some pain.

"Look, Karl, I'm not confirming anything here, you understand. But I'll need to take this back to my office. There may well be someone else you'll need to raise this with."

Baier held out his hand. "Thank you, Henry. That's all I can ask." It was Baier's turn to pause. "You must understand, I will continue to dig into this story until I'm satisfied that it will not affect our interests here in any adverse way."

"Yes, of course," Turnbridge responded. He turned to go. "I'll be in touch."

The call came that evening, while Baier was fixing his supper of soup and grilled cheese sandwiches. A bottle of Gruener Veltiner stood open and still full on the table.

"I say, Karl, good news." Turnbridge's voice crackled through the telephone wire like a radio broadcast. "My superiors agree that we should fill you in."

"Excellent. Can we meet tomorrow?"

"Well, er, that's another thing. I guess this should be good news as well. At least it would be for me."

"And that is …?"

"They want to do that filling in up in London. At our headquarters. Can you fly up tomorrow? We've arranged for a debrief the day after, and I've booked you a room at my club. Just to show there's no hard feelings over my holding out on you earlier. It's at the Caledonian Club in Belgravia, not far from Wellington's house, actually."

Laying it on a little thick, Baier thought. "Thank you again, Henry. I appreciate that. No hard feelings at all. I know the place. I've been there for dinner a few times, and as I recall, the kitchen is quite good. But how about if we move the meeting up a day?"

There was a pause. "I suppose we could do that. Any particular reason?"

"Well, yes," Baier said. "I'm in a bit of hurry to move on, and I can always fly in first thing in the morning and then head over to your headquarters the same day."

"No, that shouldn't be a problem. I'll see to it that you have a packet with the information you'll need when you arrive at the club."

"Perfect."

"Good," Turnbridge finished. "It's all set then. Enjoy the trip and be sure to touch base with us when you return."

Baier hung up and cursed his good luck. The trip to London sounded quite useful for the case. But it would delay his traveling to Saxony to pull Sabine and her parents out of East Germany. He would swing through Berlin on the way home, check in with the base there, then get a car to drive south. He did not want to delay any further. Baier had an uneasy feeling that the environment around Sabine had taken a turn for the worse, and any time lost would only increase the risk to his wife.

He also wondered if his shadow would be waiting for him when he returned. Baier had caught a glimpse of the man when he left the Interior Ministry. It was only a glimpse, and a fleeting one at that. But at least Baier knew he was not getting paranoid. Not yet, anyway. He also knew there were clearly others interested in this case.

Chapter Five

BAIER HAD BEEN stationed in London a few years back, and for him it represented excitement and vibrancy, colored as it was with the history of centuries. His plane dropped from the clouds that seemed never to leave this city, and the expanding London airport near the hamlet of Heathrow spread under its wings. Work begun just a year or so before the war was turning this small military aerodrome into a major civilian thoroughfare at a remarkable pace. It was almost as if the Germans were involved in the reconstruction.

Once he had collected his bag, Baier jumped into one of London's iconic black cabs, which sped him toward the city center at a breakneck speed of around fifty miles an hour. Baier watched the green agricultural fields slip by, dotted with spots of fluffy white wool that marked the flocks of sheep so ubiquitous in this country. From the backseat of his cab, he could see the skyline of London, and Baier wondered how much longer these open fields and the village lifestyle that went with them would survive. If this London airport out by Heathrow really did become an important traffic hub, he could see little hope for the bucolic setting. This city and Great

Britain had shrunk some in global importance since 1945, but the country remained a financial magnet, an industrial powerhouse, and a major commercial and military power, not to mention a beacon for those who inhabited the far reaches of its crumbling empire. The idea and institutions of the Commonwealth taking its place would probably allow them to keep coming, too. If Baier had to bet, he'd take just about any odds that London would remain the worldly metropolis it had been for centuries.

As these thoughts crossed Baier's mind, the cab was passing Buckingham palace and gliding along St. James Park on its way to the Caledonian Club. Apsley House, Wellington's home after he retired from the battlefield—a gift from a grateful nation—loomed off to the right. It was almost blocked from view by the monolithic Wellington Arch, a tribute to the man's success in defending the Empire. Both seemed to be standing guard over the corner of Hyde Park just behind them, not to mention Buckingham Palace, the occasional residence of the royal family. Baier smiled when he saw the bars protecting Wellington's street-level windows. They had been installed after the participants retaliated by tossing rocks through his windows in a protest march supporting the Reform Act of 1832, designed to enlarge Britain's then-miniscule electorate. Wellington had opposed it as far too revolutionary. So much for their gratitude to the hero of the Empire. Baier concluded that the great general had been a lot less astute and a lot less popular in political affairs than military ones. That seemed typical of generals who moved into politics, although Baier was glad to admit that Eisenhower appeared to be avoiding that problem.

The cabbie pulled up in front of the two-story red-brick building that housed the Caledonian Club. Baier paid him and trotted inside with his bag. At the main desk, he checked into his room, picked up his packet of instructions, and climbed the stairs past the bust of Robbie Burns to his room on the second floor. When he passed the door to the bar on the first floor opposite the reading room and just down the hall from the library, Baier remembered daring his host from MI6 to help him work his way through each of the 160-odd brands of Scotch Whiskey reputedly available at the bar. His host had demurred, but it was still a worthwhile goal. Tonight he hoped to sample a few, or at least one.

Once in his room, Baier dropped his suitcase on the bed and reached for the telephone directory. If things worked out as he hoped, he would be able to reach that particular goal at the bar and pursue some of the business behind this damn Austrian corpse at the same time. Nothing like the proverbial two birds with one stone, especially when one involved the pleasure of imbibing that fine national drink from the north. The telephone at the other end of the line rang, and a female voice with a slight Middle European accent answered. *Hooray*, he thought, *von Rudenstein's daughter is at home.* Someone who might be able to tell him more about the enigmatic Austrian aristocrat. She sounded agreeable, so he made an appointment for later that evening

It was a rare, beautiful day of sunshine in London, and Baier decided to take advantage by walking the mile or so to MI6 headquarters in St. James Square. It should be a pleasant stroll, and he certainly had the time. It was just past one o'clock, and his appointment was not until three. He might even have time to poke about in one of the haberdashery shops or tobacconists along the warren of urban pathways that surrounded the square between Piccadilly Street and Pall Mall.

The stroll through the park and past Buckingham Palace was pleasant enough. The day's temperatures could not have been beyond the low to mid 60s, and the park itself was not too crowded. With Easter already in the past, the number of vacationers and tourists remained reasonably low. The country also appeared to be getting back to work, having recovered in large part from the effort it took to win the war and overcome the systems of limitations and rationing it imposed. Sort of. There were still rations in place. It had been a costly war for the United Kingdom. But at least the Labour Government had made a point of giving everyone a stake in the country's recovery with its social programs and the National Health Service.

A little short of midway through Green Park, just as he was coming up on Buckingham Palace, Baier had the distinct feeling he was being followed. *Again, damn it.* This time, however, there was a difference. For one thing, whoever was following him was a lot less competent. Or perhaps they just didn't care as much. He couldn't be sure, and he had too much respect for his British counterparts to assume they would lay on such a transparent surveillance exercise if MI6 or whoever were really serious. He had learned to trust his instincts on certain operational matters, and by the time he approached St. James Palace, the low-slung red brick and granite assembly that backed onto the park of the same name, Baier was certain of at least one tail and possibly two, thanks to his stopping to enjoy the gamboling of one magpie, and then about fifty yards later, a second. Forget the pigeons; no one would bother to admire them unless it was one of those huge, white-throated wood pigeons that seemed almost large enough to carry off a small child. The colorful magpie with its black and white coat and bluish markings was another story. He confirmed the second tail when he entered the Dunhill tobacco shop kitty corner from St. James Palace. He quickly exited it and marched along King Street to St. James Square. Baier was tempted to stop in the Red Lion Pub for a quick pint to see how his own magpies reacted but decided he'd had enough counter-surveillance fun for one afternoon.

About a minute later, he swung right around the corner from King Street into St. James Square itself, skipped up the steps, and entered the MI6 headquarters. Turnbridge had been as good as his word, as the guard at the reception desk had Baier's name listed in his large green folder of expected visitors. "Just take those stairs to the right, sir, up to the second floor. Then go straight until you find his office door midway along the corridor. Cheerio."

Having found the door and the name plate, Baier knocked. After hearing a nasal, "Yes?" he strolled through the door and approached the large, brown-oak desk. Sir Robert Siscourt, chief of MI6's Europe Division, greeted Baier halfway to the door, then circled back behind his desk, took a seat, and motioned for Baier to do the same. Baier sat in one of the brown leather chairs facing his desk. He knew his host was a 'sir' because the man had been sure to pronounce it during the introductions. Baier couldn't help but smile. Then again, maybe this one had earned it and not been born with the title. During the war, even. If so, then he had gone to seed since. When Baier contemplated the man, he thought of circles. Sir Robert was round and plump, with a balding head and a bulb for a nose on a face set just above growing cheeks and a growing neck.

No problem with rationing here, apparently. He filled out the deep-blue pin-striped suit quite admirably. In fact, he looked about ready for a new and larger one.

"So, what is it you want me to know about your relationship with Herr von Rudenstein?" Baier asked. "And just how much of that are you willing to tell?"

"Ah, yes. Truly sorry about the muddle in Vienna. We should have let you in on our secret with the late Herr von Rudenstein from the start. It would have saved you unnecessary research."

The office had a regal atmosphere of burgundy wallpaper, well-stocked bookshelves, and high ceilings. Baier took in the large portraits of dead British aristocrats on the walls with name plates too small to read from his seat. He wondered if they were past occupants of the office or relatives of Siscourt. Perhaps both. Two large rectangular windows looked out over the rooftops and an alleyway—'mews' they called them here—onto Pall Mall. The windows framed a modest portrait of Churchill. The wartime prime minister might not have worked in intelligence, but he certainly appreciated the services it could provide. Like most Brits.

"Oh, that's all right," Baier responded. "I like doing research. I may have been trained at university as a chemist, but I've always loved history." He smiled. "Besides, I got a nice case of wine out of it."

"Indeed. Then I envy you."

"So just what was this relationship you had with our late Austrian friend?"

Siscourt heaved a sigh as he studied his American guest. "It was a relationship that began during the war." Siscourt leaned back and waved a hand. "Oh, it was nothing much at first. Just some occasional material on the popular mood in Austria. The sort of thing a diplomat would normally acquire. That is, if you have diplomats in that particular country. But there was little in the way of the leadership's views and intentions, and certainly nothing in the way of military secrets."

"I take it Herr von Rudenstein did not have the access for the former, and probably not much for the latter either. Not strategically, in any case. His role would have been rather limited."

Siscourt said nothing. He just stared at Baier, then averted his eyes.

"But that changed?" Baier prompted.

Siscourt leaned forward, nodding vigorously. "As a matter of fact, yes. After the failed attempt on Hitler's life in July of '44, he seemed to have made a conscious decision to be more forthcoming. Still very little in the way of actionable military information, though. I guess he was too old-school for that sort of thing."

"And probably concerned for the welfare of the men under

his command." Baier crossed his legs and shifted his weight. "So what did he provide that was so valuable?"

"He gave us some valuable information on the Nazis' dealings with local officials in Austria and some of the occupied territories in the east, as well as the latter's interactions with the Red Army and Soviet authorities as the front collapsed. All of it turned out to be quite accurate."

"Such as ...?"

Siscourt gazed toward the ceiling as though the information he sought might be written there. "Well, for one thing, he let us know of Karl Renner's early discussions with the Soviets about a postwar government in Austria. This sort of heads-up was invaluable, as I'm sure you can appreciate. He also assisted us with information on Soviet discussions with the Hungarians and the plans for a communist seizure of power there after the German evacuation of Budapest."

"Which no one here seems to have taken seriously."

Siscourt frowned. "I'm afraid that's true. We encountered some difficulty in getting that message through to the prime minister. As you are no doubt aware, Mr. Baier, we can only provide the information, not ensure that it is accepted." Siscourt's eyes lit upon Churchill's portrait.

"So how did von Rudenstein come to be so well informed?"

"Ah, there's the rub, my American friend. Try as we might, he never let on how he came by his information. It was one of the reasons his reporting was questioned by the higher-ups." More eye movement skyward. "There was even talk of 'fabrication' at one point." He held up his hand. "We were able to scotch that effectively, however, by pointing to the results."

"You said 'one' of the reasons."

"Well, the principal one. Another was his stellar war record and refusal to come out to safety in the West whenever we asked." Siscourt sighed. "That, of course, limited our opportunities for debriefing."

"I see. And what happened after the war?" Baier said. "It seems you Brits were pretty generous with your gratitude."

"Yes, of course. There were those of us who were very grateful and made sure Herr von Rudenstein received what he deserved to restart his old life."

"As a wine producer?"

Siscourt nodded again. "Yes, of course. Have you tried any of his?"

"Not yet. But that's the case I mentioned earlier. I am looking forward to it." Baier paused to study the room once more. "Tell me, though, did it end with the war? The relationship, I mean. Did you value him as an asset?"

Siscourt glanced out the window before letting his gaze bounce off Baier and settle on one of the aristocrats from the eighteenth century. Siscourt frowned as he said, "Not really, at least not afterward. He no longer had access to the sort of material we needed, not once his military career and the war ended."

"But there was the wine business. Certainly a convenient cover for travel, if one was needed."

"Oh, we considered that. It's the reason we helped him on that front initially. Or one of them," Siscourt added when Baier leaned forward to object. "But I'm afraid nothing developed along that line."

"I see. Then why do you think he was shot? There's nothing here that sounds like a cause or motive for murder."

Siscourt shrugged and looked directly at Baier. "I doubt there was anything in that. I suppose an unreconstructed Nazi might have discovered something of his past life. There are an awful lot of them running around Austria these days, you know."

"Yes, but I find it hard to imagine that they would jeopardize their standing in Austria today, especially on the eve of the end of the occupation, to engage in something like this."

"Yes, you're probably right," Siscourt nodded. "Have you

thought of the Austrians themselves? The official Austrians, I mean." Baier frowned. "No, probably not," Siscourt conceded. "In that case, I'd look at the Soviets. Those sods are always pulling off something like this."

"That's probably as good a place as any to start. It certainly makes sense in view of their behavior since 1945," Baier admitted. A stab of pain in his chest reminded him of the recent harassment of Sabine.

"And a good deal before then as well," Sir Robert added.

"True enough. Is there anything else that might help?"

Sir Robert shrugged and rose from his chair. "Not really. You have the general outline. And I'm sure you can appreciate that given the history, it was a sensitive case. Not even everyone in Vienna is in the know. That's why we wanted to fill you in back here."

Baier stood and reached across the desk to shake his hand. "Well, thank you very much for your time, Sir Robert, and for sharing this information."

Siscourt took Baier's hand in a tighter grip than he would have expected. "My pleasure. After all, we do have an increasingly close working relationship with you Yanks these days." He sighed again while glancing at the portraits. "And it certainly doesn't hurt to be more forthcoming after our set-to over this Maclean-Burgess mess."

"Let's not forget Mr. Philby," Baier added.

Siscourt made a show of studying the papers on his desk. There were only two or three from what Baier could see. "Yes, well, hopefully we'll get that sorted out."

Baier smiled. "Yes, let's hope so." He pivoted toward the door but stopped midway, turning back toward Siscourt. "Oh, by the way, just why did you have me followed here?"

Siscourt seemed taken aback, truly surprised as he shot up from the thin pile on his desk with a wide-eyed puzzled look and uncomfortable stance. "Followed? Why in heavens do you suspect that? And of us? We knew you were coming here, eventually. Other than that, this is an open city to you. In fact, to all you Americans."

"Well, I was definitely tailed. By a team of two, as best I could tell."

Siscourt's hands fell to his hips. "I can assure you, Mr. Baier, we were not involved. If you truly were 'tailed,' as you put it, then it must have been someone else. And if so, that should give us both reason for concern." He motioned with his head toward the window. "Perhaps you should look to our Soviet friends there as well. Lord knows there are enough of that sort here as well these days."

Baier nodded and let his smile widen. "Perhaps you're right there as well." He gave an offhand wave. "Thanks again. I really do appreciate your assistance."

As he climbed down the stairs to the ground floor, Baier wondered if Sir Robert Siscourt had dabbled in drama or amateur theatrics when he had studied at Oxbridge, or wherever the hell he went to school. There had definitely been some play-acting going on in that office, and there were clearly subjects this Siscourt fellow wanted to avoid going into too deeply. Baier suspected that the relationship between his British friends and von Rudenstein had not ended with the war. There were just too many anomalies back in Vienna for that.

MRS. HANNELORE SCHAEFER, née von Rudenstein, stood uncertainly in the doorway that led from the Caledonian Club's reception area and cloakroom just inside the front door to the main hallway, and from there to the bar. To her left, a grand staircase rose and circled to the second-floor dining rooms and lodgings. Baier approached, and as soon as he saw this thin woman clutching her small black purse in both hands at her front, he realized he had been mistaken in inviting her to the club. Membership was restricted to men, as with so many other clubs in London. After suffering through four early-adult years of semi-celibacy—no, almost total celibacy—at Notre Dame, he had no idea why anyone would want to perpetuate a similar environment. Hannelore Schaefer was trying to look proud, defiant even, but the occasional cracks in her smile and the shifting of eyes betrayed her discomfort. Too bad, because she was an attractive woman—tall, with dark-reddish hair that fell to her shoulders. She could probably hold her own with any of the crusty denizens of this club.

"Mrs. Schaefer, thank you so much for coming. Is your husband here?" Baier asked.

She stepped forward and stretched out her hand, which Baier gratefully accepted with a light shake.

"Thank you, Herr Baier. This is very nice of you. My husband is up north in York at present. But I wanted to come anyway, as you said you had some word of my father's passing."

Baier led her with a light touch on the elbow down the corridor toward the bar and to the right down a short hallway to the drawing room—the one place women were allowed.

"I apologize for the limited opportunities here. The bar, as I'm sure you're aware, does not allow women. But I think we will actually be more comfortable in here." They stood together in front of a large sofa with a floral design set against a yellow background. That and the light-blue walls made it a cheery enough meeting spot. He gestured for Mrs. Schaefer to sit. They dropped into their seats at opposite ends of the sofa.

"Would you like something to drink?" Baier asked. "I can order a tea or coffee. Or perhaps a whiskey, if you'd like something stronger."

She shook her head, studying the landscapes of Scottish pastoral scenes on the wall to either side of the fireplace. "No, but thank you. I'll be fine."

"So I gather you've spoken with the Austrian authorities."

"No," she replied, "but I have spoken with my brother."

"Well, I'm afraid I have little more to tell you about your father's death than what you already know," Baier said.

"That isn't much," Hannelore said. She set her purse to her side on the cushion and smoothed her dress over her knees.

Baier nodded. "That's almost certainly because the authorities know so little. At least that's the impression they have given me."

"What have they given you?"

"Only that his shooting was not the result of a robbery." He paused. "I'm sorry if this is difficult for you."

She shook her head again. "No, please go on. We saw and experienced some very difficult things during the war."

"Of course. Well, it seems he was shot some time before, perhaps a day or so, and then transported to the banks of the Danube near the city center. He was also wearing a Wehrmacht jacket."

"What? An old Army jacket?"

"Yes, apparently so. It certainly looked like one to me. Any idea why?"

Hannelore Schaefer bit her lower lip, her gaze firmly fixed on the floor. She lifted her white-gloved hands, which had been resting primly in her lap, and pulled off one of her gloves then the other, finger by finger. Then she looked up at Baier. "Perhaps it was a message."

"A message? From whom? Perhaps more importantly, to whom?"

She shrugged and glanced away, her hands twisting the gloves as if to squeeze all the air out of them. "Oh, I can't be sure. It's been so long. But my father was proud of his military service. His record was impressive, you know."

"Yes," Baier said, "I've seen the documents. But from what I understand, he was not a firm Nazi, or even all that committed to the Third Reich."

Mrs. Schaefer's hands flew into the air before returning to her lap. The gloves swung like small, crumpled flags. "*Ach*, no. He was not a Nazi. But he did believe in the importance of a German role in Europe."

"In the form of a Nazi hegemony?"

Hannelore Schaefer waved the thought away with a free hand. She looked impatient and frustrated. "No, of course not. I said he was no Nazi. He was much more devoted to the old empire and our Kaiser. Not the German one, but our Hapsburg one. I believe you called the state the Dual Monarchy of Austria-Hungary."

"Okay, but then why the Wehrmacht jacket?"

She leaned in. "What sort of message do you think an Austrian *Lederjacke* or a pair of *Lederhosen* would send, eh?"

"Can you give me a hint of what might be behind the jacket then? Or could it have simply been something he found and put on because he had nothing else against the cold?"

She leaned back against the arm of the sofa. "My father was not poor. He would not have been that desperate."

"Did you know he worked for the British during the war?"

Hannelore Schaefer nodded vigorously. "Yes, of course. My father told my brother and me about it after the war. It would have been too dangerous for all of us if we had known while the Nazis were still in power."

"Did he tell you what he did, exactly?"

"No. He never went into that kind of detail." She glanced away again and appeared to be studying a painting of a fox hunt on the opposite wall, apparently set in the English—not the Scottish—countryside. "It wasn't necessary," she looked back at Baier, "for us to know those details."

"And after the war? He no longer worked for the British. Did he resent being shunted aside?"

Hannelore Schaefer's eyes narrowed. "What are you talking about?" She regarded Baier with disdain, as if he were a misinformed child or simply naive. "He never stopped working for the British."

Baier suppressed a smile. He had been right about Siscourt holding out. "How do you know? That he kept working for the Brits, I mean."

"Because they kept coming by the house. And whenever they did, my brother and I were not allowed in the sitting room. The men claimed they needed their privacy. We were taught to respect that."

Baier leaned in close. "Who were 'they,' exactly?"

"My father and his British friend."

"Always the same man?"

She nodded, leaning back again. "Yes. Usually just the one. Most of the time anyway."

"You wouldn't have a name, would you?"

The look of exasperation returned. Hannelore Schaefer pulled a pen and a slip of paper from her purse. "Of course. He came too frequently for us not to learn the name of my father's special friend from London."

She wrote something on the piece of paper and handed it to Baier. He held it at an arm's length and studied the name. Professor Jonathon Hardwicke.

"He's retired now. He teaches history at St. Andrew's University in Scotland."

"Do you still see him?"

"Occasionally. Whenever he's in London. He helped bring me over here and assisted with the paperwork for my residence visa. I'm a British citizen now," she announced, straightening her back.

"I see. Did you meet your husband here then?"

"No, we met in Vienna. We became close very quickly, but we had to wait for his divorce before we could marry. That's why I needed Professor Hardwicke's assistance. I believe he was able to pull some strings, as they say."

Baier read the name again. "Do you suppose he'd be willing to speak with me about your father and their work together?"

The hands fluttered once more, and her eyes focused in on Baier. "That you have to discover for yourself."

"And for how long after the war did this man keep coming? Until 1948, when your father moved away from the estate?"

"Yes, certainly until then. But even later, when we moved to Vienna after my mother's death."

"I see. Just to make sure I'm not missing anything obvious here," Baier continued, "can you think of any reason why someone might want to harm your father? Any family disputes or problems with neighbors? Anything else from the past?"

The look of parental concern and pity returned, and Hannelore Schaefer sighed again. "Herr Baier, you must realize what we all went through during the war. There is little of a past left for any of us anymore. We all lost so many friends and family. It's hard to carry past resentments into the present after something like that. We all had to start over, or nearly so."

"Yes, of course. I'm sorry." But someone, and not just her father, had carried something into the present.

They rose from the couch, and Baier asked Hannelore Schaefer if he might treat her to dinner.

"No thank you," she said. "My husband is returning later this evening, and I'll want to be home when he gets there."

"I understand. I can't thank you enough, Mrs. Schaefer, for your help."

Baier accompanied his guest back toward the front entrance, pointing out the various Scottish-themed souvenirs and curiosities in the hallway, including the stuffed ram's head. Eventually, they stood by the cloakroom, and Baier helped his guest into her coat. "Thank you for trying to help in the investigation into my father's death," she said. "I truly wish you luck. But may I ask you one question?"

"Yes, of course. What is it?"

Mrs. Schaefer drew herself up to her full height. He guessed he had no more than three or four inches on her. "Why are the Americans interested in my father's death? Just what is your role in this? Did he have something to do with the American Embassy?"

"That's an excellent question, Mrs. Schaefer, even if it is more than one." He studied her face while he tried to think of an appropriate answer, one that would make sense to himself as well as her. “It seems I’ve just sort of stumbled onto it. It was the Austrians who first brought me in.”

“And why is that?”

He wanted to tell her he wasn’t quite sure. There was no way, though, that he was going to admit anything like that. “They’re just trying to close all avenues to make sure there won’t be new diplomatic complications before the State Treaty is signed and the occupation ends.”

“And they think my father’s death could do all that? Perhaps that’s where the real mystery lies, Herr Baier.” She smiled and held out her hand. “Goodbye.”

Baier took both her hands and gave them a light squeeze. As he watched her walk out the door and down the few steps to Halkin Street, Baier wondered how much more difficult it would be to penetrate the haze surrounding the death of Heinrich Rudolph von Rudenstein. His daughter had a point. Just why was there so much mystery surrounding this Austrian, and why were so many people holding back about his past?

Chapter Six

THE LANDSCAPE OF northern England was much as Baier remembered it. He and Sabine had traveled north several times during his tour in London, once to visit the wonderfully preserved town of York with its magnificent cathedral—or 'minster' as they called it here—and once to tour the Scottish Highlands, that majestic outlay of mountains and lakes, valleys, and heather. On the train, the fields of England swept past his window, occasionally broken by the industrial magnets of the north, Newcastle in particular. But it was the green fields dotted in the white wool of the country's sheep farms that he remembered best. Outside his window, Baier gazed upon the yellow swaths of sunflowers and mustard seed, like ponds of gold set against rolling hills of green velvet. And Berwick still seemed to be perched on the rocky crags that lined the coast of northeastern England, as though retreating to escape the predations it had suffered over and over during the border wars between the Scots and the English throughout the Middle Ages.

At Edinburgh, Baier's train pulled into Waverly Station, where he had an hour's wait for his next train to St. Andrews.

That was one tour he and Sabine had missed during their time in the United Kingdom, so this was a box he could finally check off. It hurt to do so now, with Sabine under surveillance and harassment from the damn Soviets and their East German puppets. Baier shook his head and blew out a breath of frustration and anxiety as he surveyed the great stone fortress that sat above the town on its huge hilltop foundation of rock and stone, surveying the city and all its history. As the train pulled out, he glimpsed the more modern castle of Hollywood that sat at the foot of the hill. It was the end of the Royal Mile, whose most famous—and unlucky—tenant had been Mary, Queen of Scots. He felt another pang of anxiety at the thought of the imprisoned queen and resolved to get to East Germany as quickly as possible—as soon as this interview was over.

When he arrived in St. Andrews, Baier strolled through the town, looking for a phone booth to make contact with Hardwicke. He had tried to call the number Hannelore Schaefer had provided while still in London. There had been no answer then, and there was no answer now. The walk had not been a waste, however. Baier loved history, and this town was full of it. He purposely marched out of his way to stroll through the ruins of what had once been a massive cathedral overlooking the rocky cliffs that fell from the edge of town to the sea below. After the abortive phone call, Baier wandered through the campus grounds of the university. They had to be well over five hundred years old.

Work and the mystery of von Rudenstein's death called, however, and Baier rode a cab to the address on the outskirts of town he had gotten from Hannelore Schaefer when he called after their meeting the night before. He meant only to check to see if she was all right; Baier assumed the conversation must have been a trying one for her. But she had apologized for not passing the information along the same evening at the Caledonian Club.

"That's okay. I can always look it up," Baier reassured her.

"No, there's no need for that. This will make it easier for you. I know you're trying to help."

"Do you think Professor Hardwicke will object to my sudden appearance? I haven't been able to get through on the telephone."

"I certainly hope not. He's a secretive man, but that should be understandable, given his past."

"Well, I'll try to reassure him on that point."

"I'm sure everything will be fine."

The cabbie dropped Baier off in front of a deep-gray stone cottage with a roof of slate tiles the color of night. It sat at the end of a row of similar, but not identical, houses. Each one either backed up against the coast or sat opposite on the other side of the village lane with a magnificent view of the North Sea. That water looked dark and cold to Baier, only a little more so than the cottage he approached.

Baier knocked on a wooden plank door, but there was no answer. Classes, perhaps, as the spring term was probably still underway. Baier cursed himself for not trying harder to call ahead, but he had been in such a rush to get this over with so he could leave for Germany. He was surprised that Hardwicke even had a telephone. Several houses had wires leading directly to their roofs, but Hardwicke's did not. Maybe the number Hannelore Schaefer had given him had been an office phone.

Baier knocked again, calling out the man's name and title. Silence. He tried the handle, which to his surprise, turned in his hand. The door creaked open a foot. Undoubtedly a low-crime area.

He stepped inside. "Professor Hardwicke? I'm here from the American Embassy." Still nothing. "My name is Karl Baier." He could hear the ocean waves roll in and break against the rocky shoreline below.

"I actually live in Vienna. I received your name from Hannelore Schaefer. She thought you wouldn't mind if I paid a call to talk about an old friend and colleague."

He saw a tea kettle on the stove. There was always a tea kettle on the stove in this country. Baier could not understand what these people saw in such a drink, which to his palate was watery and thin. Thank God he was an American who grew up with coffee. This kettle was also cold. There were two cups on the table, each about a quarter full of cold tea. A pot half full of the stuff sat on the table between them. There were no other dishes or food out. In fact, this kitchen appeared to Baier to be remarkably clean. Hardwicke was obviously a fastidious retiree.

He crossed the kitchen to a short hallway connected to several more rooms. The first one Baier entered was a bedroom. Probably the master. It was clearly still occupied. And now Baier understood why no one had responded to his knock or challenged his entry. He also understood why those last few dirty dishes were unwashed. And would remain so for a long time, maybe forever. Someone, presumably Professor Jonathan Hardwicke, lay stretched out on the bed, his head resting on a rust-stained pillow. Baier was pretty sure the stains were Hardwicke's blood; the back half of his skull and brain were scattered across the wall behind the bed. He or someone else had stuck a revolver in his mouth and pulled the trigger.

The pistol lay on the floor to the side of the bed by the outside wall. Baier bent down to study the weapon. Not a revolver but a Beretta semi-automatic, he was pretty sure. He was definitely not going to touch the damn thing. His being here was going to cause enough trouble as it was.

Now he wished he really had checked in first thing with London Station when he had arrived in this country. They knew he was coming up, of course. He had sent the requisite cable to keep them informed. And he hadn't planned to stay long. Just a few quick conversations, then off to Berlin.

Now this. He hadn't even imagined a trip outside London, much less to Scotland. He wondered how long this side trip might hold him up. "Shit, shit, shit …" Baier muttered as he stood and headed for the door. When he walked into the street, he turned and headed for the nearest cottage with a telephone wire attached to its roof. "I just hope the poor bastard has a phone," he grumbled. Baier was also sorry that he was about to ruin the stranger's day. Then again, the neighbor's day couldn't get any worse than Hardwicke's.

"Tell me again why you're here."

Baier studied the MI6 officer who now stood between himself and the Hardwicke house. The officer appeared to be in his mid-to-late 40s. If Baier had thought of Sir Robert Siscourt as circular, his compatriot raised images of angles—long ones. The man was tall and thin, but not bony, at least as far as Baier could tell from the overcoat that hung on his figure like a drape. He also had a full head of brown hair with a few patches of gray at the front and along the ears. They both stood in the walkway to the front of the cottage as plainclothes detectives hurried past and entered the front door. Two uniformed officers mounted an almost impressive guard on either side of the entrance.

The investigation had been underway for the last two hours, and Baier was already on his third cup of coffee of the afternoon. He'd had one at the neighbors' after he had notified the police on the man's phone, another when the investigation had begun, and a third while he waited for the MI6 liaison officer to arrive. At least no one had forced any tea on him, and the local police had stopped looking at him as though he were a magician or a recent arrival from outer space.

"They didn't explain it when London rang you? Did you speak with Siscourt?"

The MI6 man shook his head, which was bare of any hat. The wind ruffled his hair like an old rag. When the flap of his Burberry raincoat flew open in the breeze, Baier could see a plaid lining that wrapped around a slightly overweight body. Baier wondered if it was all the haggis or just the Scottish beef and lamb and black sausages for breakfast. "Not really. And, no, I did not get a call from Sir Robert. Few do."

Baier sighed as his eyes scanned the sea a short distance away. Another stiff wind blew whitecaps in the bay like patches of snow on a hillside. It felt almost cold enough. "I'm investigating the murder of an Austrian, a former Wehrmacht officer. The late professor here was an old business associate."

"In what way?"

"Don't you guys share anything? Professor Hardwicke was his handler. I'm not sure for how long, but you guys ran the Austrian during the war and afterward."

"How late afterward?" The MI6 man studied Baier. "I mean, how much do you know?"

"I was hoping to find that answer myself. I should be the one asking you the second question. Your Sir Robert Siscourt was not very forthcoming when we spoke in London. In fact, I'd say he lied to me."

"Why would he do that?"

"Well, that's for your organization to explain. I thought we were friends and allies."

"How do you know he lied?"

Baier smiled and shook his head. "No, no. You boys are the ones who have been holding back, despite our alleged friendship and close cooperation against a common enemy. You need to go first on this one."

"How do we know you didn't kill Professor Hardwicke?"

Baier stared at the MI6 officer. He wasn't sure if he should scream or laugh. He did not bother to hide his frown. "What did you say your name was?"

"Harrison. Thomas. But what's that got to do with anything?"

"In case I need to report this conversation to my superiors. And yours."

"On what grounds?"

"How about stupidity, for openers?"

It was Harrison's turn to stare. The Brit certainly looked angry.

"That's uncalled for, Mr. Baier. You know full well that I or someone else would have to ask that question. You and I can have that conversation, or we can have it with my compatriots inside." Harrison's head jerked in the direction of the house. Another blast of wind blew strands of long brown and gray hair into the air above him like a fraying halo. There seemed to be a lot of wind here.

"After all, your presence was not coordinated, and as far as we're concerned, remains unexplained," Harrison went on.

Baier nodded. "I suppose you're right. I'm sorry. But it's hardly imaginable that I would come here, make my presence known to one and all, and then do this before notifying the police. Is it?"

"Probably not."

"Probably? Seeing as how I never got the chance to question him, it would have been incredibly counterproductive, not to say plain dumb, to kill the guy. And then, to top it off, I notify the police myself, after which they contact you guys ...."

Harrison glanced back at the house, and then at Baier. "What you're saying makes sense to me, of course. But this is a conversation best conducted in London. I'm really just here to smooth things over with the locals and then bring you back to the capital."

Baier stepped in close, not bothering to hide the urgency of his task or the anxiety he felt. "Look, Harrison, I need to get back to Germany as quickly as possible. My wife may be in danger. In fact, I'm quite sure she is."

"Danger? In what way?"

"She's been visiting her parents in Saxony, and the Soviets and East Germans have begun to harass her. I want to get her out before anything worse happens. There's a history there, you see. I can't dally here in your country." He glanced at his wristwatch. "It's already going on three o'clock."

Harrison nodded. "I see." He considered Baier for a moment. "Let me see if I can square things with the detectives inside, and then we can head for London straight off. That is, if they don't object."

"Where exactly in London?"

"My instructions are to bring you to MI6 headquarters. This must be a sensitive case. It's probably why Sir Robert gave out so little information."

Baier groaned and stepped back. "I do not want to get stuck in your labyrinth. Let's do it at our station."

"I can call ahead to request that, but understand, it's not my decision."

"Yes, of course. And I appreciate any help you can provide." Baier had decided to be as polite and cooperative as necessary at this stage. But given how reserved—to put it diplomatically—the Brits had been thus far, he was damned if he was not going to press to get things back on some kind of home turf.

Harrison started to walk toward the cottage, then stopped and turned. "Do you think your wife's difficulties are related to this death?"

Baier sighed in resignation, looked at the ground, then across the bay before returning his focus to the MI6 officer. "It's hard for me to see how at this stage. But I'm beginning to think it must be."

"Then, may I offer some advice?"

Baier was surprised to feel a smile creep across his face. "Sure. Please do."

Harrison paused to consider his words before he spoke. "This is clearly a sensitive case, as I said earlier. And it's one my side cares about deeply. I can see that much. But it must have deep fractures and challenges as well, some of which appear to be unresolved." He paused again and gave Baier a hard stare before continuing. "I probably shouldn't say this, but as it involves your wife .... Well, trust no one. But then, you probably realize that already. When it does come, the answer will probably hit you unawares."

Baier could not think of what to say in reply. He wondered

why this man should give him a warning that sounded so obvious at first, but more ominous, and frankly, puzzling the more he thought about the source, especially as it was Harrison's side that was being so coy and secretive. Baier watched Harrison walk inside the house to speak to the detectives. As he waited for his return, dozens of cormorants, terns, and gulls swept the air along gray limestone cliffs that lined the shore below. Occasionally a shag or herring gull broke off and took a solitary walk along the top of the cliff. Grassland overran the hills, which seemed to tumble into the ocean and rocks below.

This scenery appeared to represent the retirement of Hardwicke far more than the idyllic environment of medieval academics.

Chapter Seven

"So, have the detectives found out anything else about Professor Hardwicke's death that might lead us somewhere?" Baier asked. The words tumbled out, reflecting Baier's sense of urgency now that he was finally back in Sir Robert Siscourt's presence.

The train ride down from Scotland to London had been agonizingly slow, at least in Baier's mind, and it had been too late to arrange any meeting with Siscourt and Baier's own Station colleagues when they finally arrived after 10:00 p.m. So Baier had spent another night at the Caledonian Club, where they fortunately still had a vacancy. Harrison had offered to put Baier up at his own place in St. John's Wood, but Baier didn't want to impose on this day-old friendship, if one could even call it that.

Now Baier wanted to move things along as quickly as possible to allow him to get first to Berlin and then into East Germany to rescue his wife. He had already lost one day and was determined not to lose another.

"Just where would you like to go?" Sir Robert Siscourt replied.

"I'd like to find the person responsible. I'm guessing Hardwicke's death was not a suicide."

"Interesting. Why that assumption?" Siscourt said.

"Well, there's not much for me to go on yet, but there were two cups of tea on the table, suggesting a visitor."

"Not necessarily related to the man's death."

"True enough," Baier replied. "Is there something else you'd like to tell us about his recent life?"

"Such as ...?" Siscourt raised an eyebrow.

"Such as his mood, his work, whether there was anyone who might like to see him dead."

Baier studied Sir Robert, unsure of how to proceed. The senior British spy had agreed to come to the American Station Chief's office in London, which suggested to Baier that the Brit was prepared to be more forthcoming. Still, he sat there in another pin-striped suit—this one charcoal gray—with a smug look of condescension on his face, as though he saw Grosvenor Square as an unpleasant reminder of Britain's declining role in the world. Brits didn't like being reminded of the role and importance of the American involvement and leadership in the war in Europe, not to mention the commanding lead in the Pacific against Japan. Or maybe he was reading too much into the man's demeanor. Like many Americans, Baier was suspicious of the upper crust who populated so much of British intelligence. At least they were prepared to draw on their best and brightest for this work.

"Like it or not, Sir Robert, we are now enmeshed in this affair. It would be best if we all played fair and open with each other."

"Well put, young, man," Siscourt responded. "Our man in Vienna, I believe you know him, a Mr. Turnbridge—"

"Yeah, sure, Henry."

"Er, yes, Henry. Anyway, he has been authorized to work with you on this matter and to keep you fully informed of our efforts with the late Herr von Rudenstein."

Baier glanced over at the CIA's local Chief of Station, or COS as they were known in Agency parlance. Jack Wainwright was from the same sort of posh, old-school background that Siscourt represented in his own country. Wainwright was from a well-to-do Eastern family with an estate on Long Island and summer home in the Berkshires. He had attended St. Paul's prep school in New England before moving along the well-trodden path of his ancestors to Harvard for undergraduate work, and then Yale Law School. He must have found work in the legal field pretty damn boring if he had left it to try his hand at espionage. Or perhaps it was part of that noblesse oblige that seemed to run through so many wealthy families on both sides of the Atlantic. It wasn't like Wainwright was going to go hungry; he probably had a trust fund that allowed him to maintain the lifestyle to which he was accustomed. And he would certainly benefit from the snobbery and connections that pervaded professional life in Washington. Baier was reminded of this class distinction all the time, considering his own humble background. He wondered how these children of privilege really looked upon a Catholic boy from Chicago who had used his four years at Notre Dame to try to launch himself a little higher on the social ladder of America.

Baier looked back and forth between his British guest and Harrison, the companion who had accompanied him from St. Andrews. He at least appeared to be more relaxed, with a navy-blue sport coat and loose black slacks. Maybe he could be an ally within MI6. He shared Baier's lack of upper-class breeding, having grown up in Manchester and attended Durham University, which was supposed to be one of the elite schools here, although they always had to suffer putdowns from the Oxbridge snobs. At least he did not appear to be a prick, like that pretentious snob Kim Philby, the subject of all sorts of persistent rumors and accusations. And there was not much love lost between Siscourt and Harrison. As he studied Sir Robert's jowls, Baier wondered what the man knew about the Philby mess.

"Of course, you can also work through my colleagues here in London." Baier looked over at Wainwright. "That right, Jack? I'm guessing you'll want to be kept in the loop in any case."

"Yes, absolutely. Thank you, Karl."

Siscourt shifted around to get more comfortably settled on the sofa. "As far as the matter of Professor Hardwicke's death, it would appear to have been the work of a professional or professionals."

"Why do you say that?' Wainwright asked.

Siscourt glanced over at the COS before returning his gaze to Baier, as though he were the real threat here. "Because the police have found so little to go on. Nothing in the way of forensic evidence, such as fingerprints, that sort of thing." He paused. "Including on the tea cups."

"And the weapon?" Baier asked.

"That belonged to Hardwicke," Harrison interjected. He had sat obediently in the chair next to the sofa throughout the conversation, and everyone in the room appeared to be surprised by his contribution. "The Beretta belonged to the good professor, apparently a souvenir he picked up during the war as an SOE operative in Italy and the Balkans."

"So that was his professional background in MI6," Wainwright said. "Interesting. Is that also when he worked with von Rudenstein?"

Hoping they were finally getting somewhere, Baier looked at Harrison, who dodged his questioning gaze by turning his own eyes on Siscourt. Baier's attempt to reach out to his new friend might have been a step too far, but it did alert Baier to a sensitive area, a disagreement or personal conflict between the two men he might want to use later.

"As I explained earlier, we worked with the Austrian primarily on internal German and Austrian affairs. Serving on the Italian front allowed the late Professor Hardwicke to build a positive working relationship with the man, a relationship we were happy to exploit after the war." Siscourt glanced at Baier. "At least in the immediate postwar years."

Baier regarded Siscourt with something close to a glare. The British officer avoided his eyes as he said, "I apologize for withholding that information about the ongoing relationship from you earlier, Mr. Baier. This is new and uncertain territory for us, as I'm sure you understand."

Baier remained silent. Siscourt glanced in the direction of the American COS.

"What else did the good professor work on for MI6 and how long ago did he retire?" Wainwright inquired.

Siscourt and Harrison exchanged glances, and both men seemed to squirm a bit.

"I'm afraid we are not at liberty to broach those subjects at the moment. But Mr. Hardwicke retired from the service three years ago. He suffered several wounds during the war, one of them serious enough to cause a recurring pain in his leg—I forget which—and that led him to seek a more sedentary lifestyle."

"Did he work on other matters?" Wainwright asked.

Siscourt nodded. "Yes, of course. He was fluent in Russian, Turkish, Greek, and Serbo-Croatian, so he spent a good deal of his career in southeastern Europe and parts of the Middle East, areas of longstanding concern to us."

"Interesting," Wainwright said. "I'm surprised our paths didn't cross at some point. I'm an old Middle Eastern hand myself."

Siscourt winced, as though having an American refer to himself as an 'old hand' for nearly any part of the world, especially one so dear to the British Empire, caused him pain.

"Yes, of course. But I gather that was an unfortunate coincidence, or lack of one," Siscourt replied.

"So his death may not have been related to von Rudenstein's passing at all," Baier said. "I mean, if he had been involved in a host of other affairs and topics, this killing could have stemmed from any one of those or several."

Siscourt and Harrison both nodded vigorously. "Yes, of

course," Siscourt replied. "But I can assure you that if we do come across any connection to the von Rudenstein affair, we will let you know."

"Well, that sounds fair enough," Wainwright said. He looked over at Baier, who had been leaning in the same spot against the windowsill next to Wainwright's desk the entire meeting. "Does that work for you, Karl?"

Baier stepped away from the wall and approached the sofa. "Absolutely. I will touch base with Henry Turnbridge as soon as I return to Vienna."

The two MI6 officers stood and shook hands with Baier. Wainwright rose from his chair behind his desk and walked over to the other three men.

"Brilliant," Siscourt announced. "I'm glad we're all working together finally, all of us on the same page in this script, as it were."

As they moved toward the door, Wainwright grabbed Baier's arm to make sure he stayed behind as the two Brits left.

"So what do you think?" Wainwright asked after their guests had departed.

"I still don't trust them. They're too damned coy and cagey about Hardwicke's work. It just doesn't fit with what's been happening on this case."

"Like what?"

"Like the indications that von Rudenstein and the British enjoyed a longstanding and fruitful relationship, one that was mutually beneficial."

"What would the Austrian have gotten out of this, aside from help with his vineyard?"

"That's what I'll need to find out when I get back to Vienna. Right now, the guy's a bigger enigma than Hardwicke and the rest of these British friends of ours."

"Don't be too hard on them, Karl. They're struggling to adjust to their new reduced global role, especially in places like the Middle East."

"Which they've made a royal mess of."

Wainwright nodded and smiled. "A mess that is far from resolved. There's all kind of turmoil in this government in London over what to do about Nasser. I just hope they don't think they can engage in the same sort of gunboat nonsense that won them the Empire in the first place."

"Well, I'm going to let guys who love that part of the world like you and Delgreccio worry about that. We're sitting on a fault line of the new Cold War with the Soviet Union in Vienna, which can break any number of ways with the end of the four-power occupation of Austria."

"And you think this death could complicate things even further?"

"I've got a hunch that's the case. There are too many troubling points on top of it all. I do not believe for a minute that Hardwicke's death stems from anything other than this Vienna caper. Those guys are still holding back."

Wainwright paused and studied the floor before looking back up at Baier. "Do you think your British colleague in Vienna, this Henry guy, will be any help?"

Baier shook his head. "Not really. He just follows orders." After a moment, he added, "Harrison might be some help. But I gather he's constrained as well."

Wainwright nodded. "Well, I'll try to keep the pressure on here in London. Believe it or not, we are attempting to build a close relationship with these guys, even after the Maclean-Burgess fiasco. It's got to be worth something, especially since this may touch on our common enemy. They seem to have gone through a pretty steep learning curve in terms of the Soviets. Some of these guys, like Eden, were positively Pollyannaish about what we'd be able to do with them after the war."

"What about Churchill?" Baier asked.

Wainwright actually guffawed. "*That* guy. He was practically delusional during the war. He kept trying to push us into southern and southeastern Europe so we could secure that flank of the Empire. Like they were still going to have an empire. I think good ol' Winston was still living in the First World War."

"That's good to know, working in Vienna. I wonder if it has anything to do with the Brits and their relationship with von Rudenstein."

"Well, that, as you say, will be something for you to pursue back there. When do you think you'll be back?"

Baier shook his head. "I'm not sure. I'll have to see how things go in Saxony with Sabine and her family first."

Wainwright took Baier's arm. "Karl, be damn sure you check in with our folks first thing. Don't pull the same boner you did here and avoid contact."

"Jack, I am truly sorry for that. But I really thought a single overnight would do it—that I could bring you guys up to speed when I was on my way out of here. I had no idea I would run into the sort of complications that have popped up now."

Wainwright gave a blithe little wave to dispel his concerns. "Don't worry about it. I understand. But seeing as how this appears to be getting serious, you need to stay straight with them. In fact, I suggested that they meet you at Tempelhof when you get in. Have you notified them of your flight schedule?"

Baier winced. "Not yet. Things have gotten kind of hectic here. I think I get in around two or three o'clock this afternoon."

Wainwright nodded and returned to his desk, where he jotted the time down on a pad of yellow legal paper. "Not to worry. I'll let them know. And Karl …?"

Baier looked at the COS, whose expression was serious and sincere. "Yes?"

"Good luck out there. And please be careful. These are not the kind of people you fuck with or underestimate."

Baier nodded. "I know, Jack. I've dealt with them before, as has Sabine. It's what has me so worried."

Chapter Eight

More memories flooded back to Baier, even more vivid than those of London. Berlin was where it had all started for him, his introduction to the collapse of Europe, the emergence of the United States as the preeminent global power, the solidifying of the front line in the confrontation with the Soviet Union. And his greatest achievement—meeting and marrying Sabine. In the others, Baier felt that he could often be only one player among many. But Sabine's situation—that, at least, he could set right now.

His plane descended slowly toward Berlin from the patch of white cloud set against the slate-gray sky he had come to know so well during his years in this city. The neo-classical columns and crescent-shaped terminal of Tempelhof stared skywards, as though assembled as his own welcoming committee. The Germans had bragged about the size of the structure when he first arrived in Berlin in September of 1945. There was little left of the city beyond piles of broken brick, shattered beams, and torn-up roads, but those locals with a little pride and life remaining had bragged that Tempelhof had occupied the largest amount of mass and space in the world when it was first built. In the streets surrounding the airport, there did appear to be more urban life and reconstruction underway, now that the city had begun to harvest some of the rewards of the Federal Republic's emergence and prosperity. At least in the city's western half. It was hard to tell from his window seat on the airplane, but the eastern half—or the Soviet zone—still had the barren, lifeless quality that had typified the entire city right after the war. As if to symbolize the change, the battered remains of the Focke-Wulf fighters that had littered the runways when he first arrived a decade ago were now gone. He wondered if some or any of the detritus from the final battle for the city had disappeared from the eastern neighborhoods. Baier doubted it.

Wainwright had been as good as his word, apparently. A driver and a car—not much different from the Jeep that had greeted him in 1945—were waiting at the edge of the runway when Baier stepped off the airplane. But the driver was a civilian this time, not an Army corporal.

"Welcome to Berlin, sir. Ted Wilson's the name."

Studying his welcoming committee of one, Baier guessed that he must be in his late 20s or early 30s. The man was roughly the same height as Baier, just over six feet tall, but slimmer and probably in better shape. Not a speck of gray in his brown hair. Baier wondered when the man had joined the Agency. His outfit was smart but casual—slacks, dress shirt, and jacket. No tie.

"The chief wanted me to bring you straight to the Mission, sir, for a quick meet and greet."

"Did Wainwright let you know I was coming?"

"I really don't know. The chief just told me what flight you'd be on and to bring you along *tout de suite*."

Baier nodded. "Thanks. I appreciate that, but I am in a bit of a hurry to head south."

Wilson took Baier's bag and tossed it in the back of the Jeep. They climbed into their seats, and Wilson nodded in turn as they pulled away from the plane and steered toward what appeared to be a garage and hopefully an exit under the terminal complex. "I understand that. But this shouldn't take long. Chief just wants to give you the lay of the land, so to speak, and see what we can do to help."

He paused as the Jeep pulled into what was a drive-through instead of a garage, and Baier saw a shaft of daylight that illuminated a line of shifting street traffic at the other end. "We've also arranged for an unregistered car, if you need one."

Baier leaned forward. "That's very helpful. Thanks." He pointed at the fading daylight and turned to watch the airport terminal fade behind them. "Don't we have to check in or anything?"

Wilson shook his head. "That's all been taken care of."

"Well, that's certainly convenient."

Wilson laughed, and Baier noted his wide smile as the man looked both ways before pulling into traffic. "It certainly helps when you're part of an Allied mission in an occupied city. We're kind of like gods here. Then again, I guess you're familiar with all that. This is my first tour, and I've been warned not to get spoiled."

Baier smiled in spite of himself. "Yes and no. A lot has changed here. But I'm also starting to remember some things."

Like the continued presence of bombed-out buildings. Not nearly as many, of course, but still enough to break the skyline created by the newer, rectangular high-rises that had been thrown up quickly to meet the massive housing shortage. They might be ugly, but they sure beat sleeping in the streets or cellars.

As the Jeep sped along the Clayallee, formerly known as the Kronprinzenallee, Baier thought of asking the driver to swing by his old house on Im Dol, now that they had entered the Dahlem area. But then he realized that he wasn't sure he could handle the memories, not with his wife Sabine facing whatever the hell was going on down south. Instead, he let Wilson pull through the front gate of the U.S. Mission, where they bounced over the cobblestones of the long circular driveway and pulled up to the front door. He climbed down onto solid ground and sent Wilson back to motor pool to return the Jeep. Baier knew the way to the chief's office.

"Welcome to Berlin, Karl." Bob Wheeler, the local Chief of Station, or COS, stood behind his desk, hand outstretched. "Or I guess I should say welcome back."

It was the second time in less than an hour that Baier had heard that greeting, but it felt good all the same. Baier shook Wheeler's hand. "Thanks, Bob. It's good to be back. Sort of."

Wheeler walked over to the open window, which looked out onto a courtyard of green lawn and yellow daffodils, and sat on one end of couch below it. He motioned for Baier to sit as well. Baier had met Wheeler once before, back on the Mall as both were preparing for their current assignments in Vienna and Berlin. Wheeler was also a Midwesterner, a Chicagoland boy, to be exact. But he had grown up in River Forest, an area on the border between city and suburb just off the city's southwest, not the near north side like Baier, where so many German immigrants had settled. Wheeler had sought Baier out to pick his brains on the operational environment and assets in Berlin—the few that were still active from Baier's time, most having escaped to the West already. Baier invited him to dinner at his place in Arlington to meet Sabine, sure that she could add to the conversation. And she had. Wheeler had sounded sincere in his appreciation for the food and the information.

Wheeler was not wearing a tie either, although he did have on a navy-blue suit.

"How did things go with the pick-up at Tempelhof?"

"Oh, fine," Baier answered. "Wilson seems like a good officer. New, I gather."

"But good," Wheeler confirmed. "He came to us a couple years out of law school. Said he couldn't stand working with all those other lawyers and sitting in an office all day." Wheeler smiled. "I think we've been able to offer him something else."

"Well, that's good to hear. And thanks for agreeing to see me and help on such short notice."

Wheeler waved his gratitude away. "Not a problem. I remember Sabine well from that night back in Virginia. She was great, and you are a lucky man, Karl. We'll do whatever we can to get things straightened out down there. Things are getting hairy here again, and I don't want to see her caught in a crossfire, as it were. Especially not with her personal history."

"How do you mean, 'hairy'?" Baier asked.

Wheeler sighed. "Well, you no doubt know, Karl, our Soviet friends wax and wane in terms of how friendly and cooperative they can be. Right now we're in a pretty ambiguous situation."

"How so?"

Wheeler leaned forward. "It has a lot to do with your hosts in Austria, Karl."

"Wait a minute. It's been a lot of love and kisses from what we've seen in Vienna. The Austrians have wanted all of us, but mostly the Russians, out of their country so they can be free and independent again. And the Soviets have been willing to negotiate to make that happen. Some in Vienna are even hoping this could be the harbinger of an easier and more open relationship between East and West, post-Stalin."

"That's not how things look up here, Karl. That's a very Austrian—and I might add parochial—view."

"Because the real target of the State Treaty may be Germany? Yeah, I've heard that."

Wheeler nodded with enthusiasm. "Absolutely. At least, if you ask people like Adenauer and the U.S. Military. There are a lot of people shitting bricks here in Germany—Germans, Americans, Brits, you name it—who are very concerned about Adenauer's upcoming visit to Moscow."

"Fearing that he might agree to a similar deal? The end of

occupation and reunification as long as Germany remains neutral?"

"Yep. Or that he might be pressured into it by his constituents here at home." Wheeler sighed again. "Can you imagine how bad we'll look if we try to block that?"

"That's dreaming, Bob. I know something about these Krauts and their neighbors. It's hard for me to imagine anyone to the east of here accepting a reunified, not to mention rearmed, Germany under any circumstances. With the Federal Republic already in NATO and integrated into the Western economic system—and profiting nicely from it, I might add—there are links being built that will be awfully hard to break."

"Come on, Karl, you also know as well as I do that far too many people are not prepared to trust the Germans, which includes those in Washington. And they won't be for generations yet. So, very few are comfortable with the thought of the West German chancellor heading off to Moscow on his own." Wheeler reached out and grabbed Baier's arm. "And you are also aware, I'll bet, that the Austrians pretty much ignored the instructions and entreaties the Western governments gave the chancellor and foreign minister as they were dealing with the Soviets."

Baier leaned back. "Yes, I am. But as I've said, they saw their goal of regaining their independence and sending the Russians home within their reach. And they were not going to be deterred."

"Assuming everything comes off as planned."

Baier nodded. "True enough. But if the Soviets really are aiming for a similar deal in Germany, they won't let this one get away. I would expect them to see to it that this treaty gets signed and delivered."

Wheeler sat back in turn. "True enough, as you say, Karl. But that will make the following weeks and months very interesting." He paused. "How does all this affect the case you're working on?"

"I wish I knew, Bob. It's what I was hoping to find out in London."

"And didn't, I gather."

"No, not entirely," Baier admitted. He shook his head and stared out the window for a minute or two before continuing, "Why did you speak of Sabine being caught in a crossfire, Bob?"

Wheeler sat upright again. "Jeez, I'm sorry, Karl. I don't have anything specific to go on. I was just thinking out loud. You know what pricks the Russians can be."

"But if they are acting down there with a purpose, it could have as much to do with the past as the future. Not that that is any more comforting," Baier added.

"You mean your past in Berlin? Or her past?"

"I guess I'd say both." Baier looked up at Wheeler. "It looks like there's only one way for me to find out, Bob."

"You're right, Karl. We really won't know until you get down there and find out for yourself. You'd have to ask yourself what purpose harassing your wife would serve in terms of current Cold War politics." Wheeler seemed to weigh alternatives. "They're probably just harassing her because she's married to an American who works for the U.S. Government, and they have an opportunity right now to be assholes."

Baier took a deep breath and blew it out. "Well, let's hope that's all it is."

"When did you want to get underway? We've booked a room for you at the Harnack House for tonight."

Baier shook his head. "I'd just as soon leave now. I can always spend the night with Sabine's family if necessary. I've lost enough time as it is. Besides, I don't think I'd be able to sleep."

Wheeler stood and nodded. "All right then. I can appreciate your concern. Let's get Ted, and he can bring you around to motor pool and fetch your travel papers. I think we've got a nice beat-up Mercedes for you to lower your profile. We've also got documents that put both of you with the Allied authorities here in Germany in case anyone decides to stop you and ask questions."

Baier started for the door. "The car is still comfortable and reliable? That's what counts right now."

Wheeler put his hand on Baier's shoulder as they navigated down a hallway crowded with new office furniture, judging by the smell and gloss. Some of it was still wrapped in plastic. "Absolutely, Karl. Absolutely. Sabine deserves a comfortable trip home."

BAIER SPED ALONG the Autobahn south in the direction of Leipzig. He figured he was averaging about 80 miles per hour. Then again, that's what these roads had been built for: speed. And not just for Hitler's tank divisions either. There was little or no scenery to distract him, since shortly after he left Berlin at around eight o'clock, the sky had turned from the gray of dusk to the coal black of night. There was really only farmland in Brandenburg and northern Saxony anyway, and not a lot to see there. At least not for Baier, whose Midwestern upbringing made him familiar with that sort of landscape.

It took just over two hours to bolt around Leipzig and propel himself for another thirty minutes to the historic town of Erfurt in Thuringia, a region just to the southwest of Saxony, and thankfully, closer to the West German border. Sabine's parents always told people they came from Leipzig, and the family had indeed come from there originally. But now they lived closer to Erfurt, having fled from the larger city in hopes of avoiding Allied bombing raids. They had survived the war, so apparently their plan had worked.

Baier cursed as his car bumped over the cobblestone exit ramp. It felt like his internal organs were being rearranged by the hundred feet or so of jolting. He hoped that as the U.S. constructed its own highway systems—allegedly inspired by what Eisenhower had seen here during the war—those in charge would make sure the exit and entrance ramps were well paved.

He drove down the dark country road more carefully now that that he was no longer on the vaunted German highway. He was on the final stretch to the home of Sabine's parents, the Schillings. He had been here before, but only once. He and Sabine had thought his visits invited too much risk and had always insisted that her parents come to Berlin when they had lived there after the war. He'd therefore thought it wise to bring along the address and review a map of the region with Bob Wheeler before leaving the U.S. Mission.

"And be damn sure to run some counter-surveillance, or at least check your rearview mirror periodically, Karl."

"Yeah, yeah. You're not dealing with a novice here, Bob. I've done this kind of thing before."

Despite his protests, he had forgotten to do so in his rush to reach the Schillings.

The house was a neat little stucco building, more of a cottage than a house, with two stories that rose to a triangle of more slate tiles at the top. The original white had been stained gray by the smoke that emanated from the soft brown coal the locals burned for fuel and heat down here because it was plentiful and cheap. The walls looked like they could use a decade's worth of power washing to get that original white back. The other houses along the street all looked the same: neat and trim but filthy. Baier wondered what the air pollution had done to the Schillings' lungs. Just one more reason to get Sabine out of here. And the in-laws as well, if they would consent to leave.

He parked the battered old Mercedes that the Station in Berlin had provided in front of the house and walked across the stamp-sized lawn to the front door. Sabine's father, Kurt, stood in the doorway. He must have seen Baier drive up. His eyes struggled to focus on the strange car and its driver who now approached his house. Kurt Schilling was perhaps three or four inches taller than Baier, a stature accentuated by his thin angular frame. It looked as though he had not shaved or even combed his hair in several days. His ragged red sweater and loose brown slacks added to the general impression of dishevelment.

"Ach, Karl, it's you. Come in, son, quick."

Baier slipped past his father-in-law and deposited his coat on the wall rack that hung next to the door and opposite a set of stairs that ascended to the upper floor. Kurt Schilling led the way through the short hallway that served as an entrance and through a doorway that opened onto a small sitting room. Off to Baier's right was a compact dining room surrounded by shelves that held a set of china and glassware, various knickknacks, and a handful of books. Directly in front of him, a set of glass doors in a thick wooden frame peered out over a small stone patio and a yard that had been transformed into a vegetable garden during the war.

"Where's Sabine?" Baier asked.

Kurt Schilling fell into a plump armchair, and his wife Gretchen rushed in, wringing her hands in agitation. "Sit, Karl. We'll try to explain."

"Explain what? Isn't Sabine here? What's happened?"

"Kurt," his wife exclaimed, "please be careful." She took up a post just behind his armchair. A loose flowered frock hung from her shoulders covering what appeared to be a well-worn brown dress. Baier recalled that she had brought the frock to Berlin whenever they visited, as she would insist on doing the cooking and cleaning up in the kitchen afterward.

Her husband waved his right arm in the air, as though wanting to dismiss this affair and the entire postwar history of Germany in the bargain.

"*Ach*, Gretchen, she's his wife. I don't care what they say. They can all go to hell. Karl wants to find Sabine, and I'm going to tell him what I can."

Baier was beside himself. He realized he was unconsciously pacing the room and rubbing his hands over his arms. "What the hell is going on?" He halted before the Schillings. "Where the hell is Sabine? What has happened?"

"They've taken her away. They say she has been arrested for espionage," Kurt Schilling explained.

"Who has? And where have they taken her?" Realizing his fists were in tight balls, he relaxed the muscles and unrolled his fingers. Lord knew he didn't intend to threaten his own in-laws. Sabine's arrest was clearly the last thing they wanted. He could only imagine the shock and anxiety they must have felt—hell, that they were feeling even now—when Sabine was taken away.

"The secret police. The Gestapo … er no, I mean the Stasi and those fucking Russians." Baier wondered if Sabine had learnt the phrase from her parents, or if she had taught them those endearing words.

"Do you have any names or offices? Is she being held in Erfurt or Leipzig?"

Kurt Schilling shook his head, while his wife continued to wring her hands. Tears had begun to roll down her cheeks. Baier was shocked to see how pale and thin she looked, how illness had taken its toll on both parents. This certainly didn't help. Sabine's father looked weak and much older than Baier remembered.

"I don't know," he responded. "They didn't say. They just shoved some papers in our faces and took her away."

"Did Sabine say anything?"

"She told us to be sure to inform you. That you would take care of everything." He thought for a moment. "She also said to remember the Russian."

"Russian? What Russian?"

Kurt Schilling shrugged, his face creased with frowns and fear.

Russian or no Russian, I will damn sure take care of things, Baier thought. He would drive straight back to Berlin tonight to get to the bottom of this. It looked as though he would have to use that room at the Harnack House after all. Before the war, it had served as a sort of faculty club for the many scientists at the Berlin University's scientific facilities set up in Dahlem. The Americans had seized it for their own use because of the dining and lodging facilities, which had survived the Allied bombing largely intact. It was also located close to the American headquarters on Clayallee. Baier remembered the rooms as comfortable, if pretty basic. There was the noise issue, given its function as an officers' and non-commissioned officers' club. He doubted he would get much sleep tonight anyway.

"I'm going to find your daughter." Baier leaned forward toward his in-laws, his hands resting on the arms of Kurt Schilling's chair. "And I'm going to get her out of here. Then I'm coming back for both of you."

"Don't worry about us, Karl," his father-in-law responded. "We've lived through a lot here. We'll survive. And the journey would probably be too much for us anyway." Baier saw the tears in his eyes as well. "But please find Sabine and make sure she's safe."

I'll do more than that, Baier thought. *I am going to rip those motherfuckers apart.*

"I'll let you know one way or the other what I find out. But I will get her free, whatever it takes."

Baier shook Kurt Schilling's hand and kissed his mother-in-law on the cheek before embracing her. He could feel her body shake with fear and worry as the bones seemed to rattle under the fabric of her dress. Then he rushed to the door, grabbed his jacket, and headed for the car. Right behind his own Mercedes sat another one, this one slightly less bruised and covered in dark-blue paint in contrast to the dirty white of the car he had driven down from Berlin. Ted Wilson stood next to the passenger door.

"What are you doing here?" Baier demanded. "And how did you find me?"

"Bob has the map. Remember?"

"Yes, of course …. But why?"

Wilson held out his arm. "Hurry up. We don't have a lot of time. I'll take the car you drove back to Berlin with me after we meet up with some local contacts at the border. Then you can take this one across with a new set of papers."

"What border? I'm driving back to Berlin. The bastards have taken Sabine."

Wilson nodded. "I know, I know. But she's not in Germany anymore."

"What the hell …?"

Wilson pointed at Baier's car. "Come on. We're going to get you over the border and into Bavaria. It'll be quicker than taking the official route through Berlin. We figure it's worth the risk to save time."

"Why Bavaria?"

"Because we need to get you back to Vienna. I'm pretty sure I was not followed. I drove here like hell to catch you, so I wasn't as careful on my counter-surveillance as I should have been." Baier winced. "We really can't linger here, man."

"But why back to Vienna? Is that where Sabine is?"

"Not according to our sources."

"Where is she?"

"They've taken her to Budapest."

Chapter Nine

"RALPH, YOU'VE HEARD? About Sabine?"

Delgreccio nodded and pointed to the chair in front of his desk. Baier had come in to work at 7:00 to get as early a jump on the day as possible and was surprised to find his boss already at his desk. "Yes, of course. Karl, we will get her out. One way or another, we will get her out. How long do you think she can hold up?"

Baier ran his hand through his hair. He had gotten very little sleep, not arriving home until the early hours of the morning. Adrenaline seemed to be all that was driving him now. That and a lot of coffee. "Hard to say. If only I knew what those bastards were up to. I mean, she's dealt with those fucking Russians before, as you know. But this is something new entirely. I just don't see what they get out of this move."

"All right, let's walk through this, piece by piece. Any problems at the border crossing into Bavaria?" Delgreccio asked.

"No, and from there I sailed right into Austria. Just outside Salzburg. Like any other tourist," Baier replied.

"Nice try, Karl."

Baier forced out a smile. "Yeah, I know. I guess I'm trying to lighten the moment with a little bad humor. Relieve some of my anxieties about Sabine."

Delgreccio stood and walked around his desk. He put an arm around Baier's shoulder. "Oh, hell, I understand, Karl." He gave Baier's shoulder a squeeze. "The humor wasn't all that bad. Just not very funny."

Baier sighed and settled back into the chair across from Delgreccio's desk. Looking out the window at the rooftops of Vienna, he thought of how Sabine had come to love Vienna for its old-world charm. They had talked of it as a living history museum, an imperial capital that had somehow found a way to retain its former splendor even after losing its empire, its *raison d'être*. He looked over at his boss, who had returned to his own chair.

"Yeah, well …. Crossing into the West was easy enough, if unnerving."

"How so?"

"They didn't seem all that suspicious. They studied the papers and passed them around, as usual. And of course, there was a long wait while those assholes went through every document of every person in line with that proverbial fine-toothed comb." Baier seemed to spit out the words that followed. "I don't think they expected to find a spy or anything truly threatening. I suppose their only target was some poor sap eager to start a new life in the West and to enjoy freedoms he or she had been denied for most of their life. That would be a prize enough for them. Just a chance to show their power and make someone suffer."

"Did it work? Did they find any of those?"

"Not on this go-round. They didn't seemed to suspect me either. They didn't even search the car. They were content to force me and the others to wait for a really long time, to make us extremely uncomfortable. You know how it is with those clowns. They had to let us know who was in charge."

"Makes you wonder the difference between them and the last bunch of assholes who ran the place," Delgreccio commented.

Baier nodded. "Yeah, no shit."

"So what did you have in mind for the next steps?"

Baier didn't answer at first. He fixed his eyes on the wall to his right, where for some reason a crack in the plaster reminded him of the Rhine—maybe because it ran the length of the wall, almost to the ornate wooden paneling just above the floor. He turned back toward his boss.

"I want to go to Budapest, of course. That's my priority. I'm sure you can understand that."

Delgreccio came forward and sat on the corner of his desk. His pants were hiked up enough so that Baier could see the black argyle socks beneath his black woolen slacks. "I don't think so, Karl. Not yet anyway. Not right now."

Baier couldn't believe what he was hearing. "You really expect me to sit on my ass here in Vienna?"

Delgreccio shook his head. "Of course not. But you can't go running off half-cocked to a city like Budapest, a city you not only don't know but also is located behind the Iron Curtain."

Baier threw up his hands. "What am I supposed to do?"

Delgreccio kept his voice low and even, as if hoping to calm Baier. "You wait until we have more information on who is holding Sabine and where and why. And you help us all by staying out of trouble in Hungary. There's plenty for you to do here."

"Like what?"

"First tell me what happened in London and Scotland."

"Hasn't Wainwright sent anything in?"

Delgreccio nodded. "Sure, but I want your version."

Baier sighed and shifted his weight in the chair. He relayed the gist of his travels and conversations, rushing through the account as though that would shorten the time spent in Vienna and waiting to be released into Budapest.

"So, do you trust the Brits now? And do you have any ideas

how this guy Hardwicke's death could tie into what you're investigating here?"

Baier scratched his head. "Not really, Ralph. Not on either count. I think MI6 is still holding back, and the Hardwicke death is a new and puzzling wrinkle. It does suggest that the von Rudenstein killing goes deeper than we originally thought."

"Wasn't there a Soviet officer in your group when the Austrians gathered all of you at the riverbank to brief you about the death of the old Austrian? You know, when they wanted to show everyone his corpse?"

"Yeah, but he never said a word. Neither did the French guy."

"You know full well that doesn't mean he doesn't know anything. It's a place to start, anyway."

Baier sighed. "I suppose you're right."

Delgreccio frowned. "You know damn well I'm right. And what's the meaning behind Sabine's clue about the Russian? Have you given any thought to that? Maybe this guy can shed some light."

Baier nodded. "Actually, I have. That's one thing I've had time to do … think about her last words to her parents."

"And …?"

"Well, I can't be sure, but there was one Russian we encountered in Berlin. He had infiltrated her black market and smuggling ring, and had also come across her husband and his money laundering and black-market activities as a Wehrmacht officer in Greece. That is, he had come across them when he captured Sabine's husband after the battle for Budapest."

"What do you mean by 'infiltrated'?"

Baier smiled and laughed—a small, bitter 'hah!' "He wanted part of the profits from the smuggling operation. There was a lot of money to be made in that business back then."

"So, how much of a threat could he be?"

Baier shook his head. "I doubt it's the same guy. I mean, this one fled to South America with some Krauts we knew. I can't imagine he returned in good graces."

"Any significance in the Budapest angle?"

Baier shrugged. "Hard to say. Certainly not with this guy. Like I said, the last we saw of him was when he boarded a ship for South America. He was hoping to cash in on some of Sabine's husband's ill-gotten gains and reunite with his family in the new world."

"Could he be back?"

Baier shook his head. "I seriously doubt it. Even if they had leadership changes over there, the guy would almost certainly be hung as a traitor if he returned. Not only did he try to get rich like a good capitalist, but he also spied for the Germans. Then he fled Europe and his Soviet spymasters. The guy was NKVD and blew the whole thing off. He'd be nuts to come back here. They're more likely to be hunting for him there."

"They probably were … and still are, if they haven't found him yet."

"My guess is they have. That's one thing they're good at," Baier noted, "unfortunately."

"Then who else could it be?"

Baier looked out the window again and in the direction of Berlin, as though he could see his and Sabine's past in that city from where he sat. "Hell if I know. I can't get my head past that 'fucking Russian,' as Sabine used to call him." He blew out a breath. "I'll tell you one thing, though."

"What's that?"

"I'm not sure how I'd react if he did walk into our lives again. I might embrace him, but then I might blow his head off."

"Don't do anything that could make it harder to find Sabine and bring her home, Karl."

"No, you're right, Ralph. I'll think of a reason to approach the Soviet who was there at the riverside that night. That could open some things up."

"And what about the Brits? Any way you can get them to more helpful?"

Baier uncrossed his legs, stood, and brushed the wrinkles

from his slacks before looking up at his boss again. "Hard to say, Ralph. Like I said, they were clearly holding back in London. I think they thought they could throw us off the scent with a condescending nod and sentence or two. At least until Hardwicke turned up dead. They were really thrown for a loop by that one. But I'm still not sure how forthcoming they're prepared to be, even after Sabine's disappearance."

"Well, that's another avenue to pursue."

Baier nodded. "Yeah, I suppose so. Jesus, but things are piling up here in Vienna."

Delgreccio stood and retreated to the window, where he took a seat on the sill. "Bear with me Karl. That also brings us back to the Austrian."

"Which one?"

Delgreccio's forehead wrinkled in confusion. "The older, dead one, of course. How many are there?"

"There's that prick who showed up at my house that first morning insisting I get involved in the investigation and warning me about Sabine. He has to know more than he let on."

Delgreccio's face cleared and he nodded. "That's right. We need to follow up with that one as well. But I was thinking of the mystery surrounding old Herr von Rudenstein. Do you still think his background and history lie at the center of this mystery?"

"Yes, I do." Baier moved toward the door. "I plan to trace his roots as well. He has a son here, I understand. Now that you mention it, I'm going to look him up, too." He paused on the threshold to read Delgreccio's face. "Before I go to Budapest, that is."

Delgreccio grinned. "Fair enough." The grin disappeared. "And, Karl …."

"Yeah?"

"Lean on these guys as much as necessary. Someone crossed a line when they grabbed Sabine. Be as tough and mean as you need to. I'll take care of Washington if anyone squawks."

"Thanks, Ralph. I appreciate that." Baier shut the door on his way out.

Lean on them, he would, and he would start with the Soviets.

Chapter Ten

THE MORE BAIER thought about it, the more he was convinced Delgreccio was right. *Go right to the source*. It made the most sense to start with the silent Soviet officer from that night on the riverbank. He now regretted having avoided the company of the Russians throughout his tour in Vienna, and as a result, he wasn't sure how to start. He decided to call Huetzing, the Austrian police officer, to see if he had any contact information. If there was anyone in the government here who promised to be a solid connection to the investigation and the people involved, it was this guy Huetzing. Probably the most honest, too. Baier was not about to go knocking on the Soviets' door asking blindly for "the guy from the riverbank."

"Herr Baier, how nice of you to call. How can I help?"

"Thank you, Herr Huetzing." Baier was grateful for the strong telephone connection. Most people in Austria still had to make do with the system installed right before the war. "I was wondering if there have been any developments in the murder case you called me and my Allied counterparts about. Any new leads or information?"

"*Ach*, no." With those few words Huetzing conveyed his

disappointment and frustration over the telephone. "We've been stymied at every turn."

"Stymied? What seems to be the problem? I hope the Americans have been cooperative. I know I'm prepared to help wherever possible."

Baier could hear a sigh escape through the wires. "Actually, you Americans have not been involved at all. Aside from your brief appearances, that is. The case is a difficult one, you see, as there were no witnesses that we have been able to identify. Nor is there much in the way of forensic evidence. We had hoped to trace his movements and activities leading up to the killing, but that has not been possible. At least not in any detail."

"Why not? Surely, you have access to any records or documentation you might need."

Huetzing continued as though he hadn't heard the American. "You know, Herr Baier, it is fortuitous that you called this morning. Your British and Soviet colleagues have not been forthcoming, and perhaps you can help."

"How so?"

"Well, they have refused to provide access to their document files that might reveal Herr von Rudenstein's movements on the eve of his death. In fact, they have not even returned our phone calls. We know the man had some sort of association with both sides during and immediately after the war, but they have been reticent in communicating with us."

"Really? What sort of association? And with whom?"

"We have reason to believe that he worked for the British right before the war's end, perhaps assisting with some surrenders in Italy."

"And the Soviets?"

"Ah, well, Herr Baier, that's where it gets murkier. And more interesting, I might add."

"Go on."

"We think he may have been meeting with the Soviet authorities here in Vienna and down in Steiermark to the south of Vienna. It's actually next to Burgenland, where the von Rudenstein estate is located."

"Yes, I know."

"And he made numerous visits to Hungary and Czechoslovakia."

"That doesn't mean anything in itself." Baier did not want to reveal his own knowledge about von Rudenstein's work on behalf of British intelligence. "Remember, he was a vintner. Business could explain his travels there."

"Herr Baier, perhaps with the Czechs and Slovaks, but the Hungarians are very proud of their own wines. I doubt he was able to sell much there."

"And the evidence about his meetings with the Soviets here?"

"Apparently there had been some surveillance by our own intelligence services, and also by the British. They refuse to confirm that, however."

Their own intelligence services? "I see."

"In any case, Herr Baier, there may well be an intelligence connection to this killing …"

No shit, Baier thought.

"… which will severely restrict our ability to investigate. That is where I was hoping you could help."

"What would you like me to do? I mean, I do not have any authority to engage in law enforcement activities here, as I'm sure you are aware."

Huetzing paused, perhaps to consider his words … or his options. "Er, yes, I am aware of that. Could you make a few discreet inquiries among your Allied friends and colleagues?"

Bingo, Baier thought. "Sure, I'll see what I can do." It was Baier's turn to pause. "Perhaps there is something you can do for me in return. To help get things started, that is."

"Please. What might that be?"

"First, though, Herr Huetzing, I would like to know if there is anyone else in your government investigating or even interested in this case. Someone not in your office."

"Do you mean in the Foreign Ministry?"

"No, I mean elsewhere in the Interior Ministry, or even in Austrian intelligence. You mentioned the surveillance activities on von Rudenstein. I wonder what else they might have or know."

"Herr Baier, you are better placed to inquire into that than I."

"Perhaps, but it would help if I knew where to turn. A name would help, of course."

"I see. I will see what I can do. Perhaps when we speak again."

"Yes, of course. In the meantime, can you give me the name of the Soviet officer who was at the river that night? He was a silent one, and I never got the chance to ask."

"Of course. That was a Major Igor Nuchyev."

Baier thanked him and hung up.

Later that afternoon, sunlight sparkled against the steeple of Saint Stephen's Cathedral as Baier strolled past the front of the church toward a bench set before a row of shops. The area around the cathedral was crowded with late afternoon shoppers, many of them Austrians who had left work early to buy groceries or other household items. Major Igor Nuchyev sat upright against the back of the bench closest to the church, his face locked in a gray grimace as Baier approached. Periodically, he glanced to either side, and once he even shot a quick look behind him at the shop window filled with antiquarian books, clearly concerned about meeting Baier here on neutral ground in the city center. He had to be nervous about not having the Four-Power Allied patrol to provide cover for his meeting with an American officer. Or perhaps he was suspicious of the way Baier had reached out to him, working through the Soviet office in the Allied Control Commission.

"Major Nuchyev is not on duty yet. He called in sick this morning, but he is supposed to arrive at noon today," the enlisted man at the desk had explained. "I will tell him of your call. May I inquire as to why you need to speak with the major?"

"No," Baier had replied, simply. "Just tell him it's important."

If Soviet intelligence had been doing its job, which Baier never suspected they were not, Nuchyev would learn quickly enough who Baier was. Let the Soviets fill any gaps all by themselves. He was not in an accommodating mood. Baier made sure, though, that he did not have a tail. He had taken a circuitous route to the cathedral, stopping to study his fellow pedestrians at streetcar stations and in the reflections from shop windows. Then he lingered just outside the square to check further for any possible surveillance. There had been no sign of his mysterious shadow since the return from London, which was a mystery in itself. He recalled his friends from St. James Park in London and doubted they had been Austrians. The British had assured them that if he'd had a tail, it was not set by them. Several small trips in and out of the cathedral had given him one last opportunity to see if he was being followed, as well as to make a final search through the crowd for familiar faces that reappeared periodically. Only then did he turn the majority of his attention to Nuchyev.

The man did not look well to Baier. In addition to the gray pallor and grimace, the Soviet had heavy bags under his eyes, and his shirt collar and tie hung loose. The military jacket appeared not to have met an iron in about a month. The boots retained their shine, however, probably thanks to the diligent efforts of some enlisted man. A quick check at the office on Nuchyev had revealed little about the man, other than that he appeared to be real military, infantry actually. That explained why there was so little in the file.

"Thank you for coming, Major," Baier said by way of introduction. "I appreciate you taking the time."

"Yes, of course." Nuchyev started to stand, but Baier rested his hand on the Soviet's shoulder.

"You look nervous. Perhaps we should go inside the cathedral."

The Russian frowned. "Do you really think that is necessary?"

"It might be better for you. Although I can understand if you're worried about a sudden conversion to the opiate of the people."

Nuchyev stood, facing Baier. "My people are religious, Mr. Baier. They have retained affinity for faith despite Soviet prohibitions. I have no fear of Roman church."

"Good, then. Why don't you go inside and take a seat in a pew in the chapel just off to the left of the entrance. I'll follow after a minute or so to make sure no one else goes in after you. Vespers are underway, which should help mask our conversation."

Baier found the Russian slumped in a pew in the second row of the chapel. His gaze was frozen in the same frown he had worn outside as he pondered the image of the Virgin Mary receiving the news of her Immaculate Conception. Baier slid into the pew behind him.

"You look like you've had a rough night of it. Or even a rough few days." Baier leaned forward. "Have you been working hard to prepare for your withdrawal from Austria now that the treaty is almost in place? We're just about a week away from the scheduled signing on the fifteenth. Rumor has it that your side will be the first to leave, unless someone in Moscow comes up with an excuse to delay." Baier was tempted to say that the Soviets probably had little to do, since they had shipped most of the surviving industrial equipment in their occupied zone east years ago. But then, he did not want this conversation to end before it had begun.

A shy grin replaced the frown on Nuchyev's face. "Actually, we have been celebrating imminent departure. Unfortunately, too much vodka does not make for happy morning after."

"No, I suppose not." Baier smiled to show he was trying to be friendly. "Why drink vodka, though, when you have all this good beer and wine here in Austria?"

Nuchyev shrugged. "Vodka is national drink. And tea, of course. Is what we grow up with." He shrugged again and smiled in return. "Besides, we drink beer and wine, too."

"I see. Well, that is certainly understandable." Enough chitchat about Russian drinking preferences. How to move the discussion on to more sensitive matters? "So, you are really preparing to leave? There is no sleight of hand or tricks up Moscow's sleeve now?"

Nuchyev sobered quickly. "Is that why you wanted to speak to me today?" He took a quick intake of breath and surveyed the rest of the church. "Is this back-channel approach from your government? Does Washington have new concerns about State Treaty?" The Russian frowned. "You people have complained enough. We finally gave in to objections about making Austrian neutrality part of treaty."

"Ah, but we know the Austrians have promised to enshrine that in their law anyway. So you get what you wanted in the end."

Baier tried to disarm the Soviet with another broad smile, while he glanced around the cathedral to see if Nuchyev had reason to be alarmed. So far so good, as best Baier could tell. "No, no. I can assure you that as far as I know, we have every intention of fulfilling our obligations under the Treaty. We will sign it, just like our other Allied friends, and we will withdraw our forces as well. Besides, this question is really just a personal one. I mean, it seems strange to me that you're willing to break with your past practice in the region."

Nuchyev's frown deepened. "What do you mean?"

It was Baier's turn to shrug. "Well, you have to admit that this is not the pattern you followed in Prague or even Budapest and Bucharest. Have you really given up any hope of incorporating Austria into your system of alliances in Eastern Europe?"

Nuchyev leaned forward and studied the wooden planking at his feet before looking up at Baier with a pained expression. His skin had a greenish tinge. Baier wondered if the man was about to vomit.

"May I be honest, Mister Baier? Can I trust that my words remain between us?"

"Of course. My superiors do not know I am here," Baier lied. "So I am under no obligation to report back what you say."

Nuchyev nodded, his gaze focused back on his boots. "That is good. Because I do not have energy to spar with you, Mister Baier. Perhaps I should stick to beer and wine."

Baier said nothing, not wanting to interrupt the man. He waited for Nuchyev to talk himself out, to see where the Soviet would take the conversation.

"You see," Nuchyev continued, "we are actually happy to leave this country behind."

Such a bald admission came as a surprise to Baier. "How so?"

The Soviet looked up at Baier and caught his attention with a half-smile, half-frown. "Well, for one thing, we realized we would never win popular approval or support we hoped for. You are aware of voting results, I'm sure."

Baier nodded. "Yes, something like five percent for the Communist Party each time the Austrians went to the polls."

Nuchyev nodded. "That is correct. I'm afraid we have behavior of Red Army troops after liberation to thank for that."

"Not to mention the expropriations and deportations in the years that followed. You also don't have control of the entire country." Baier simply could not let these points pass without comment.

Nuchyev ignored the last item. "Yes, we have already taken, quite frankly, what we needed—and deserved, I might add—after Nazi destruction in our country."

"Fair enough," Baier replied, hoping to encourage the Soviet to continue talking. "But what about that conglomerate of Austrian companies you expropriated that you've been running in your zone? I think it's called USIA now. There's over four hundred companies in that group from what I've heard. Weren't they supposed to establish Soviet style state-managed industrial production here in Austria? Are you telling me you're giving up on that idea?"

Nuchyev waved him away as though disputing Baier's point entirely. "Those things are practically bankrupt. In fact, we pay thirty to forty million shillings a month for our presence here. And we are victors!" He blew out a long, slow, stale breath. "We simply cannot afford to stay."

Baier leaned forward and touched Nuchyev's arm. "So there really are no tricks in play?"

The Soviet shot him a puzzled look, the wrinkles on his forehead deepening. "Of course not. Why play tricks? This is glorious day for all of us, exactly what Comrade Khrushchev wants." He shook his head in disbelief. "Stalin is dead, gone."

Baier sat back again. "And there is no link between the death of Herr von Rudenstein and the State Treaty?"

If anything, Nuchyev's confusion appeared to increase. "Why … why do you ask that?"

"Didn't you kill him?"

Nuchyev's mouth fell open, and his eyes grew wide with confusion and disbelief. "Wha … What are you saying? Why would we kill old man?"

Baier leaned in close, then backed off a bit from the stench of his breath. "You tell me. Somebody did, and you guys are my best bet for it."

The Russian's head shook almost enough to set the pew trembling in this small, isolated chapel of Vienna's famed cathedral. "No, no. I know nothing about that. Believe me, Mister Baier."

"Well then, what have you found out about his death? Have you spoken with the Austrians?"

Nuchyev shrugged. "Why should we? Is their matter. What do we care if someone shot old Nazi? It wasn't us, I assure you."

"But have they approached you for assistance?"

Nuchyev's hands spread wide, then came together again in his lap. "They made initial inquiries about old man to see if we had information for them. I passed those along myself. But I was instructed to tell them we had nothing to offer."

"Did you check with your colleagues in military intelligence or the KGB?"

Nuchyev didn't respond immediately. "As I said, we had nothing to offer. What about yours?"

Baier paused, then shook his head. "Look, I haven't found anything. That's why I asked to speak with you. You were there that morning by the Danube. I thought you might be in charge of whatever liaison work there was with the Austrians."

The Soviet officer blinked a few times. It was difficult to believe he knew more than he was letting on. "There hasn't been liaison work with Austrians on this case."

"Is that because you have nothing to share, or because those are your instructions?"

The Soviet gave him a long, hard look. His eyes appeared slightly glassy. "There has been no liaison work with Austrians or anyone else on this case."

Baier began to fear that Nuchyev was slipping away. Perhaps he was sobering up. "I see. Well then, can you tell me why you people have abducted my wife?"

"Wha … What are you saying?" Nuchyev stood and moved farther down the wooden church pew, taking a position several feet away, as though he wanted to put a safe distance between himself and this crazy American.

"My wife was taken from her parents' house in a village outside Leipzig, Erfurt actually, by East German and Soviet authorities."

"Then why ask me, and here in Vienna?"

Baier could feel the blood rising in his cheeks. He rubbed his sweaty palms together to avoid balling them into fists. "Because she's been taken out of that country, probably to Budapest. I want to know why. And I want your side to know that I will be getting her out."

If the Russian knew anything, he wasn't letting on. "What are the charges?"

"I don't know if anything has been filed formally, which

would be odd if she has indeed been taken to another country. But something in Leipzig was said about espionage." Baier stood and leaned forward to bring his face closer to where Nuchyev had taken refuge. "I want to know why and who is responsible. If it has anything to do with von Rudenstein's death or this damned State Treaty, I want to know, damn it."

"Yes, yes, of course. I understand your concern. "I'll see what I can find out."

"Good. And thank you. You can reach me at this number." Baier passed a slip of paper with his office number at the Allied Command written on it. "I'd like to know as soon as possible." He looked in Nuchyev's eyes, trying to gauge the impact of his words. "Do you have a family back home?"

Nuchyev nodded. "Yes. So? Are you threatening me?"

Baier shook his head. "Not at all. I simply wanted you to understand my concern, my anxiety."

Nuchyev nodded, and even offered his hand. "Yes, of course. I'll see what I can do." Baier grasped it and shook.

"One last question." Baier added.

"What?"

"Does the name Sergei Chernov mean anything to you? Have you heard it before? I believe he held the rank of Colonel."

Nuchyev thought for a moment before shaking his head. "No, I don't think I've ever heard it before. Why?"

"He's somebody I remember from Berlin. One of your colleagues." *For better or worse.* "I wonder sometimes what happened to him."

Nuchyev was quiet while he considered first Baier, then the long row of arched, gray columns that lined the cathedral's interiors and the people wandering through them and along the walls and past the large gothic doorway. When his gaze returned to Baier, the Soviet spoke in hushed tones. "Would you like me to inquire into his whereabouts as well?"

Baier's smile was faint, almost imperceptible. "No, that's okay. It was ages ago. Probably doesn't matter anymore."

Baier turned to go but then ambled over to the set of pews underneath the ornate pulpit with its carved figure of a medieval pilgrim. Perhaps he would stick around to catch the rest of vespers. He knew that regardless of what he said, an inquiry would be made, and not just about his wife. Maybe that would shake things up. For better or worse.

The von Rudenstein son was a bit harder to locate. Fortunately he had settled in the French district, which made contacting him much easier than if he had lived in the Soviet zone.

"I prefer living in the French sector," Thomas von Rudenstein explained. "I chose this address on purpose. I moved here after the occupation zones were established."

"Did you live in the city before this?" Baier asked.

Von Rudenstein Junior, as Baier had silently dubbed him, nodded. Almost eagerly. "Oh, yes. Actually, I lived in the American sector, but I wanted to avoid your GIs."

"Why is that?" Baier had taken an instant dislike to the man. The light-blue sport coat and gabardine slacks were not too pompous, given the prosperity that had come to Austria, especially with the country's access to the Marshall Plan. But the red silk cravat and handkerchief in the breast pocket struck Baier as something you'd find on an insecure aristocratic unsure of his place in a new world. And the crack about American servicemen definitely rubbed Baier the wrong way.

"Oh, they're generally too loud and pushy."

"So you prefer the sedate and refined French, especially with their more restrained behavior here in Austria since the war." Baier hoped this clown would pick up on the sarcasm.

Rudenstein junior shrugged as he refilled his tea cup. "More or less. Granted, the French policy here has not been what one might call 'enlightened,' but—"

"It has been anything but."

Rudenstein Junior paused and glanced from his tea to Baier,

as though offended by the interruption. Baier kept his face as blank as possible to hide his contempt. Rudenstein returned to his tea, stirring in the sugar and cream.

"Still, their history does give them certain advantages."

"And baggage," Baier added. They were seated at a table by the window of a small café in the same block as the apartment building where the younger von Rudenstein lived. Baier noticed the Rococo interior design and wondered if his host had chosen this locale for its old-world extravagance. "Did your father share your affinity for the French?"

"Oh, heavens no. He considered them our eternal enemy."

"The Germans' eternal enemy?"

Rudenstein Junior set his cup back on its saucer and regarded Baier with an enigmatic smile. "Oh no, they were our enemies as well. The Austrians', I mean." He paused to observe his tea then looked up at Baier again. "You obviously never met my father, which is too bad. You would have liked each other. I clearly don't know you well, having just met you, but I think you two are similar in some ways."

"How so?"

"He was what some might call a man of the people. A very solid man of the earth, not given to the finer things in life. *Kaiser und Krone,* we would say, devoted to our emperor and the crown. But it also meant in his mind service of both on behalf of the people. It made him very direct and frank."

"Is that why he disliked the French? Because they had long been competitors of the Hapsburgs in Europe?"

Rudenstein Junior nodded, this time eagerly. "Yes, yes. I can see you know some European history. Have you studied it?"

"As a minor. I concentrated on chemistry at university. But history has always been my second love."

"Second?"

"I am married." Baier almost stumbled over those words, thinking of Sabine.

"Yes, of course. Well, my father would not have approved

of my move to this sector. He would have insisted I stay in the British zone, or even the American one if necessary. He always admired the British, you see, as natural allies for our monarchy and empire. I think that was one of the things that so infuriated him about the Nazis. Their inability to see where the German Reich's natural allies lie here in Europe, at least in his view."

"What can you tell me about your father's views of the British after the war?"

"May I ask you a question first?" young Rudenstein asked.

"Sure. What would you like to know?"

"Well, you initially said that you wanted to pass along information on my father's death. Do you have something to add to what the police have told me, or is there another reason for our meeting? So far you have not told me anything."

Damn, Baier thought, *this guy is smarter than he looks. Don't be deceived by appearances*, he reminded himself. Baier had assumed the younger von Rudenstein would be the type who liked to hear himself talk, that he would be easy pickings. *Alas.*

"I'm trying to assist the Austrian authorities in their investigation, and I was hoping you could fill me in on your father's background, his outlook. What have the police told you?"

Rudenstein Junior frowned as he tasted his tea, which appeared to have gone cold. "Not much. That he was shot, but that it did not appear to have been a robbery. They claim he was also wearing a Wehrmacht jacket, which seems odd to me."

"Why? Your father had a distinguished career during the war. He appears to have served with distinction, especially in Italy."

Young von Rudenstein nodded, more slowly this time, as though weighing his words. "That's true enough. But my father would hardly cling to a relic of that regime and period. Besides, it wasn't his jacket."

So I understand," Baier added. "I suppose if he had something that harked back to the imperial period, that would have been more appropriate."

"Perhaps. But my father was more than just a nostalgic old man. He had a vision for the future as well, you see."

Baier leaned forward. He shoved the coffee, which he'd ordered only to be polite, to keep von Rudenstein Junior company, to one side. It was going cold as well. "What sort of vision?"

"Well, my father always thought that the breakup of the Hapsburg Empire was one of Europe's greatest tragedies. He claimed it was the only way to keep this part of Eastern Europe prosperous and stable."

"Surely he did not think the various people and states that had inhabited the Empire would really be happy to welcome that ruling house back. The Hapsburgs never understood the national aspirations that broke the Empire apart."

"Oh, absolutely," young von Rudenstein agreed. Then he chuckled. "Did you ever see or hear what the old parliament, the Reichsrat, was like before the Great War?"

Baier shook his head. "No, not really. I can't imagine that it was very effective."

Rudenstein Junior laughed out loud this time. "Oh, from what I've read, it must have been a circus. The various national parties all yelled and sang and marched about, and the rules would not allow the speaker to discipline anyone. It was an exercise in the absurd." His frown returned. "Some say it was a lesson for Hitler in how to disrupt parliamentary government that he learned from his time here as a vagabond."

"How could your father ever hope for a return to that sort of state or confederation even?"

"He realized that mistakes had been made. But he still wondered if a new version, some kind of substitute, couldn't be found. I mean," von Rudenstein Junior pointed out the window, "look at what has come to replace it. A Soviet empire." The finger shifted toward Baier. "And you are apparently our only alternative."

"I'm so sorry to hear that," Baier replied. "I'd say your country, not to mention the rest of Western Europe, has benefited nicely from our presence and the policies of my government."

Young von Rudenstein sipped his tea and suppressed a grimace. "Yes, of course. I did not mean to sound ungrateful—"

"Which you do, by the way."

"Yes, and I'm sorry. But my father would have agreed with me. That's why I believe he retained his relationship with the British after the end of the war. He saw them as the best counterweight to you and the Soviets." He raised his hand, palm out to stop Baier from objecting. "Not that they in any way have the resources and power that you now enjoy. No, no. But he saw them as a necessary player nonetheless."

Baier was silent while he considered this new side of the dead man. He even took a gulp of coffee while it lingered on the underside of warm. At least the cinnamon topping gave it some flavor, almost like a pastry with the foam of cream resting on the top.

"How far had your father progressed with this dream of a resurrected Austro-Hungarian state?"

Young von Rudenstein's smile returned. "Oh, it never reached that stage. Not that I know of, anyway. My father was not the sort who would be in the position to bring it about. But there again, you would have had to speak with him. Or the British perhaps."

"You think he discussed it with them?"

"I can't say for sure. I believe so. He believed quite strongly in this."

"Did he think London would play along?" Baier said.

Rudenstein Junior shrugged. "He never said. Perhaps he thought he could just influence their policy in the right direction."

"And what did he think of the State Treaty?" Baier said.

Young von Rudenstein sat back and rolled his eyes. "Oh, my!" The smile widened. "He said it was a catastrophe. Not that he wasn't happy to be rid of the Soviets, mind you, and I doubt he regretted that the rest of the Allies would depart as well. "

"Then what was the problem?'

"He said it was the end."

"Of what?"

"History. Or what he understood as history." Baier frowned. "You see, it will cut Austria off from its natural hinterland to the east and south."

Jesus, the old guy had been a real throwback. The Austrian drained the last of his tea. Baier rose to his feet. He tossed a small pile of schillings on the table—enough, he figured, to cover the cost of the tea and undrunk coffee.

"Well, thank you for the refreshments and conversation," von Rudenstein Junior said. "I should get back to my office. Unless, of course, you have anything else on my father's death to impart."

Baier looked up at his guest and shook his head. "Not at the moment. I thought you worked at home, managing your export-import business, as it were?"

"Oh, I do. That is my office."

"And what is it you import and export?"

"Wine, of course. It's in the blood. Someday I might even begin to export our family's wine again."

"But who will grow and harvest the grapes? You're barely staying afloat as it is, and that, thanks to the old groundskeeper."

"Well, we haven't worked that out yet. But may I ask another question?" He did not wait for Baier to respond. "Did any of this help in the search for my father's killers?"

Baier stared down at the notes on the table. "I'm not sure. I think it may have. A little bit at least."

Baier reached out as the young von Rudenstein turned to leave. "Now, may I ask you a personal question?"

Von Rudenstein junior shrugged and nodded. "Oh, I suppose so. Then again, many of your questions have been personal. Of a sort."

"It's about your relationship with your father. You do not seem all that disturbed by his death. Or maybe I'm expecting a certain type of reaction, which isn't really fair to you."

"Go on."

"What sort of relationship did you have with your father? Were you close?"

"And how does that help you solve his killing?"

"It gives me a better picture of the man and his environment."

Von Rudenstein Junior considered Baier's question and sighed. "We were not close. But what can one expect when you have a Nazi occupation of your country—"

"So to speak."

"Yes, well there was also the war. He was away for most of that, of course, and I imagine he did and saw things that have a profound effect on a man. They are bound to change one, often for the worse."

"And in your father's case?"

"It made him more withdrawn, which he had always been in any case. But it also made him more determined."

"Determined about what?" Baier pressed.

"Determined to do what he thought was right for Austria—as he understood it—and Europe."

"Did he ever discuss that with you? Do you know what he was trying to do?"

The younger von Rudenstein shook his head. "No, my sister and I had to rely on guess work. You'll have to take that up with your British friends." He smiled. "And good luck to you with that. They're not always forthcoming, I've discovered. Please let me know if you learn anything."

"Yes, of course. Good luck to you as well."

Baier watched the younger von Rudenstein slip out the door and cross the street to his apartment building. He thought more highly of him now.

Chapter Eleven

THE FOLLOWING MORNING, Baier met with the Englishman Turnbridge again, this time in the Volksgarten. Delgreccio had endorsed the idea, which was no surprise. Not that Baier needed much in the way of permission or prodding. He had assumed a pretty free hand by now.

"Did you accomplish anything yesterday?" his chief had asked regarding his long day interviewing the Russian and the dead man's son.

Baier shrugged and wandered over to the window in his boss's office. "Some. I established contact with the Soviets and planted a bug in their butts."

"How so? You didn't threaten them, I hope." Delgreccio smiled. "Not yet, anyway."

"I asked about the von Rudenstein caper, of course. But then I brought up Sabine's abduction. That seemed to shake the Russkie somewhat. I also inquired about the Russian we knew during our time in Berlin to see if he's resurfaced."

"What was his name? I can have a search run on the guy back in Washington as well."

"Sergei Chernov. And good luck. I'm guessing he's fallen off the face of the earth. I hope so, at any rate."

"Good," Delgreccio interjected. "Did he have anything on the dead Austrian?"

Baier shook his head. "Nope. Nuchyev claimed the Soviets were as innocent as babies on this one. He said his side wasn't even looking into it, that it wasn't their affair."

"Do you expect anything to come of your mentioning Sabine?"

"We'll see. But I don't plan to wait long." Baier paused and turned toward Delgreccio's desk. "Afterward I learned some more about von Rudenstein from his son."

"And …?"

"And the guy is turning out to be a lot more interesting than I realized. For one thing, I think that Wehrmacht jacket is nothing more than a red herring."

Delgreccio frowned. "That doesn't help clear things up at all."

Baier smiled and strolled to the front of the desk. "From everything I've heard, it's pretty clear the guy was no Nazi, nor was he some rabid Kraut nationalist. If anything, he was a throwback to the old Hapsburg Empire."

"Than what was he doing serving the Reich so earnestly and successfully?"

Baier shrugged and leaned against the chair set in front of his chief's desk. "I didn't say it cleared things up. I said it was a red herring, a path we shouldn't waste time on." Baier snorted. "Hell, Ralph, he was serving his country like anyone else would in his position. It was the only one he had, and it would have to do until something better came along."

"Like what?"

"I'm not sure. But that 'something better' may have led to his death."

"A Hapsburg variation? That sounds like the stuff of fantasies."

"To us, perhaps. Given our backgrounds, just about anything in this part of the world could sound like an old man's fantasy. I mean, it's not like anything else has popped up."

"How do you plan to find out?"

"By calling in some chits with our British allies."

"Chits? What the hell leverage have you got with them?"

"Sabine, principally." Baier frowned and turned toward the door. "And the fact that they've been holding back from me while my wife sits in a KGB jail, as best we can tell."

Baier was not really surprised that Turnbridge had readily agreed to meet him again while passing once more on his suggestion of the Belvedere Park. He was, however, taken aback by his British colleague's insistence as soon as he arrived that they begin walking across town to the section of the Ringstrasse that ran in front of and opposite the Vienna Rathaus. The city hall, with its dark red, neo-Gothic façade, was meant to remind passersby that this was once part of the headquarters of a mighty empire, one that stretched back hundreds of years to the thirteenth century. Granted, the new city hall had been built in the second half of the preceding century, but its towers and curved archways seemed to recapture some of the town's medieval elegance and power. It was also one of the locations where the forces that tore that empire and Europe apart had found their voice and political form in the shape of the city's pre-World War I Social Christian mayor. Karl Lueger had made an art of appealing to his countrymen's anti-Semitism and concentrating their hatred and sense of victimization on an allegedly alien minority.

"Why are we here?" Baier asked.

"Because there's someone who wants to meet you." Turnbridge stopped at the edge of the curb and across the street from the Rathaus. He pointed to the arches that ran along the ground floor of the building. "He's back in there. You'll know him when you see him."

"Where will you be?" Baier asked.

"Back in my office, where I belong."

"That doesn't sound very encouraging. Are you guys backing out of your offer of support?"

Turnbridge laughed. "Hardly. I'm sure you'll be pleased."

Baier waited for a break in the traffic, then trotted across the street to the monument to the city's history, its successes and failures. He wondered what von Rudenstein had thought of the building and the institution it housed. He wondered what other Austrians thought of the building and the history it represented.

Baier watched Turnbridge disappear along the wide boulevard that ran in front of the opulent Burgtheater just across the square, on his way to the neighborhood on the other side of the imperial palace where his embassy and desk waited. Turning back to the deep red limestone archway, he found himself about five feet away from Thomas Harrison, the MI6 officer from St. Andrews and London, standing at the opening to a tunnel of Gothic-styled arches. He was outfitted in a traditional beige Burberry raincoat, even though the sun bled yellow and white across the columns that surrounded them both.

"Good Lord, Harrison, to what do I owe the pleasure?"

The MI6 man smiled and shrugged as he, too, glanced across the street. "I wanted to follow up on our offer and make sure some new information got into your hands."

"Well, that's certainly nice of you. But you didn't have to travel all this way, did you? Couldn't you trust Turnbridge to deliver the message?'

Harrison shook his head. "Not this one. Turnbridge is a good man whose heart is in the right place. But as I'm sure you've noticed, he has his limits."

"Which the rest of you do not?"

"Do you want this information and assistance or not?"

Baier smiled and held out his hand. "I'm sorry. I'm sure you can also imagine the pressure I'm under these days. I have not been sleeping well."

After shaking Baier's hand, Harrison reached into an inside pocket and brought out a slim book.

"And that would be …?" Baier asked.

"I gather that when you discovered Hardwicke's body, you did not search his lodgings," Harrison said.

"No," Baier replied. "I didn't want to generate any more suspicion toward myself than necessary. I figured you guys would be able to see if I had, and there was already enough anxiety as it was."

Harrison nodded. "Right. We appreciate your discretion. But if you had, you might have found this." He held the book out toward Baier. "It's a diary. Hardwicke's."

"Kind of private, isn't it?"

"Not anymore," Harrison stated. "Besides, you don't get that sort of privacy when you work in this business, especially once you've been shot."

"I suppose you're right. This does involve a murder. But won't your people need it as evidence?"

"Not anymore," Harrison said. "Besides, not that many people in the investigation had access to it. Just enough to convince the chief investigator that there was no direct line pointing to a specific culprit. And it's not the sort of thing we like to leave in others' hands. I'm sure you can appreciate that."

"You guys do have leeway. More than us, it seems." Baier took the book and began thumbing through the pages. "What period does it cover?"

"The last three years, basically the time since Hardwicke's retirement from the Service."

Baier scanned a few pages at random. "He wasn't a man of many words, was our Professor Hardwicke? Some of these pages have little more than times and places. Others appear to be in some kind of code."

Harrison nodded and took the book. "You're absolutely

right. Which helps us justify keeping it out of the hands of law enforcement. It just wouldn't help a prosecutor much." He smiled. "Then again, if you were a trained intelligence professional, would you lay everything out in black and white for any stranger—or opponent—to read? Still, the code is easy enough to decipher, probably because Hardwicke never intended for it to remain a mystery forever. It's simply a combination of letters and numbers to create mildly confusing abbreviations."

"Just what did he intend?" Baier said.

"We, and especially I, believe he simply wanted to use it as a reminder when it came time to bring this information to light."

Baier took the book back. "And what information would that be?"

"I believe it was information about his continuing contact with von Rudenstein, contact he was no longer supposed to be pursuing."

"Why and why not?"

"Because," Harrison continued, "the man had retired to a life of academic bliss and ignorance. And because he was supposed to have turned his asset over to a new handler."

"Who was that?"

When Baier looked up he saw Harrison's broad smile. "That would be me. Or at least, it was supposed to be me."

Baier smiled back, only slightly more reserved. He appreciated the move by his British colleague. "Excellent," was all he could say at first.

"I thought you'd be pleased. So you see, I have a direct interest in this case as well. It's why I was selected to meet you in St. Andrews." Harrison paused to give his next words more impact. "We're not always so stupid, you know."

"Nor so arrogant either." Noting Harrison's frown, he clarified, "Sorry. I was thinking of your colleague back in London."

"Of course you were."

"How is Sir Robert, by the way?"

Harrison sighed. "Sir Robert has been shaken by Hardwicke's death far more than you realize. Certainly more than I realized."

"How so?"

"It seems they were at school together in Winchester at the cathedral there. Hardwicke went off to Exeter University, while Siscourt studied at Oxford. But they stayed in touch throughout their careers."

Baier held up the book. "Well, I'm sorry for that. But thank you for this. Do you mind if I take it home for a night?"

Harrison waved at Baier. "Be my guest. But I can give you the important bits right here."

"Sure. Go right ahead."

"It seems that our late friend Professor Hardwicke not only continued his contact with Herr von Rudenstein, but he continued to task him as well."

Baier looked down at the book in his fist, turning it over and back as though inspecting it for flaws. "How can you tell that from this slim little volume?"

"As best I can tell, he followed and reached out to von Rudenstein almost monthly, sometimes more frequently. And the dates on the contact always came in sets of two, like he was following up on his instructions. I'm pretty sure they matched von Rudenstein's travels behind the Iron Curtain. We can check with the Austrians investigating the case to see what they have on the old man's movements to make sure."

"Fair enough. We can even do that today."

Harrison nodded vigorously. "Absolutely."

"But what was he tasking the Austrian to do …" Baier paused, "and perhaps more importantly, was this what got the old man killed?"

"Or both of them?" Harrison added.

"Damn straight." Baier looked the MI6 man straight in the eye. "But tell me, why all the mystery on this meeting? Why meet me out here, away from your place and away from Turnbridge or anyone else in your office? And why not mention your role in all this when we met back there?"

Harrison sighed and glanced up and down the Ringstrasse once more. "I'm afraid these sorts of precautions are necessary these days. One can't be too careful when you work in MI6 or MI5."

"Trouble at your headquarters again?"

Harrison's sigh was even more audible this time. "Yes, it would seem so. As you Americans know already, we have yet to get to the bottom of this whole Burgess-Maclean-Philby conundrum. And as far as I'm concerned, we will work together on this, just you and me. Can you trust all your people?"

Baier stood back, shocked by the question. "Yes, of course I can." He paused. "At least, I think so. No, I'm pretty sure I can. Besides, I only need to keep my boss informed. And I planned to keep it that way in any case. We call it 'need-to-know.' "

"Good." Harrison held up his hand. "It's not that I don't trust your compatriots, but one can never be sure to whom they'll talk. We really do need to move cautiously if we are to find out not only about these killings, but also locate and free your wife." Harrison held up his index finger when he saw Baier frown. "Cautiously does not mean slowly."

"Okay. I'm sold," Baier said. They shook hands again. "But who knows you're here from your side? You didn't just disappear and then re-emerge here, I hope. You have to have some cover back home."

Harrison nodded and chewed his lower lip. "Only Siscourt knows from my end. I had to tell him to get his approval. And he has taken a personal interest in this case. Besides, he would have found out anyway. No doubt he had to get clearance from someone higher up—I'm not sure who. Maybe even a chap we refer to as 'C.' "

"How mysterious. And Turnbridge knows, of course," Baier said. "Anyone else here in Vienna?"

"No. Just our chief of station, like your own."

Baier narrowed his eyes. "Good," he said. "That way, if anything happens to Sabine, I'll know whom to blame. And who to take it out on."

The two men quickly made their way to the Herrengasse and the Modena Palace for the Ministry of the Interior, where, as luck would have it, they ran into Inspector Huetzing in the lobby. The Austrian was wearing a long raincoat over a light-gray suit, which struck Baier as odd, given the bright sunshine that had lit the day so far. Baier had not consulted the weather forecast from the newspaper or radio, and now he wondered if he was in for a wet surprise later this afternoon. Or maybe Huetzing, like Harrison, had something hidden within the folds of his coat.

"Gentlemen, to what do I owe this pleasure?" Huetzing asked. "And Herr Baier, I do not believe I have met this gentleman before. Is he a colleague of yours from the embassy?"

"Actually," Baier replied, "he's a British colleague."

Harrison leaped forward and held out his hand. "George Harris," he proclaimed. "A pleasure to meet you, sir."

Baier stared at the MI6 man for a few seconds before realizing the Brit must be offering a pseudonym to provide cover for his presence here. The name must have popped into his head without much forethought, it being so similar to his real one. He had clearly not been declared to the Austrians. That made sense if he was not going to stay and planned to run a unilateral operation of some sort.

"I assume this has to do with our late friend, Herr von Rudenstein," Huetzing continued. He held out his arm in the direction of the stairway. "Please, allow me. I was just on my way out, but I can take a few minutes for you. We can talk upstairs."

Once in his office, Huetzing pulled off his raincoat and hung it on the coat stand by the door. "Please sit down. How can I help you?"

Baier took his place in one of the chairs directly in front of Huetzing's desk, where he could look out at the blue Vienna sky. There was not a cloud in sight. He leaned forward. "When we last spoke, you mentioned that your investigations had turned up some information on the travels of von Rudenstein behind the Iron Curtain. I believe you mentioned Prague and Budapest in particular.

Huetzing nodded. "Yes, that's correct."

Out of the corner of his eye, Baier saw Harrison lean forward. Baier jumped in before Harrison scared Huetzing away from his cooperative mood. "Would it be possible to share those dates and locations with us?"

"Why?' Huetzing inquired. "What good would that do? Is there a diplomatic or security angle to this killing?"

Baier nodded, as did Harrison. "There may be," the MI6 officer interjected. "It's one reason I'm here."

"We're exploring all angles ourselves, Herr Huetzing," Baier added. "I'm afraid at this point I can't say more."

"But this man was an Austrian citizen, and the crime was committed in Austria," Huetzing noted.

"Yes, yes," Baier said. "You are absolutely right. And I promise that if we find anything that sheds light on this crime, you will be the first to know." He sat back. "You've been very cooperative thus far, Herr Huetzing. That has been noted and appreciated. But I should also remind you that it was your side that called us into this affair."

Huetzing swiveled his chair in the direction of the window, where he joined Baier and Harrison in gazing out at the rare blue sky. A few small patches of white cloud had gathered, drifting lazily over the gabled rooftops of the city. They reminded Baier of the soft dollops of white cream that one found on the tops of many of the coffee servings here, like an invitation to the sweeter things in life. Then again, clouds often brought rain as well.

Huetzing again faced his visitors. "Just a moment." He

walked to a cabinet on his left and pulled out a file from the second drawer, leaving it slightly ajar. Returning to his desk, he shuffled the papers in the file, pulled a blank writing pad toward him along with a fountain pen, and proceeded to jot down a list of places and dates that he found on the sheets from his file. After filling two full pages, he passed both to Baier.

"Our findings only go back six months," Huetzing explained. Those," he pointed to the sheets, "are what we've been able to discern from the records held by our customs and border security people."

Baier glanced at the pages, then shoved them toward Harrison. The MI6 man took them and began to read, while Huetzing studied the Brit's facial expressions, which alternated between intense interest and delight.

Turning his attention to Baier again, Huetzing said, "There is one other thing, Herr Baier."

Baier glanced up from Harrison to the Austrian. "Yes?"

"The last time we spoke, you asked about the identity of a certain Austrian official you had seen in the building." Huetzing wrote something on a slip of paper, which he passed to Baier. "This may be the man you saw." After a weighty pause, he added, "I can't be sure, but logic dictates that this man has the same kind of interest in this case that you two gentlemen appear to share."

Baier read the name on the note in his hand. 'Friedrich Stein.'

"And," Huetzing added, "you did not get that name from me."

Baier and Harrison stood, and the three men exchanged hearty handshakes. "Thank you, Herr Huctzing. I really do appreciate this." Baier studied the Austrian. "But why the name and why now?"

Huetzing stared back at Baier. "Why do you think, Herr Baier?" Another pause, with a silence thick enough to slice.

"Because you don't like interlopers from either side, is my guess."

Huetzing said not a word but simply nodded as his visitors walked toward the door. Then he called Baier back. "Just one more thing, Herr Baier." Huetzing bent low over his desk and wrote on a slip of paper, which he passed to the American. "This is for you," he glanced in the direction of Harrison, "and you alone."

Another name. "Helmut Meyerhof?" he whispered. "Who's this?"

Huetzing smiled. "It's the name that was sewn into the lining of the Wehrmacht jacket von Rudenstein was wearing when we found his body. You might want to speak with this gentleman as well."

"Why? What have you learned?"

Huetzing sighed. "That we were to drop all contact with the man. But he was very interested in speaking with you."

"Why?" Baier was too stunned to ask more detailed questions.

"Because he has information he believes you might need and want to know. You may not like it, however." Huetzing motioned toward the door. "You will have to find him yourself and alone. That is, if he doesn't find you first."

Once outside, Harrison grabbed Baier's arm. "Wait a minute, Karl."

"What's the matter? Did we forget to ask Huetzing something?"

"Give me the diary a second, please. There's something I need to check." Harrison held out his hand, his eyes fixed on the side pocket of Baier's suit jacket where the book resided.

"Sure." Baier offered it to his British colleague. "Just what do you hope to find?"

Harrison paged through the diary, stopping a little over halfway. "Here. Look at these dates, and then at this entry from Huetzing. It's not Prague or Budapest. I don't know why he didn't point this out. And the same entry from Hardwicke gives only a date, not a place."

Baier grabbed the sheet and checked the dates and places on the list Huetzing had given them. "Holy shit! The son-of-a-bitch was in Moscow. And if memory serves me right, that was when the Austrian delegation was there to finalize the terms for the State Treaty back in April. As I recall, there were four long, hard days of negotiations with a sudden breakthrough at the end. That's when the Austrians were finally able to come home with a draft of the Treaty acceptable to all."

Harrison nodded repeatedly, enough that Baier was afraid he might injure himself, sprain his neck or something. "So what could our friends have been up to?" Harrison asked.

Baier added, "And could it have gotten them killed?"

Chapter Twelve

TO HELL WITH *the paperwork*, Baier thought the next morning. He hadn't slept well, not even after draining a bottle of the von Rudenstein wine. He was finding it increasingly difficult to fall asleep at night with the thought of Sabine locked in a Hungarian cell tormenting him. He knew he wouldn't be able to sit still at his desk in any case. And Delgreccio continued to urge patience, as planning for a rescue operation proceeded. Washington would only approve it once all other options had been tried. Unfortunately, Baier did not expect much from the diplomatic approach. For all he knew, this could have been some kind of rogue operation of which the Kremlin was unaware. At the very least, Moscow was likely to deny all knowledge of the affair. It would conflict with the charm offensive underway since the death of Stalin.

So that afternoon Baier drove back through the rolling green countryside of Burgenland to the von Rudenstein estate. The place looked more deserted than on his original visit, if that was possible. He parked his Ford in front of the main entrance and marveled at the silence as he stepped out of the car. He expected some noise at least—movement back in the barn, voices of people at work. Someone was obviously making wine, no matter how little. He had a case at home to prove it. But there was a not a single sound of human activity. It was almost as though the war had just ended and the guns had fallen silent again. Or, given the surroundings and history of this place, it was as though he was slipping back in time, but had yet to arrive at a particular moment in the past.

Baier wandered around the side of the main house and back toward the barn and storage buildings. The smell of stale alcohol drifted into the courtyard, mingling with the scent of honeysuckle and gardenias. He called out to the groundskeeper, Carl Joseph Leibner, several times, his only answer the sound of humming bees and a slight breeze that ruffled his hair. When he gazed toward the acres of vines stretching into the hills, Baier noticed that their branches had begun to fill with the clusters of grapes and the small pointed green leaves that would eventually blossom along the stocks in a few months. The wiring and posts still looked to be in good repair, as though awaiting another harvest.

Giving up on the yard, he strolled back to the front and pushed on the door, surprised to feel it give under his soft pressure. Dust particles swam in the sunlight that had broken through the windows above the door and in the rooms on either side of the hallway. The wooden floor was bare of carpets. To his right was the living or receiving room with a massive portrait of some ancestor sitting atop the mantelpiece in a Baroque-styled picture frame, gold leaf rimming the curved outlines. The fireplace was shrouded in an ornate piece of carved dark wood, cherry maybe. The furniture—two sofas and two sets of armchairs plus small end tables and two large bookcases—looked as though it hadn't been used in years. At least it hadn't been dusted in that long. The sheets covering the chairs and sofas were a pretty good clue.

He marched across the hallway and into what appeared to be a dining room, the large wooden table and twelve chairs around it another solid clue, covered as they were with white sheeting. A huge china cabinet stood against the far wall, across from the two front windows. Two sideboards held their posts on the other walls. Baier walked over to the cabinets and checked the drawers and shelves to see if there was any silver or dishware still there. He was surprised to find both. He marveled that these possessions had not been looted at the end of the war when the Red Army swept through. Probably too busy raping the locals and stealing watches.

Baier glanced into the back room behind the dining area and found a kitchen that looked as though it were still in use. Carl Joseph, Baier guessed, and probably no one else, unless there were laborers who came to work in the vineyards and needed to be fed during the day. As he headed for the front door and was about to pass through the entrance, Baier decided to take a look upstairs.

The steps groaned under his weight, as though they hadn't been asked to work that hard in decades. Carl Joseph was a diminutive man and probably tried to avoid any intrusion into the family's private quarters. Even when no one was left around to populate the estate.

Bedrooms that Baier would consider small by American standards lined the hallway to his right, along with two full baths that looked as though they had been installed around the turn of the century. The curved bathtub and brass plumbing looked inviting, but Baier hadn't come here for the hygiene or to relax.

Rudolph Heinrich von Rudenstein had become a truly interesting enigma. Baier was more and more certain that his actions were at the heart of the killings and his own wife's abduction.

In the opposite direction lay the master bedroom. It was more of a suite, really, with a large bathroom attached. The age appeared the same as the other. This room also featured a canopied bed, still fully made, as though the master would return any day now. The mattress was at least queen-sized, maybe larger.

Directly across from the bed was a roll-top desk that Baier assumed von Rudenstein had used for his personal correspondence and possibly his business interests. Cherry, or whatever similar dark wood, was clearly the preferred material for the furniture here. Baier pulled out the chair, took a seat, and began to rummage through the drawers. In the bottom right-hand one, he found several notebooks that looked like account ledgers. Business correspondence was folded and stuck between several of the pages. There was also a diary. These Europeans sure liked to keep diaries. And that was turning out to be a good thing, he realized, as he turned the pages and became even more familiar with von Rudenstein's thinking and views.

Von Rudenstein's truest and deepest loyalties clearly had lain with the Hapsburg monarchy, which to Baier's American mind seemed like such an anachronism. Every day's entry began with a comment on or praise for the Hapsburg Dynasty, its role in European history, or simply a greeting of *"Hoch"* to the family and throne. But von Rudenstein had not been blind to the troubles plaguing the Empire in its declining years. The Crown and Country had been stretched to its limits in the later decades of the nineteenth century and the first two of the twentieth. Nor had he been unaware of the burdens the legacy of that Empire had left on this part of the world. The entries reflected the evolving sentiments of a young man whose political views and version of history had been shaped by the world of his father.

"Father was right. These nationalists and anti-Semites around Lueger and the so-called Pan-Germans of Schoenerer proved to be the death of our land and rule," was one passage that leaped out at Baier. And not just because it was underlined in deep-red ink. "If only we could have limited the immigration of the Jewish rabble from the East and integrated the Hebrews already resident in the Empire, things would have gone more smoothly; the Pan-Germans and hate-mongers would have had less to work with," read another.

Baier skimmed the pages, pausing to read a passage here and there, figuring he would have more time later to peruse the volume in depth. Several minutes later, though, toward the back of the book he found this comment: "I find it difficult to sympathize with the Jewish element of our population, but there are many who served Crown and Country. Many did not belong, but how will we ever live down the crimes we committed against this race? Father had not foreseen this sort of thing, not the extremity of it all." At least he had admitted, if only to himself, where the Austrians' anti-Semitism had led once given free rein by the Nazis.

So, where did von Rudenstein sit at the time of the Anschluss? Had he really wept, as the groundskeeper had claimed, and if so for what?

"Away, away with this socialist menace!" was another phrase that was repeated several times. "Men like Adler have no sense of loyalty to our crown and society! His successors show the same lack of principle!" Words of anger that repeated that same sentiment. Well, von Rudenstein had clearly not been a left-winger. But what was his true attitude toward the working class? Was von Rudenstein simply another out-of-touch aristocrat, or had he held a more corporatist view of social order and hierarchy, one which the inter-war government in Vienna had exploited in the absence of loyalty to a crown that no longer existed? The quotations would seem to put him in league with the Nazis, and Adler was a Jew to boot, although he had begun his career as a Pan-German who was eventually expelled from the movement when the anti-Semitic component intensified and took on an ethnic base to replace the medieval religious one.

What had it meant for his work with the British over the past decade? And his death? Baier resumed his search.

"Can I help you? Is there something here you are looking for?"

Baier jumped in his seat and swung around to find Carl Joseph Leibner at the door to the bedroom. He shut the book and placed it on the desk.

"Where have you been? I walked all over the grounds outside calling for you. Or anyone, for that matter."

"I must have been in the fields," the groundskeeper replied. "I try to do some tending of the vines every day. I would hate to see the entire holdings slip into ruin."

"What will you do when it comes time to harvest and process the grapes?" Baier asked. The man seemed to accept his intrusion with equanimity, so Baier did not bother to apologize. He was simply grateful he didn't find himself staring at the muzzle of a rifle.

"There are still people in the village who know the work and are happy for the employment."

"But can you make enough to pay them, to keep this property going?'

Leibner sighed and shrugged. "We shall see. I take it one day at a time."

Baier was surprised at how concerned he suddenly felt. "What about the son and daughter? Will they be able to help?" he went on. "Do they show any interest in the family business, the estate?"

Leibner glanced out the window. "They haven't thus far. The son has probably inherited the estate, but we have not heard anything yet." The groundskeeper looked back at Baier and motioned with his head toward the desk. "There is nothing in there that will give you an answer to that question." He paused. "And no one has said anything to me."

"Is there any chance someone else might purchase the property, get it going again commercially?"

"I would not know about those things, sir. You had best ask the son in Vienna. No one I know of has come to view the property."

"How long has the family held this property, Herr Leibner? And how long have you been here?"

"The von Rudensteins were awarded this property in the seventeenth century, after the battle for Vienna. The original Herr was rewarded for his distinguished service against the Turks in relieving the siege in 1683."

"So there was a history of military service and honor in the family that the late Rudolph Heinrich von Rudenstein felt obliged to represent?" The groundskeeper nodded. "What did you know of von Rudenstein's relationship with his father?"

"The Herr obeyed his father, as would any proper son. His father was master of the family and estate until he passed away."

"But what about their politics? Did your master's father share his son's attitude toward the Hapsburgs and their country's history?"

Leibner considered Baier as though the American had arrived from a different planet. Then he nodded. "Of course. That is where the Herr received his political tutoring and perspective."

"And you?" Baier asked. "What's your story here?"

"My family has been working on this estate and in this house since the time of my great-grandfather."

"Do you have any family of your own?"

"My wife became ill and passed away before the war."

"I'm sorry, Herr Leibner."

"And my older son was killed during the fighting at Kursk. My second son returned from a Soviet prisoner-of-war camp in 1948 but died several years later." Leibner moistened lips that appeared to have gone stiff. "He came back a very sick man from working in the mines."

Baier was silent. He wasn't sure what to say. Although Leibner tried to hide his emotions, his face seemed to have aged decades in that single moment. His eyes were wet and cloudy and his cheeks had sunken in toward the skull. Baier had decided to leave the man to his memories and sorrow when Leibner suddenly spoke.

"Is there something you were looking for?" His eyes moved in the direction of the diary. "Or have you found it already?"

Baier was happy that the man had broken the emotional stalemate between them. He took the slim volume in his hand. "I wasn't looking for anything in particular. Just something to help me understand the man, in case it would lead us to his killers." Baier looked out the window. "Have the police been here to speak with you?"

Leibner shook his head. "No, only you. But why do you speak of his 'killers'? How many were there?"

Baier smiled, in spite of himself. "Oh, I'm only speaking in generalities. But I suspect it was not some random act. So there probably was more than one. I think his extracurricular work after the war had something to do with it."

"What sort of work?" Leibner inquired.

"Political work, mostly. I'm afraid I can't say more than that, if only because I still know so little." He raised the diary. "Perhaps there's more in here that will help. I've already found some enlightening things." Baier's gaze shifted from the book to the groundskeeper. "The man truly was a Hapsburg patriot."

Leibner nodded. "Yes, he was. And he hated the Soviets and the Nazis—"

"Although he fought for them, and well."

"Yes. He did so because it was his duty. And he hoped something more could be done after the war."

"About what?" Baier asked.

"It would have been best to ask the Herr, but it's too late for that. I do know he did not believe our country should be confined to the little tourist site that the victorious powers had planned for it."

"Really? That's enlightening. What do you think he meant by that?"

Leibner drew himself up, as though aspiring to a height superior to his own, something approximating his late master's. "He said that our country had played a great role in

European history and should continue to do so. Perhaps one of the victors, such as the Soviets, killed him because of that."

"Why do you suggest the Soviets?"

Leibner shrugged. "It could have been any one of them if it resulted from his 'political work,' as you call it. Even the Americans."

Baier leaned forward and stared hard at the groundskeeper. "If you truly believe that than you've been spending far too much time on this estate." He sat back. "What did he plan to do about Austria's diminished status?"

"The Herr never confided in me. I only know how he felt, what he believed in." Leibner pointed at the book. "Perhaps you'll find more in there."

"Yes, maybe I will. That is, if you have no objection to me taking it back to Vienna."

Leibner shook his head. "It is not mine to give or keep, now that Herr von Rudenstein is gone.

Baier rose to leave. "Thank you, Herr Leibner. You've been very helpful.

Halfway down the front stairs, Baier stopped and turned to look at the groundskeeper, who stood at the top of the stairway. Baier could not read his expression, but he imagined how he must look to the man—a stranger from the New World departing for the foreign lands from which he had come.

"I wish you good luck with your harvest. And with the future of the estate."

"Thank you, sir."

It didn't sound like the old man really meant it.

Before driving back to Vienna, Baier retraced his path along the von Rudenstein vineyards to the border to see how the construction was coming. The Soviets had appeared to be way behind schedule when he last drove through the area, although the presence of the Soviet captain had prevented Baier from making a thorough study of the area.

The captain and his colleagues were nowhere in sight today. Baier parked his car and walked over to the edge on the opposite side of the road to get a clearer view of the plain below. The People's Republic of Hungary stretched out in the distance, running to Budapest and beyond. The construction work at the border looked to be nearly finished, although there were still patches where the fencing had yet to be put in place and where the guard posts stood unfinished or there was simply an empty hole. The poor conscripts and local Hungarians would probably be putting in plenty of overtime.

Then again, that wasn't his problem. Once the State Treaty was in place, those poor people would be stuck behind a new wall that would finalize the division that had split the continent in two. Some hoped the State Treaty and Austrian neutrality would launch a diplomatic effort that might prevent that very development from unfolding. Best as Baier could tell, things were already well along that path. It was difficult to see how a single treaty or a small country in the heart of a tried and battered continent could change that now, especially the tourist attraction that von Rudenstein allegedly had feared it would become.

About half a mile down the road, as Baier was looking for the turn off that would bring him back to the road to Vienna, he encountered that very same Soviet captain standing in the road, waving his right arm for Baier to slow down and stop. The Soviet officer appeared to be alone this time. Baier rolled to a stop as the captain marched over to the driver's side window. Back at the estate, Baier had already rolled down the window in his old Mercedes to allow for a better flow of springtime air.

"So, Mr. American, you have returned." He took a step back, as though to admire Baier's car. "You've improved your standing since you were here last. This automobile is much more impressive."

"Oh, I suppose it's all right. One of the benefits of capitalism, I guess."

The Soviet nodded and smiled. "Have you been studying our work below?"

"Just doing some sightseeing, you might say," Baier responded. "Too bad this beautiful countryside will be scared by the border fencing and towers."

The Soviet glanced in the direction of the border and sighed. "*Ach*, yes. But politics today demands it."

"Not from our side," Baier offered by way of correction.

"That's a matter of interpretation, Mr. American. And it's an interpretation that will be made in our respective capitals, not here. Don't you agree?"

"Unfortunately, yes. But it really is too bad that we can't do more ourselves here on the ground. I mean, those of us on the front line can see the human dimension of these politics, as well as the costs and the opportunities. True?"

The Soviet leaned low to the window and brought his face level with Baier's. "Yes, I suppose there is truth in what you say. But for now I have my orders, which are very clear."

"And those are …?"

"To keep strangers from interfering with or observing our work below." The captain paused to study Baier for a long moment. "You haven't been taking photographs, have you?"

Baier smiled and laughed. "No, I haven't. I didn't even think to bring a camera. I was just visiting a family estate some miles back, looking for more of their wine to purchase."

The Soviet office glanced at the backseat. "Did you find any?"

Baier shook his head. "Unfortunately not. They can't produce in the volume they did formerly. At least not yet."

The Soviet stood. "I'll take you at your word, Mr. American. By the way, what is your name … in case we meet again?"

"Karl Baier. I'm with the American Military Command in Vienna." The Soviet's eyebrows arched. "I work out of the Embassy in Vienna." Baier stared at the Soviet officer in turn. He wasn't sure if the wry grin that appeared was one of friendship or condescension. "And yours?"

The Soviet officer smiled and shook his head. "Not today."

"That's too bad." Baier smiled back at him. "Perhaps we will meet again someday."

"Tell me, Mr. Baier, are the streets of America really paved with gold?'

"Not all of them. Why?"

The captain shrugged. "Just curious. I always test the propaganda of the other side."

"Perhaps you should also test the propaganda from your side," Baier shot back.

The Soviet stood up straight again. "Have a safe drive back to Vienna, Mr. Baier. And please do not stop in this area again, or suddenly remember your camera." He stepped back and saluted. "Until we meet again. Perhaps then we shall have something that will allow us to work together more effectively."

As Baier drove off, he wondered if indeed they would meet again. And just what the hell had the Soviet meant about working together? Looking back toward the captain and the fields below, he'd had an idea about how to move Sabine out of Budapest and back into the West. If the Soviet officer was still around, his plan might even test his taste for cooperation.

Chapter Thirteen

IT HAD BEEN three days since Sabine's kidnapping, and Baier's anxiety was growing worse by the day. He found it impossible to spend any time at his desk. When Baier did show up at the office, Delgreccio would only shake his head at the obvious and unspoken question that hung in the air between them. Baier's face said it all. When could he, or anyone for matter, move on Sabine's captivity? To hell with the growing pile of paperwork in front of him. He had needed yet another bottle of wine to dull the pain and get to sleep last night. And that had only gained him a mere four hours of sleep. If he didn't do something about Sabine's kidnapping soon, he'd turn into an alcoholic.

This morning, he'd decided to put in an appearance with just a quick call. Perhaps he'd shuffle some papers and then poke his head into the chief's office to let him know he still worked here. He'd ask, of course, if there was anything new to report from Washington or Budapest. But as for sitting and working through his cases and catching his breath in this confined space, well, that seemed virtually impossible. It was the uncertainty, not knowing what Sabine was going through, tough as she was, that drove him to distraction.

He had shoved his door almost shut, leaving just a crack for air to circulate in from the corridor. Warmth from the sunlight piercing the windowpanes was already building up, even though it was only mid-morning. Regardless of the heaviness in the air, he wanted to send a clear signal that he did not want to be disturbed.

It had also been almost two weeks since that night at the Danube had launched this entire affair with the discovery of von Rudenstein's corpse. When would he get the break he needed in that case? And would it spring anything loose on Sabine's kidnapping? He trolled through the Rolodex and telephone listings. Friedrich Stein was not easy to find. Baier had respected Huetzing's request to protect the source of his information, which restricted just how much he could say as he inquired after the mysterious Mr. Stein. His contacts were better and more numerous in the Army Intelligence Service and the Austrian military's counter-intelligence wing, the *Nachrichtendienstliche Aufklaerung*, and the *Nachrichtendienstliche Abwehr*, respectively. They were the principal agencies pursuing foreign intelligence targets and the most likely partners for Baier and his office. Baier had hoped that his contacts in their services who worked the Soviet and Warsaw Pact target with him would be discreet as well as forthcoming. But they had claimed never to have heard the name before. Baier was determined to limit his interrogation, claiming a vague need-to-know restriction—to which he wasn't really sure the Austrians paid much heed in their own business dealings—for his brief and superficial questions. He did not want to discuss his concerns over the von Rudenstein death, not yet at least, much less the abduction of Sabine. He wasn't sure yet how far he should let his investigations go within the Austrian Government, or how many people he should bring into Sabine's case. Too many cooks, and all that.

His luck was not much better with their civilian counterparts. Huetzing worked within the State Police division of the Ministry of Interior, the ominously named *Staatspolizei* or *Stapo*, as they were commonly known. Since protecting Huetzing was one of the guiding operational principles here, Baier did not want to delve too far and too fast in that direction in the very office where Huetzing worked. That left the *General Direktion fuer die Oeffentliche Sicherheit*, or the Directorate General for Public Safety. The primary focus of their work was domestic threats and security, but they also functioned in a form of oversight for intelligence operations within Austria. That particular office made a lot more sense to him, and it was here that he had his first success. Not that it was much. He did place the name, but only with some vague, meaningless designation attached to a general office with operational oversight and one without any regional or functional focus. It suggested to Baier that Mr. Stein was either well hidden or that he was fairly high up in the service's hierarchy. In any case, he was not in when Baier tried to call, and the woman on the telephone would not give Baier a direct contact number.

"Glad you could make it in." Delgreccio's greeting had only a mild touch of sarcasm as Baier passed through his boss's office door with a slow, considered gait and a mind that was elsewhere. He bumped into the chair in front of Delgreccio's desk before pulling it back and taking a seat. "You making any headway?" his boss said.

Baier shrugged and looked out the window before fixing his gaze on Delgreccio. "I'm sorry, Chief. I've mostly been trying to find out more about this von Rudenstein character."

"Any luck?"

"Some. I feel like I know the man a whole lot better now, but I'm not much closer to why he was killed. The guy really was a Hapsburg patriot and pretty unhappy with the turn of events here after the First World War and into the Nazi occupation.

It would explain why he was willing to work for the Brits, especially after the last war."

"But does it explain why he served the Nazis so admirably?"

"Yeah, actually, it does. That is, once you understand the guy's family history. He served the state and its rulers, whatever its form, since his preferred alternative was not a realistic option at the time. He was a German patriot of sorts, and a pretty committed anti-Communist."

"But it's not getting you any closer to why he was killed and why the Austrians solicited your assistance."

Baier nodded. "Yeah, exactly. The more I learn, the less I seem to know about the truly relevant motives in this case." He paused. "By the way, have you heard of some guy named Friedrich Stein?"

Delgreccio's his gaze roamed to the ceiling and back. Then he shook his head. "Can't say that I have. Why?"

"Well, it seems that's the guy who paid a visit to my place the morning after von Rudenstein's body was found. He made the initial warning about Sabine. I'd really like to find the son-of-a-bitch and grill the bastard."

"Have you placed him within the government here, or is he working this case on his own—some kind of freelancer? Or maybe even a Kraut—from the East, that is."

"No, he's definitely an Austrian, and his name is known over at the Public Safety Directorate. He does appear to work there, although it's not clear in what capacity. I'm guessing he's fairly high up in their operations branch."

Delgreccio leaned forward. "I'll see if I can find anything else out. How'd you come by the name?"

Baier leaned forward in turn and lowered his voice, as though the very walls of his chief's office posed a threat to Baier's future cooperation with the Austrians, and Huetzing in particular. "I got it from that cop who's been working the von Rudenstein case. He asked me to protect him as the source of the name."

"Why did he come forward with it?"

Baier tapped his chin in thought. "I have the suspicion that it was more of a personal grudge. Like he didn't appreciate the interference and obstruction from another branch of the government."

"Well, it does sound pretty mysterious." Delgreccio smiled. "You gotta love those bureaucratic squabbles, and then exploit 'em when you find 'em. They do help sometimes. All the same, I wonder just what this Stein guy does. And why we haven't come across the name before." Delgreccio glanced at the door, and then back at Baier. "How have the Brits been? Are you getting the cooperation you need?"

Baier brightened. "Yeah, that's going pretty well. They've sent down that guy I met in St. Andrews when the locals were investigating the death of Professor Hardwicke. As it turns out, the dead guy had a diary, which they've shared with me. And this new fellow here in Vienna—"

"Turnbridge?'

Baier waved a hand in denial. "No, no. That's the guy they had here before. Nice fellow, but kind of limited in terms of his capabilities or initiative. I'm not sure which. Anyway, the new guy in town is Harrison. He was supposed to be von Rudenstein's case officer after the war, once Hardwicke retired."

"How long ago was that?"

"I'm not absolutely sure, but several years ago. Anyway, the interesting thing is that it appears Hardwicke hadn't given up his asset, which left Harrison high and dry."

Delgreccio sat back. "You mean the son-of-a-bitch was still running the old Austrian? What the hell for?"

Baier raised a finger in the air. "That's what we're trying to find out."

"We?"

Baier raised his eyebrows. "Yeah, this Harrison guy is very open and cooperative. It seems he's as pissed about the way things are going as I am. He wants to protect his own back, here and in London."

"Which is understandable, given all the crap they've been going through."

Baier stood to leave but asked one last question. "What's the word from Budapest?" Delgreccio frowned. "Ralph, you know I'm going to keep hounding you. I can't stand it anymore."

Delgreccio stared at his deputy. "We're working on it, Karl. Noting definite yet, but we'll get there. I promise."

Baier raked his hands through his hair as he paced the room a few times then stopped at the door. "I know you guys are trying, but I'm at my wit's end. I'm giving it a day or two more, tops. Then I'm going in and bringing her out by myself if I have to."

"Oh? What did you have in mind?"

Baier's expression was tight and determined. "I'm still working on that. I'll have a plan soon enough."

Delgreccio stared hard at his deputy. "Don't let your emotions get the better of you, Karl. Make sure you work with us on this. We've got good people working in Budapest."

Baier smiled for the first time that morning. "Oh, I will, Ralph. I'm not that crazy. Not yet, anyway."

Harrison suggested they meet at the opera house this time. He claimed it was the perfect location for counter-surveillance.

"Are you really that worried about being tailed and overheard?" Baier had asked when they met at the back corner of the Operngasse and across the street from the famous Sacher Hotel.

"Shit, yes, mate. I don't trust my own people, much less those Soviet bastards." He took Baier's arm and led him around the front of the building, through the innumerable archways that seemed to hold the building up, and toward the front of the opera house, where they strolled through the ornate entrance and up the marvelous baroque staircase. Called the Grand Staircase, it was embellished with statues, elaborate marble handrails, and fronted by a series of huge paintings that depicted the muses of opera and ballet. He couldn't be sure if these allegorical figures were those that traditionally portrayed the finer arts. Baier did know that whenever he and Sabine had visited the place since its re-opening after being rebuilt following its bombing in 1945, it always left him breathless. Understandably, there were mobs of tourists and locals eager to see it all for themselves and probably even purchase tickets for the upcoming performances. Baier wondered how he and Harrison would ever be able to identify possible tails in that fast-moving crowd. "You know what we've been going through with that Philby bastard."

"So you're convinced he's really guilty?"

"Yes, believe it or not, there are a few of us around. Besides, I can't stand those snotty Oxbridge pricks. But it's the Austrians that have me worried now. On reflection, I probably shouldn't have gone with you to see that cop. It's best that I stay as far as possible away from those people."

"Is that because you guys kept running a unilateral operation with von Rudenstein?"

"Yes, that and the fact that at the moment we, or I, know so little about that operation. There may have been Austrians involved, or at least aware of it, but until I know more I'll need to move cautiously." Harrison held his right forefinger up in the air. "Do you suppose that fellow following you in St. James Park could have been Austrian? Possibly the same fellow who accompanied us from the Rathaus? I believe I saw him again today. He kept about twenty yards behind us.

Shit, Baier thought, *he's back*. "I'd really be surprised if he was in London, especially an Austrian. I wouldn't expect them to have that kind of reach, not to mention the resources." He sighed. "I wonder where he picked us up."

Harrison glanced over at his American companion and grimaced.

Baier shot a look backward down the front staircase. "I have to confess that I missed this one. I've been kind of preoccupied lately. Can you describe him?"

"Sure," Harrison replied. "Several inches shorter than you, but stockier and broad-shouldered. Rough but short-brown hair and dressed like a day laborer who just got off work."

"Thanks. If he isn't Austrian, he certainly outfitted himself to fit into the Viennese background."

"I suppose you're right." They resumed walking. "My guess is that it is a Soviet operative or one of their satraps acting on instructions."

"Why the Soviets?"

"I figure them for the von Rudenstein and Hardwicke killings," Harrison said. "It fits their M.O. The problem is, I can't fathom their motives."

Baier considered his approach to Nuchyev and the alarm bells he had hoped to set off by referring to Sabine and Chernov. "Well, there was that trip to Moscow, remember?"

"True," Harrison replied. "But at this point it's simply one more piece of this mysterious puzzle, at least until we know more about it. I get the feeling that after all this time, we're just scratching at the surface."

"Does the name Friedrich Stein ring a bell for you?" Baier said. "I've been able to place him in the Public Safety Directorate, but that's it."

"Is this the chap who paid that call the first morning?' Baier nodded. "Well, at least it sounds as though he isn't in counter-intelligence, which takes some of the heat off."

"Not that we know of," Baier said. "Hell, I'm not sure what he's involved in at this point."

"True enough. But even if he had a counter-intel interest, that would hardly explain his approaching you shortly after the murder of our Austrian friend."

"True, he wanted to make sure I didn't walk away, which would have been my natural instinct in a case like this."

"And you say he gave an early warning about your wife and her safety?"

Baier nodded. They reached the top of the stairs and started to move off toward the stalls. "That's right. Which raises the question of what he may have known about Soviet plans in East Germany as they prepared to move in on Sabine."

Harrison halted in the corridor and grabbed Baier's arm again. "You don't suppose the prick is a double agent or some kind of Soviet plant? Lord knows there seem to be enough of those bastards running around these days."

"If that's the case, then why have me followed by a tail? Besides, most of those double agents seem to speak English with a posh Oxbridge accent," Baier reminded him. Harrison's expression was pained. "Sorry," Baier said. "I couldn't resist."

"Well, please do. I think you realize that it's difficult enough as it is. At least for me."

"I have been learning a lot more about the character of von Rudenstein, though. Visiting his estate and talking with the groundskeeper proved enlightening. It even explained why he worked for you guys. Somewhat at least."

"How so?" Harrison asked.

Baier stopped before they entered one of the stalls to the right of the stage. Directly to their front, a small sea of plush red color arose and spread to both sides through the carpeting, seats, and curtains. "Do you really need to ask me that? I mean, your country represented the fight for freedom and justice in Europe, right? At least it did until we entered the war." Baier grinned. For some reason, he enjoyed ribbing this British colleague, perhaps because Harrison was dedicated and capable and might also prove to be a valuable friend.

Harrison rolled his eyes. "Oh, please. It took your lot long enough to jump in as it is. And now it's people like me who want to make damn sure you don't run away, back across the pond, like you did last time."

"Not much chance of that." Baier studied the luxurious

interior of the opera house. He had yet to see a performance here. He'd wanted to wait until Sabine returned. "It's funny, but when you stand in a place like this, you can almost forget how much this continent has suffered and how much power and authority it has lost, despite the rich history and traditions. You needn't worry, Tom. We can't just pack up and leave now."

"It isn't just the continent in need of your patronage," Harrison said. "We still have our rationing system in place, you know."

Baier patted him on the arm. "Yes, I do. But I can still understand why someone like von Rudenstein might have seen the need to work for your service to do what he could, to make a contribution to restoring some of that."

"Why not you Yanks? You're the new big boy on the block, even if you have only moved in recently."

Baier considered the ceiling and its massive crystal chandelier before turning back to his British colleague. "He may have been one of the many who consider us interlopers, ne'er-do-wells." He shrugged. "I'm just guessing here. The man remains an enigma. Besides, you guys still want and have a role to play. He probably felt more comfortable working with you."

"Karl, your observations on European history are fascinating, but do they get us closer to solving the puzzle of one dead Austrian? Have you had a chance to read through Hardwicke's diary?"

Baier shook his head. "No, not yet. But it occupies some prime real estate in a drawer of my night table. And what I keep driving at here is motives for the actors involved."

Harrison started for the passage back into the corridor. "Well, as far as the diary is concerned, I can't help but think that there's more in there than we realize. Or certainly more than I could find."

"You mean about why von Rudenstein continued to work for you, or why you folks continued to have an interest in him and what he might be able to do for you?"

"Both, actually," Harrison replied. "But, once again and more importantly, some direct indication of why he and Hardwicke were killed."

And who might be behind Sabine's kidnapping. "If you haven't been able to find the answer to the first, what makes you think you can find the answer to the second? Or that I can solve either mystery? After all, Hardwicke was your officer."

Harrison pointed at Baier. "You certainly know the saying about two heads being better than one. Well, that may apply here as well." He sighed. "I mean, your stature as an outsider could reveal something I've missed."

"In the meantime, you'll let me know what you find out about Stein?"

Harrison continued his stroll down the steps of the Grand Staircase and toward the front entrance. "Yes, yes, of course. You're aware that I am constrained against inquiring too broadly back home. But I'll ask Sir Robert if the name means anything to him."

"Thank you."

Baier took one last look around the wonderful old building before he headed into the bright sunshine. He recalled hearing that the architects had been widely criticized for their design, and that one had even died of a heart attack or committed suicide before the grand opening, thus missing the adulation that followed shortly thereafter. Baier wondered if there was some kind of parallel to von Rudenstein and Hardwicke and anyone else involved in this case.

At least he had not seen anything resembling a tail in here. He wondered if Harrison would say the same.

Chapter Fourteen

THIS CITY—NO, THIS part of Europe—could not make up its mind which season of the year it was in. Later that afternoon, Baier watched the sun flee behind roving clouds of white and gray vapor in a cool, darkening sky as he sat on a bench a little over a block down from the Ministry of Interior. He had no way of knowing, of course, whether Stein would use this particular entrance. There were probably several others at the back or along the sides through extensions to the main block. Seeing how he had little choice, Baier thought it was worth a try. He couldn't cover them all, so he chose the main one.

After an hour that seemed like two, Baier was rewarded for his diligence. Stein strolled casually through the front set of glass and steel doors. His full-length beige raincoat was open at the front and pressed to his sides by hands thrust into the front pockets of the slacks in a black woolen suit. The man was exactly as Baier remembered him: tall, thin, and angular, with dirty-blond hair that flapped down across the tops of his ears and his collar. Stein's face remained thankfully exposed enough to give Baier a clear view of his profile with the hair pushed from his forehead like a stiff mop.

Stein strolled down the street away from Baier, who had to hustle up from his seat to make sure the Austrian did not lose him along the broad pedestrian boulevard that led through the heart of Vienna's old city center. Surveillance was easy enough despite the man's long, looping strides. Stein ambled along the sidewalk and crossed the city's busy intersections like a man out for an evening stroll. Not once did he pause or double back to check for a tail. But then, why should he? Why would he suspect that anyone, much less an American intelligence officer, would be following him?

As he approached the Stefansdom, Stein angled around the front of the cathedral and proceeded down the street that ran along the left side of the church. He passed the gate tourists could use to view the common burial tomb in the church cellar. It contained the skeletal remains of the thousands of paupers from the city's rich history—those too poor to afford their own burial plots. Mozart was even reputed to have found his resting place there, although Baier doubted it. Baier also doubted Stein would enter the afterlife from such a common and forlorn departure point. From all that he had seen, this was a man able to adapt to almost any circumstances, any political or social environment, and not only survive, but prosper. Whether that talent would pass muster with St. Peter once Stein arrived at the pearly gates was another matter and not Baier's problem.

Just shy of the back alley that led to the house where Mozart had resided during his longest sojourn in Vienna—three of his thirteen years—Stein cut to his left along Stobelgasse and followed the meandering pathways to Baeckerstrasse. This route brought the two to the city square that had been renamed for Ignaz Seipel, one of Austria's interwar chancellors who hadn't been quite as unsuccessful as most of the others. So now he had his own square to remind people. Stein halted only momentarily, then marched into the Jesuit Church in front of him.

Baier doubted the man intended to say a prayer or light a candle. Perhaps he suspected surveillance and decided to see if anyone followed him in. Baier sure as hell was not going to do so. Across from the church entrance was a small café that appeared to accommodate no more than twenty-five or thirty customers, while also providing a good vantage point of the church itself, an eighteenth-century reconstruction the Jesuits had consecrated as their local headquarters because of its proximity to the old university. The Jesuits had long been known for their academic prowess, leading the Vatican's charge into the Counter-Reformation, and their church conveyed that sense of purpose and power. Baier and Sabine had visited it once, hoping for a break from the elaborate and ornate Gothic decorations in St. Stephen's only to find the overwhelming gold ornamentation that typified so many Baroque churches in Europe. At times Baier had wondered how there could still be any gold and marble left in the world.

After about five minutes, Stein returned to the street and retraced his steps to another café in Baeckerstrasse. Baier hurriedly threw some money on the table to pay for the coffee he hadn't touched and hustled back to Figlmuellers, the famous schnitzel restaurant across the street, where he planted himself at a table by the window. Stein had taken a seat at a table near the rear with a clear view of the entrance to the square outside. He ordered a coffee. Baier did likewise. His goal was simple: get some sense of the man's life, his style, his behavior, and if possible, his home address.

To his surprise, it was not long—perhaps another ten minutes—before Stein had company. That in itself was no great surprise. But his company was: the Soviet officer Nuchyev. Baier sat nearly dumbfounded as Nuchyev took a seat opposite Stein, his back to the entrance. Fortunately this also blocked Stein from seeing any further into the street or the café where

Baier sat. So far Stein had shown no sign of detecting Baier's presence. The down side was that Nuchyev also blocked Baier's view of the conversation—not that he could hear anything anyway. He did observe as both men became increasingly agitated, their arms extending and fingers pointing. Their faces glowed with patches of red.

Occasionally, Nuchyev or Stein would lean forward over the small glass-topped table separating them as though to make a point. After another ten minutes Nuchyev jumped up, his head shaking and his arms waving. He very nearly upset the waiter's tray teetering with cups of coffee and glasses of water. Then he stormed out, his face frozen in a grimace. He had never bothered to order a coffee.

This did not seem to bother Stein. He finished his own cup, ordered another, then sat back in his own iron-rung chair and lit a cigarette. He was also smiling. Baier could see that much now.

The second shock of the day came when Stein received his second visitor. This shock easily surpassed the first. The newcomer was Thomas Harrison, the British intelligence officer Baier had come to think of as a trusted colleague. Harrison demonstrated a bit more professional savvy than his Soviet predecessor by pulling a chair from a nearby table over to Stein's and placing it at the side so he could also keep an eye on the street and the entrance. Baier tried to press his body almost literally into the wall behind him to become as inconspicuous as possible.

The progress of this conversation went in almost exactly the opposite direction as the previous one. Harrison ordered his own coffee and a piece of Sachertorte. It was Stein who appeared to lose his composure after about five minutes, as he squirmed in his chair, thrust out his arms, and ran his hands over his slicked-back hair. Stein's mood seemed to ebb and flow, but Harrison remained calm as he chewed, swallowed, sipped, and smiled. It was the smiling that seemed to aggravate

Stein the most. After fifteen minutes where he did most of the talking, Stein jumped up and marched out the door and down the street, thankfully in a direction away from where Baier was sitting.

There was no way he was going to follow the Austrian now. Not with Harrison still in that café. Baier watched as the Brit sipped another cup of coffee, lit his own cigarette, paid the bill, and departed. The smile never left his face.

Harrison moved off in the direction of the Stefansdom, while Baier headed for his office. He stumbled several times, distracted by his efforts to come to terms with this discovery, this new and troubling information, over the course of a long, slow walk.

BAIER FINISHED THE afternoon in his office before heading home shortly after six o'clock. He had managed to get some work done, even if only administrative stuff like personnel evaluations and approvals for cable traffic to Washington. The streets were beginning to empty themselves of commuters as he made his way back to his house. The solitude comforted Baier as he tried to work through the information he had assembled and all that had happened. What disturbed him most was how little he knew at this point about the one event that had pulled him into this mess to begin with and the link to Sabine's disappearance, if there even was one. All this confusion, just as he'd thought the picture was becoming clearer, at least the picture of the sort of man von Rudenstein had been.

When he glanced down the sidewalk that ran in front of his house, Baier saw a familiar figure in a dark woolen suit and beige raincoat. He was bare-headed, and stood two houses down, waiting for Baier to return.

"I understand you've been asking around about me."

"I have," Baier replied. "I'm glad you at least waited outside for me to come home this time."

Friedrich Stein smiled and waved at Baier's front door.

"There was no need for the same dramatics this time, Herr Baier." He approached Baier in a casual glide.

Baier paused at the entrance to the walkway that led to his house. "I suppose I should invite you inside." He gestured with his head toward the door and stepped toward it as Stein fell into line behind him. A chill raced down Baier's spine with this man so close behind him. He quickened his pace.

"No need to hurry, Herr Baier. You're safe."

Baier pushed open his front door and held out his arm by way of invitation. Stein stepped through and waited in the foyer. "Thank you." Stein smiled. "And no, before you ask, I would not like a coffee."

"I was not going to offer you one."

"However, a beer or a glass of wine would be nice."

"Really? Is that your price?"

"For tonight, yes."

Together they strolled back to the kitchen, where Baier pulled down two wine glasses with their green stems and clear bulbs, then walked over to the counter across from refrigerator, where he pulled out a bottle of the Blaufraenkisch from Burgenland. He poured two glasses and offered one to Stein.

"Thank you again, Herr Baier. Again you make it worth my while to visit you at home." He picked up the bottle to study the label. "I see you have been doing your homework on our man." He glanced from the bottle to Baier. "At least some of it."

"Let's hope you help make it worth my while. And while we're on the subject, just why do you prefer to meet me here and not at your office? And just where and what is your office?"

Stein sipped the wine. When he spoke, his focus remained on the rim of his wine glass. "Suffice to say, Herr Baier, that I have a wide operational latitude and very high-level access. I operate on the orders and with the knowledge of few men."

"Well, that's certainly convenient."

"Yes, it is. And you can understand that this is a delicate subject, and there is a need, I believe, to keep the circle of those who know of our interest in this affair very small." Stein shifted his gaze to Baier. "I'm aware that you have been investigating Herr von Rudenstein's background and history, in part at my instigation."

"That's one way of looking at it."

"Yes, well, it is my way of looking at it."

Baier took a seat opposite Stein and sipped his own wine. Finally he said, "You can understand that I have another incentive these days, one that takes me past the mystery of a dead Austrian." He sipped again. "In fact, it was an incentive you gave me just as this thing was getting started."

"Ah, yes, your wife. I did try to warn you, you know."

"But how did you know to warn me? That's what I find so interesting."

Stein drank more of his wine so that the glass was almost empty. Baier stood to fetch the bottle from its post next to the sink over to table and refill Stein's glass. While he was it, he topped off his own as well.

"You can appreciate that this is a delicate matter, Herr Baier."

"As is my wife's situation. So get on with it."

Stein studied his glass, then raised his eyes again to Baier's face. "I had no foreknowledge that your wife would be seized by the Communist authorities. But I did believe she was in danger where she was, and that it would be best to get her out of there."

Baier leaned across the table to bring his face closer to Stein's. "How did you know she was in danger?"

"What I did know for certain was that the death of von Rudenstein signaled how seriously they took this business."

"What business? Who are 'they'?"

"They, Herr Baier, are elements of the Soviet security services, and presumably their allies behind the Curtain. I am fairly certain that they are responsible for the death of von Rudenstein."

"And the 'business,' as you call it?"

Stein relaxed back in his chair and gave an elaborate shrug. "That I cannot say for sure. It's one reason I wanted you involved. I hoped that would bring their intentions and plans to the surface."

"But why this certainty about the Soviets and the death of our aristocratic friend?"

"He clearly presented a threat to their interests."

"That sounds pretty damn vague, Stein. In fact, it sounds like you're holding back some important information."

Stein waved his free arm in the air, the one not holding the wine glass. "No, no. Not at all, Herr Baier. I can tell you that I knew the British were 'running' von Rudenstein, as you Americans like to say. But for what purpose I was never sure. I can also say that I was aware from their activities here in Austria that the Soviets were also well-informed. And very concerned."

"What else?"

"What else do you need to know?"

"Why my wife? Why take anyone at all?"

"Because, Herr Baier, they wanted leverage. Given their brutal history, are you really so surprised that they would make that sort of play? Have you no idea of the stakes involved? For them, for Austria, for the West?"

"But why Sabine?"

Stein shook his head, as though marveling at how obtuse this American could be. "Because she was vulnerable." Stein paused for another sip of wine. He pursed his lips and said, "This is really very nice." He raised the glass. "My hat is off to our dead friend."

"I'm so glad you like it. But again, why Sabine in particular? Why would they need leverage over me, or even over an American if they were so concerned about what the Brits were doing with von Rudenstein?"

Stein stared at his glass as he said, "That is a question I can't really answer. Perhaps because they assumed you Anglo-

Saxons are all one and the same. If so, they wouldn't be the only ones."

"And why take her to Budapest and not just back to Berlin? It would be much easier to arrange an exchange up there."

Stein frowned, as if trying to work out the logic of Budapest. "That's what I originally thought as well. It suggests the other side is not interested in a simple exchange of prisoners. A contact of ours in the Hungarian service passed along some interesting information when we started inquiries on behalf of your wife." He looked up at Baier. "You see we are also trying to help. This affects all of us. It's why you saw me speaking with that Russian this afternoon."

Goddamn you, Baier thought. "What were you talking about?"

"Nothing that you need to be concerned about. Certainly not regarding your wife's safety. My intention is to help."

"How can I be sure?"

"You can't."

Unsure of how to show his appreciation, Baier hesitated to speak. He didn't hesitate long. He still wasn't sure how much to trust this enigmatic Austrian.

"I thank you for your good intentions at least. What did he say?"

"The Hungarian or the Russian?'

"Either one."

Stein rolled his hand over the table top. "The Russian claimed to have no knowledge of the entire affair."

"Do you believe him?"

"Does it matter? I have no leverage over the man." He paused and studied Baier's face. "Fortunately, the Hungarian was more forthcoming. He mentioned the presence of a certain Russian in Budapest, the one who is running this operation. The Hungarians are being kept in a supporting role, for the most part."

"Did he have a name?"

Stein leaned back again and pondered his wine glass. He drank some more. The glass was now about half empty, but Baier did not bother to refill it.

"Unfortunately, he did not. Not that he was willing to pass along at any rate. We are trying to reach out to him again to help ascertain just where they are holding her and what can be done. You know, we still have a few friends over there from before. Not all have been shot or 'retired.' "

"Did he say anything else about this Soviet officer? Was he KGB or GRU?"

"I believe he is KGB. But even here we are not certain. Then again, does it really make a difference?"

"Perhaps. How can we find out more?"

Stein sat forward, his body resting against the edge of the table. He picked up his wine glass, studied the nectar against the fading sunlight outlined against Baier's kitchen window, and nodded. He drained the remainder and sighed with satisfaction. Then he leaned over the table close enough for Baier to smell the scent of the grapes.

"That, Herr Baier, you will have to determine for yourself. I would suggest you travel to Budapest to discover what you can and confront this Russian officer yourself. I believe that is the best way to determine just what they want and what you must do to free your wife."

"That sounds a little too convenient. Do you really think it will be that easy?"

If Baier ever intended simply to walk in and open a conversation with Sabine's captors, he was not about to discuss those plans with this man. Hell, he was not about to discuss anything he planned to do to Sabine's wardens with anyone outside of the Vienna and Budapest stations. "And what did you talk with Harrison about?"

"Ask him yourself. The British are your special friends now."

"He did not look like he was your friend at the café."

Stein shrugged. "I never thought he was. But I'm not going

to help you there. You need to follow up on those issues on your own. And believe me, there are definitely matters you need to discuss with your *friends*." He spat the last word out as though it were an insult.

Baier said nothing. He stared at Stein, and he could have sworn that a smile escaped the man's lips, although it passed quickly, quicker even than the wine that seemed to evaporate from his glass.

AFTER STEIN HAD passed from his sight down the street, Baier refilled his glass and walked with it to his bedroom. He set it on the night table and pulled Hardwicke's and von Rudenstein's diaries from the top drawer. Leaning back against the pillow, he opened first one slim volume, then the other. The shock was slow in coming, perhaps because the revelation only came after ten minutes of reading in each of the diaries. But it made a lot of sense. It was almost as though a new door, no, a new building, had opened before him.

"You son-of-a-bitch, Stein," was all he could think to say. But he said it out loud, and he said it twice.

Chapter Fifteen

"OKAY, RALPH, IT'S time. It's been four days, and that's four days too many. I'm going in."

Ralph Delgreccio studied his deputy as Baier took his usual seat opposite his boss's desk. Delgreccio swung his own chair around, away from the window and back toward the pile of requisition forms awaiting his signature. The chief of station appeared taken aback at first by his deputy's determined expression. Baier's entire body was rigid, as though cast in concrete, tense with anxiety and anticipation.

"Actually, I was hoping to keep you out of it." Delgreccio said.

"What the hell for?"

"Because," Delgreccio explained, speaking slowly and enunciating his words carefully in hopes of calming his deputy, "you know it's best to keep emotions out of an operation like this."

Baier narrowed his eyes. "That's not gonna work here, Ralph, and you know it. I've waited long enough. I'm not sure there's much more I can find out here that will help, or if I can concentrate long enough to do my job properly."

"You mean find out more on the von Rudenstein case?"

"Yeah, that. But only in part. Sabine's my priority now, Ralph."

"I thought you saw the two cases as linked." Delgreccio stood. "Don't get me wrong, Karl, I'm not trying to prolong Sabine's incarceration. I want her out and back here, too. We've made good progress putting a team in there, and our folks in Budapest have located the place where they're holding her. But I want to make sure we don't get ourselves wrong footed by going in too soon."

"I'll just have to take that chance, Ralph. I can't wait any longer. This is driving me crazy."

Delgreccio's gaze shifted from his deputy to the desktop and then back to Baier. Then Delgreccio nodded and slapped the edge of his desk. "Okay, then, we'll move on it now. And you're in as well." He regarded Baier in silence, then added, "But before you go, we need to set things up with our folks there, and I will need to square this with our chief in Budapest."

"Of course." Baier leaped up, then sat back down, his right leg pumping with nerves. "Once we can get Sabine free, I have a pretty good idea of how and where we can cross the border—"

"I'll let you discuss that with the Station in Budapest. But let me also pass along some information about our friend Stein that I discovered after paying a call on the director of the General Security Directorate yesterday."

Baier's eyebrows arched. "So you went right to the top? I'm impressed. And grateful."

"Yeah, well, they owe us a few favors, several hundred in fact, considering all the stuff we're leaving behind and all we've done to get their show up and running."

Baier leaned forward. His leg movements had slowed but not stopped entirely. "What did you learn?"

"That our friend Mr. Stein has an interesting and complicated history. He is definitely Austrian, from the Tirol actually, which is about as Austrian as you can get."

"I suspected as much from his accent."

"Well, he was a devout Catholic, like most there, and he struggled to come to terms with the new Nazi state after the Anschluss. But when he did, he must have gone in whole hog, as they say in Iowa—"

"I thought you grew up in Brooklyn."

Delgreccio nodded and frowned. "A mere technicality. As I was saying, he dived right into the new regime and ended up working for the Gehlen Organization during the war. You know, Fremde Heer Ost, the military intelligence arm that focused on the Eastern Front."

"Yeah, I know all about those guys, Ralph, the Wehrmacht's intelligence arm. At least we know he's a real professional. Can we assume he's still a committed anti-Communist, like Herr Gehlen?"

Delgreccio nodded. "His boss, whom I spoke with, was pretty confident about his opposition to the Soviets. It looks like he retained that anti-Commie edge from his war experience. It may have been what motivated him under the Nazis in the first place."

"Can we assume that since 1945 he worked at some point for Kurt Fechner?"

"Oh, he most certainly worked for Fechner. He reportedly worked under the guy when Fechner ran the Gehlen organization's *Leitstelle II Sued-Ost* operation here in Vienna during the war, collecting all that intel on Eastern Europe and Yugoslavia. And afterward, too, when the Austrians set up the same sort of operation under Fechner—with our help, of course. Stein has apparently been instrumental in overseeing the turnover of the archives to us—the information they have here on the Soviets and their buddies from Gehlen's organization."

"And just what does he do now?"

Delgreccio blew out his cheeks. "Oh, he does a lot. And in the prime minister's office. Apparently, you received a late-night visit from the PM's personal intelligence advisor."

"In that case, we should be able to trust him on this. Wouldn't you say?"

Delgreccio frowned again. "Yes, if that's all there was. But he apparently spent several years in Soviet captivity—three to be exact—returning home in 1948."

"Are you going to tell me he did something then that raises suspicions about his loyalty?"

Delgreccio shifted toward the window and then back to face his deputy. "I wish I knew, Karl. The Austrians claim that period remains an open gap in their records and their assessment of Stein. At the same time, they claim that they've never had any cause to question his commitment or loyalties to Austria and the West."

Baier leaned back in his chair, looked sideways at the wall, then blew out his breath. "Shit, Ralph. That makes what I'm about to tell you seem even worse."

"Oh, Christ. What is it now?"

Baier shook his head, then pushed out the words in a stream of frustration and anxiety. "I waited for Stein yesterday outside his office—or what I thought was his office at the Interior Ministry. Fortunately, he either works there or spends a lot of time in the building. So I tailed him for a while. I mostly wanted to see where he lived, where he went, what he did. You know the story, establish a baseline on the guy's credibility."

"And …?" Delgreccio sat rigid, staring hard at his deputy. Shadows dipped through the window, cutting the desk into streaks of morning light and shade.

"Well," Baier continued, "after about twenty minutes out walking through the old town behind the Stefansdom, he met with my friend—no, my acquaintance—the Soviet officer Nuchyev at some café."

"The guy from the riverbank? The Soviet rep when this whole thing got started?"

Baier nodded. "That's right. I couldn't hear what they said, but the conversation seemed to start off amicably enough.

After a few minutes, though, there was a lot of hand wringing and finger pointing on both sides. Then the Soviet jumped up and left."

"So?" Delgreccio said. "What did our friend Mr. Stein do?"

"He sat and finished his coffee." Baier cleared his throat as he gathered his thoughts. "Then it got even more puzzling. My pal Harrison showed up next."

"Motherfucker! How did that go?"

Baier grimaced. "Worse. The finger-pointing and red cheeks were there from the get-go. But this time Stein was the one to storm out."

"What did Harrison do?"

"He just sat there, smiling. And then he ordered another coffee."

"I think you'd better hold off on Budapest, Karl," Delgreccio said in a low voice. He had turned quite pale.

"Fuck it, Ralph, I don't care at this point." Baier slapped his thigh for emphasis. "I'm not waiting any longer. I understand why you're concerned, but you can certainly understand where I'm coming from. What I really need to know is whether there's something else you're not telling me."

The chief threw up his hands in frustration. "Hell, Karl, I wish I knew if there was anything else. But there isn't, not that I can see right now. It's that gap that troubles me. I have a very bad feeling that you're going into the lion's den, as it were, knowing all this. You know the kind of organization you'll be up against. Not just the Soviets."

Baier's jaw hardened and his eyes narrowed. "Hell, yes, Ralph. I know. I'm aware of the kind of shit the Hungarian security service, the AHV, pulled after the war. Those bastards were as bad as any of the Soviets' henchmen, if not worse. I mean, deportations, torture, show trials, executions—and not just of potential opponents, but whole, extended families. That was all standard stuff for those creeps."

"Yeah," Delgreccio said. "The reformer Imre Nagy was able

to tame them some after 1953 when he became the prime minister, but who really knows what the hell is going on inside an organization like that? That prick Erno Gero is still around as head of the Hungarian Communist Party, so you know they've got some real bastards working in their security services. Our penetrations have not gotten very far. And despite what the Austrians think, neither have theirs." Delgreccio considered his deputy for a moment. "I'm sorry to say all this, Karl. It's almost like you want the Soviets to be running this particular show. It may be your only hope."

Baier stood, recalling Stein's comments from the night before. "Well, that means we can't waste any time, and going in there is a risk I'm going to have to take. Why do you think I've been lying awake at night trying to figure a way to get Sabine out of there? You know the saying, 'There comes a time ....' Well, this is it."

Delgreccio rose to his feet as well. "Just be sure you check back in with the Brits before you do anything further. I asked Wainwright to press them again on their handling of von Rudenstein and what the hell this Hardwicke guy may have been up to with him."

"And ...?"

Delgreccio shook his head. "Nada. So you need to get things straight with your buddy here before you go. He has some explaining to do."

Baier nodded and reached out his hand. "Thanks, Ralph. I was planning to do just that."

Delgreccio took his deputy's hand. "And stop back in here so we can set you up before you leave." The chief stared hard into his deputy's eyes. "Be careful, Karl. For Sabine's sake, if not your own."

HARRISON LIVED ON one of those streets that seemed to have escaped the ravages of Vienna's periodic bombings during the war and the brief battle for the city as the Red Army swept in. The bay windows, the chiseled, Baroque façades with their bright-yellow colors and classical window frames of gray concrete and gabled rooftops harked back to a preceding century when the city and country had been a real player in European and world affairs. Harrison's flat was located on the second floor above ground level. It looked out over a courtyard at the back surrounded on all sides by rows of balconies that rose to the skyline like stairs to the clouds. But it was a sky the Austrians and their former compatriots no longer ruled. It was a new era, although these buildings seemed to indicate that the inhabitants had been able to insulate themselves from the passage of time.

Harrison was the odd duck in this neighborhood, at least as far as Baier could tell from their brief and episodic meetings. "Come in, Karl, come in. To what do I owe the pleasure?"

Baier shook Harrison's outstretched hand and marched into the apartment's foyer. "I'm just happy I caught you at home. I also thought it might be better to meet here occasionally, rather than have me constantly calling at your office."

"Absolutely. Grand idea, and I might add that you are welcome anytime. As for this morning, well, I'll just say you're in luck there. It seems I had a bit too much of that *huerige* stuff last night and was trying to sleep it off before heading into the office."

"Would you rather I came back at a later hour?"

Harrison ushered Baier into the apartment's living room ahead of him. "No, no. This will do fine. I've just made coffee. Can I get you a cup?"

Baier smiled "That would be great, Thomas. This shouldn't take too long, but a *cuppa*, as you Brits say, would be very helpful this morning. Just so long as it isn't tea."

Harrison laughed. "No need to worry there, old man. I've developed a real taste for coffee after all those years working with you Yanks. And now to live in this city …." He spread his arms wide, as though to embrace the entire café culture of Vienna. “Cream?”

Baier nodded. He took a look around as he waited for Harrison to return with their coffee. The temporary nature of Harrison’s assignment was obvious from the absence of any wall hangings or even pictures of family and relatives. Just the bare furniture, which gave the room the feel of an emotional desert. Baier suddenly realized how little he knew of his partner, his personal and professional history. He began to reconsider how much he should divulge about his upcoming trip behind the Curtain, but then decided that Harrison was probably well informed in any case. It would also be necessary to mention it if he was going to press the Brit on his relationship with Stein.

“Here you go, Karl.” Harrison handed Baier his cup on a saucer. They sat on opposite ends of the sofa, which looked over toward the bay window and down onto the street. He peered over at the book in Baier’s hand, which his guest then set on the table. “What’s that little volume you’ve brought? Not taking up any of the Austrian literary masters from the older imperial days like Joseph Roth or Stefan Zweig, are you?”

Baier sipped the strong coffee. Harrison had added a touch of cinnamon in the Viennese style. That would explain why he hadn’t offered any sugar, which was fine with Baier. He took sugar in his lemonade, not in his coffee. Baier picked up the book, glanced at the binding, then set it back down. “No, nothing like that. It’s von Rudenstein’s diary, and it makes for interesting reading. I’d offer it you, but I think there’s someone else who has a more pressing need at the moment.”

“Enough said, Karl.” Harrison slapped the sofa cushion next to Baier’s seat. “Now, what can I do for you?”

“Two things. First, I wanted to raise the subject of your service’s relationship with von Rudenstein again. Have you found out any more about what Hardwicke was up to with our Austrian friend?”

Harrison set his cup on the long coffee table. His lips pursed as he seemed to consider how much he should divulge. Then he sat back, ran his hand through his hair, and looked at Baier as though he had just made a momentous decision. "I can say that the good old Professor Hardwicke appears to have been running some sort of operation with von Rudenstein to undermine Soviet control in the Eastern European countries they occupied."

"How so? What sort of operation?"

"They had been working on building a network of access and influence agents from von Rudenstein's previous contacts during the war."

"And how extensive and successful was this?"

"Well, it seems von Rudenstein did succeed in assembling a network of sorts among former military officers in some of these countries, principally Hungary and Czechoslovakia, and he had argued for greater cooperation among the former states of the Hapsburg Empire."

"I take it he came up against the proverbial wall in Yugoslavia," Baier said.

Harrison held out his hands, palms up. "Oh yes, very much so. He had succeeded in getting some nibbles in Romania, though."

"That all sounds pretty fantastic. What did they think was actually going to happen with all this?"

"I'm not really sure. Hardwicke, at any rate, may have had his doubts. But if it served to undermine Soviet rule and create room for future possibilities, he might have decided it was worth the effort."

"He was being pretty cavalier with von Rudenstein's safety," Baier noted.

Harrison retrieved his coffee and top a long sip. "Oh, I agree. I can assure you I played no part in this little drama. If Hardwicke were still alive today, you can be certain that I would have expressed my displeasure forcefully and in person." He sipped again and replaced the coffee on the table. "It's all highly unprofessional. Then again, von Rudenstein was no babe in the woods, as they say. He probably knew full well what the risks and the prospects were."

"Yeah, you're probably right, given what I've learned. How many in your organization were aware of this operation?"

"That's where it gets exceedingly difficult. I haven't been able to determine that. I gather, although I can't be sure, that Sir Robert must have been aware. But beyond that, I really can't say. It may all have been a rogue operation by Hardwicke and von Rudenstein."

Baier realized he was still holding his cup and saucer, so he took a long sip and set them on the table. "Why would Hardwicke do such a thing? I mean, the guy was retired. He had a nice sinecure at a well-respected university where he could have lived out his life in quiet, well-meaning contemplation."

"Well, he may have simply been playing along. You will learn, if you aren't already aware of it, that many in our profession find it hard to let go. After years of excitement, anxiety, and anticipation, one can be hard-pressed to find the contentment you seem to think Hardwicke had stumbled onto."

"So this was all an adventure?"

"Oh, I wouldn't say that. In fact, I've gotten the distinct impression that von Rudenstein was the driving force behind this operation. Is that consistent with what you've discovered of the man's personality?"

Baier nodded and leaned forward to take another drink from his cup. "Yes, it is, now that you mention it. Very much so, in fact. But is it also consistent with Hardwicke's personality? You spoke of a general inclination to cling to past practices and that way of life, but would this fit Hardwicke in particular?"

"Yes, I believe so. The man was fully committed not only to von Rudenstein, but to all his assets, of which he had collected a considerable stable."

"Unfortunately for him, in the end." Baier drained his cup,

then placed it on the table and sat back. "The Moscow trip … what do you make of that?"

"A final throw of the dice, as it were. Von Rudenstein apparently wanted to attend as a military advisor to the Austrian delegation. They were having none of that, however." Harrison sighed. "Just as well, I suppose, since I'm sure he was pursuing his own agenda, which did not sit squarely with that of his government."

"How did the visit to Moscow fit into that?" Baier watched Harrison carefully, trying to read between the lines. "You have no further information on just what he did there? I mean, it looks like it may well have sealed his fate. As a matter of fact, I wonder how much the Soviets knew of this operation through their own sources."

Harrison winced. "Oh please, Karl, not that again."

Baier smiled and waved at his colleague. "No, it didn't have to be you guys." He thought of Stein, perhaps unfairly. "It could have been the Austrians, or a penetration somewhere else."

"Well, thank you for that consideration, at any rate. I'm not sure how much the Austrians knew of this, though. And as for Moscow, we can only guess that Herr von Rudenstein said the wrong thing at the wrong time."

"But to whom? And what about Hardwicke's killing? Can we assume it was the Soviets? That's whom I'm tapping for the von Rudenstein murder."

"Excellent question, Karl. Do you have any way of finding out?"

"I'm not sure, but I will certainly try. How about you?"

"I promise to try on my end as well. Will you be here in Vienna for the next week? I might have to return to London for a few, and I'll press on there."

Baier looked out the window, then at Harrison. "I may be traveling in the very near future. I'll be in touch when I return. I have one more question before I go, Thomas."

"That's right, you said there were two things. What else is there, Karl?"

Baier shifted his weight to resettle himself on the cushions. "It's about you, actually. I'm wondering if you have an additional agenda here, Thomas." Harrison's brow furrowed. Baier smiled as he dropped his bombshell. "You see, I saw you meeting with Stein yesterday."

Harrison sat back hard, as though trying to bury himself in the cushions of the sofa. "Oh, dear." He stared at the coffee table, avoiding Baier's eyes. "That does seem suspicious. May I ask what you were doing?"

"That's hardly material at this point. I was not tailing you. I stumbled upon the both of you merely by chance." Baier leaned in close. "Imagine my surprise."

Harrison finally looked up at Baier. "Yes, I can imagine." The room seemed suddenly too warm and small. "I assure you, Karl, it was nothing untoward, and certainly nothing to undermine your efforts."

"So what was it?"

"Karl, believe me, Stein called our office and insisted on the meeting. I had to go to find out what he wanted. It seems he knew something about the von Rudenstein operation and insisted that this sort of thing had to end. He gave me a lot of guff about the State Treaty making all that unnecessary. I admitted to nothing, of course, and refused to respond to his claims about the future." Harrison sat back. "In effect, I told him to sod off."

Baier studied the man he wanted to trust and had come to regard not just as a colleague, but as a friend.

"So, the Austrians are aware of what was up with von Rudenstein."

Harrison nodded. "To a degree. Not the whole story, mind you, but a good part of it."

"Did my work come into the conversation?"

Harrison waved his arms in protest. "Absolutely not, Karl. Absolutely not. I think you're safe there."

In the end, Baier realized he had little choice but to let the subject drop. If he discovered that Harrison had done anything to jeopardize the Budapest rescue, Baier would hunt the man down. He wasn't sure what he would do beyond that. He would definitely have his revenge.

Harrison reached out his hand. "I am truly sorry for the misunderstanding, Karl. I hope I haven't undermined our cooperation."

Baier took the Brit's hand. But his mind was already on the road to Budapest.

Baier had one last stop to make before reporting back to his office and departing for Budapest. He found the white, turn-of-the-century apartment building that housed the younger von Rudenstein's home and office, climbed the stairs to the third-floor, and rang the bell. A woman's voice called out that someone was at the door—"perhaps a customer at this time of day"—and footsteps approached the door. "But no one has called ahead," came the muffled reply.

Baier was mildly surprised when the door swung open to reveal an obviously relaxed Herr Thomas von Rudenstein in shirtsleeves and rumpled hair. It was not at all the image the man had fostered in their first encounter.

"*Ach, der Ami.*" The American. Von Rudenstein Junior blinked a few times. "Baier wasn't it, or something like that?"

Baier nodded and smiled. "Yes, you've got it right. Both ways. It is Baier, and I am an American."

Von Rudenstein retreated from the doorway. "Come in, come in. I'm sorry if I sounded rude. That was certainly not my intention."

"Thank you." Baier stepped in just over the threshold. "This will only take a minute." He pulled the diary out of the side pocket in his jacket. "I wanted to give you this before I left." He held the slim volume out to the son.

Von Rudenstein took the book in his hand with a puzzled

frown and turned it over several times, as though expecting pages to spill onto the floor. "What is it?"

"It's your father's diary. I found it out at the estate in Burgenland. I have to confess that I read it through, searching for some clues to your father's character. I thought it might help in the investigation."

"Yes, yes, of course." He looked up at Baier. "And did it?"

"Yes, it did. I think I understand the man much better now. I'm not sure it will lead the investigation to his killers, although I have a pretty good idea who they may be."

"And will they be prosecuted?"

Baier shrugged. "That's hard to say. We have to catch them first."

Von Rudenstein nodded absentmindedly. "Yes, well good luck with that, Herr Baier." He held out the book. "Won't you need this for later use?"

Baier held out his hand, palm up. "No, that's all right. I can always come back for it if necessary. I just thought you should have it for now." Baier studied the young Austrian for a moment. "It might help you get to know your father a bit better. He was an interesting man."

Von Rudenstein clasped the diary to his chest. "Thank you for that, Herr Baier." He offered his hand. "I'm glad we met."

Baier shook his hand. "Me, too, Herr von Rudenstein. Me, too."

"Perhaps we shall see each other again someday," von Rudenstein Junior said as Baier walked to the door.

Baier looked back at the young man. "Yes, I think we probably shall."

Chapter Sixteen

"When does your train leave?" Delgreccio stood in the doorway to his office.

"Later this afternoon, at four thirty."

"Good. I'll let Budapest know you're on the way. Hopefully, we'll get some contact instructions before you leave. Do you know anyone there in Station?"

Baier shook his head. "Nope. So I can't be sure I'll recognize anyone if we don't hear back before my train leaves."

Delgreccio sighed. "I'll send them a description of you and what you're wearing." He inspected Baier's gray flannel slacks, blue dress shirt, and linen jacket. "You shouldn't be all that hard to pick out of a Hungarian crowd."

"Which, as I understand it, fits perfectly with my cover."

"That it does. Lucky you." Delgreccio strolled around behind his desk, reached into the middle drawer and pulled out a Manila envelope. He poured the contents out on his desk. "I hope you appreciate how quickly our technical staff and support people were able to pull this package together."

Baier did not say a word. He simply stared at the pile of documents.

"Okay, we've got a West German passport that claims—"

"You mean 'proves,' don't you?"

Delgreccio smiled. "Yeah, right. 'Proves' you are a citizen of the Federal Republic from Stuttgart. I figured your Swabian-like accent would help make the case if any overeager Hungarian customs or security types tried to press you in German. I gather quite a few still speak it there." He drew a finger in the air, as if the name were written on a placard: "Mister Wolfgang Meyer."

"Go figure."

"Absolutely." Delgreccio passed the bundle to his deputy. "Your other documentation says you are a sales representative for firms in the machine tools industry, working for an import-export company headquartered in Stuttgart. You are visiting to explore export opportunities for rebuilding the Hungarian industrial base. They need that sort of thing, you know, if they're ever going to evolve into a working-class state." He paused to study Baier, who was focused on the desk, sifting through the small pile of documents. "We've even made an appointment for you at a local firm for the day after tomorrow, in case they want to check up on you. It's in your little black notebook, but don't ask me to pronounce the name of the company."

"Don't worry. I'll just pretend to be an arrogant Kraut who couldn't be bothered. It will be entirely in character."

"Good. We did not get a hotel room for you."

Baier gave a small wave of indifference. "That's fine. If necessary, I'll just walk toward the city center and find someplace that looks appropriate for a visiting German businessman. I'll book a room for the week, in case they check to see how long I'm staying."

"Good, good. Our people there should have some kind of operational plan in the making. They've known about Sabine's presence there, and that we want to get her out as soon as possible. They have a contact inside the service there—"

"The AHV still?"

Delgreccio nodded. "Yep, those same Stalinist clowns, trained and controlled by the KGB. Anyway, the source has tried to keep them up to date on her condition and the service's plans for her."

"I thought you said we weren't well plugged-in there."

Delgreccio waggled his eyebrows. "Need-to-know, buddy. And we're not really. It's tenuous, what you might call a 'developmental,' if you're being generous. But so far, your wife seems to be in pretty good shape."

Baier looked up at his chief and then out the window. "That may mean they've intended to use her as bait for some kind of swap all along. I wonder who's calling the shots here. You pretty sure it's the Soviets?"

Delgreccio watched him carefully. "Yeah, that's still my guess."

"Do you think they're waiting for me?"

"That's a very strong possibility, Karl. It's why we held off on a hotel room, to reduce their leads as much as possible. They must know you want her out, and I'm sure your Soviet buddy here has kept them informed of your interest."

"I just hope Stein hasn't sent a warning of his own."

Delgreccio gripped Baier's forearm, but quickly released it in favor of resting his hand on his deputy's shoulder. "Just make sure the other side doesn't end up with two people as bait or trading material."

Baier couldn't help but think of his German namesake, Sabine's first husband, as his train sped across the Austrian countryside and headed for the border with Hungary. He still could hardly believe they'd shared a name. The other Baier—the German one—had been stuck in Budapest, sent there with a legion of German reinforcements in yet another vain attempt to stem the tide of war that was sweeping toward the Fatherland, with all the death, destruction, and rapine in its wake. The Germans succeeded in virtually destroying the city in a vicious battle that halted the Soviet march only briefly. It was during his predecessor's escape from the city as it fell to the Red Army that the German Karl Baier had suffered such grievous injuries from a Soviet artillery barrage that caught his retreating band in the open. Still, the man had struggled on, trying to reach his home and his wife to present her with his own plunder and stories of a hidden horde that would secure their futures. Nothing ever seemed to go as intended in this part of the world, however—not in this century. There always seemed to be a bigger picture that interfered.

Baier wondered how much Sabine had dwelt on these very same thoughts sitting in a prison cell in Budapest, as she underwent interrogation at the hands of the Hungarian AHV and their Soviet puppet masters. He shifted uneasily in his seat as the Hungarian border came into view, and the train rolled to a stop for the border crossing and inspection. A short while later, he could hear the tramping boots, the harsh voices, and the sliding of the compartment doors as the Hungarian customs and border guards made their way through the carriage.

When his own door slid open, the two guards stared at him for what seemed like a full minute before holding out their hands for his passport. Baier occupied the compartment on his own, which made sense, since there was not a whole lot of reason to travel in an easterly direction these days. The reforms Imre Nagy had tried to implement to make life a little more open and free in Hungary had been scaled back ever since the country's original pro-Soviet satrap, Rakosi, had gotten Nagy discredited and replaced. That was one reason he wasn't sure how much to trust the press reports that claimed the Hungarian service was much more humane these days. In any case, another occupant might have helped deflect some of the guards' attention or ire, if they had any toward a Westerner. One never knew where the sympathies of the individual

Hungarian you were dealing with would lie these days, with the Nagy reforms or the Rakosi reaction.

To his surprise, the two men paged through his passport, mumbled something like "*Willkommen in Ungarn*," or 'Welcome to Hungary,' and handed his passport back. Their faces remained stoic and expressionless, which was no surprise. Baier immediately suspected that they were aware of his arrival and simply letting him into a trap. Seconds later, he scolded himself for allowing his nerves to drive him into useless speculation. He was committed. He had no intention of turning back. And maybe these guys were Nagy fans, Hungarians who had hoped the previous premier would be the harbinger of a new day for their country. Maybe their long stares could be explained by his dapper Western clothes. Maybe, maybe, maybe.

So much for that. Shortly afterward, two more men in uniform, this time members of the Army, marched in and gave the compartment a thorough search. They pawed their way through Baier's luggage, kicked the seats, and looked in every possible crevice. Baier was tempted to ask if they truly suspected someone of trying to sneak into this godforsaken place. Although he did have to admit that any goods from the West would probably fetch a small treasure on the black market, if there even was one in Budapest. Then again, there had to be. The black market existed wherever the opportunity presented itself.

Over the next few hours, the train crawled toward Budapest, swinging through the verdant and plush green fields and rolling hills of the northern and western Transdanubian region. Baier even saw some mountains in the distance, presumably part of the Alpine chain that stretched into this part of Hungary. Eventually the skyline of Budapest loomed in the distance, and the train pulled into Keteli station, the principal rail link with the West. Baier pulled his bag off the rack, made sure the two Army clowns had refastened it correctly, and made his way through the carriage and onto the platform. He had not heard anything from the office here before he left Vienna and wondered if or how contact would be made.

As he walked toward the center of the railway station, looking for an exit, Baier sensed someone alongside him. When the man grabbed for his suitcase, Baier instinctively pulled his bag closer to his body and turned to face the individual.

"It's okay, Herr Meyer," the man said in accented German. "I've been sent to pick you up and deliver you to your hotel."

Meyer studied the figure more closely. The man winked. And smiled, while he tugged at Baier's suitcase. "It's okay," he said again, this time in English. "Come with me. It's all taken care of." Back in German now.

Baier released his grip on the bag and followed his new companion to a small black sedan of Eastern European make—Baier had no idea which—waiting out front. The driver tossed Baier's bag in the front seat on the passenger side, then held the door open for Baier to climb in the back. Once they settled in, the driver sped away from the curb and out into the city's light traffic, which was actually a blessing, in Baier's mind. It would make it easier to see if they had a tail.

"Sorry about the little bit of drama back there," the driver said, as his eyes repeatedly searched the rearview mirror. He spoke in American English now, which Baier had pretty much expected. "We didn't have enough time to pass along any contact instructions before you left, so we threw this together at the last minute. I'm going to drop you off at a hotel across the street from the museum of some kind of art, which will give us a good location. It's also pretty nice—the museum, I mean—as a building, anyway. I've never been inside. It's one of the buildings that is supposed to exemplify the local nouveau style, and it wasn't too badly damaged in the war, so they were able to restore it pretty quickly." He paused. "It should give you something to talk about this evening, at any rate, in case someone decides to chat you up."

"How is it looking as far as company on our route is concerned?" Baier asked.

"I think we're in pretty good shape. The short notice may have helped in that regard—ironically, since it didn't give the other side much time to catch on to our plans. When we get there, just go inside to check on a room, and then come back for your bags. You can tell me then which room you're in."

"Sounds good. Are you comfortable using German further? From what I've heard, yours seems passable."

"It's good enough. We can speak it in public."

"Great. Is there any kind of a plan yet?"

The driver turned to face his passenger. "I guess you could call it a plan. That's the downside of not having much time. But we have to move tomorrow."

Baier's heart leaped. "Why is that?"

"Our contact tells us that they're planning to move your wife to one of the camps tomorrow. I guess they've been expecting something, and they've only been able to arrange transport now."

"Who's running the show? The locals or the Soviets?"

"Oh, we're pretty sure this is a Soviet operation. Our contact claims they've been running it since they picked her up in East Germany."

Baier paused long enough to blow out his breath in a light whistle and watch the city of Buda pass by. When he spoke, it was to no one in particular. "Man, I really hate those fuckers."

"I can certainly understand that." The reply was equally general.

The car rolled over the Danube and passed the parliament, a massive building that hung on a hillside overlooking the river like an ancient fortress. After about five minutes of navigating the streets behind the parliament and the government square at its rear in Pest, the driver swerved toward the curve and halted in front of a relatively prosperous-looking establishment, the Buda City Hotel. It looked relatively new, with the metal frame and rose-colored glass paneling that seemed to represent the architectural style of the Communist Bloc. Baier jumped out and trotted inside. Fortunately, they had a room for him, which was no surprise, given the eagerness to acquire hard currency in this workers' paradise. Baier then returned to the car and showed the driver his key with the number of his room, 428.

"What's the plan for tomorrow then?"

The driver set Baier's bag in front of him, then looked from the street to Baier. "Someone will be by in the morning to pick you up. There really isn't time to go over things in any detail, and we'd like to minimize contact, just in case you are being watched." The driver surveyed the street once more. "They may have tumbled onto your presence since you've crossed the border, although I know your cover looks pretty solid."

"That's fine. It's always good to be safe. Just make sure that whoever comes by lets me know what I need to do. Is there an exfiltration plan?"

The driver nodded. "I'm sure they'll want—and need—your help. You can discuss that with the team tomorrow, but I'd say that's still a weak spot in the operation. Again, that's one of the downsides of having to move so quickly. It's going to be a snatch operation. We've got a pretty good plan to grab your wife, but after that, it gets kind of iffy." He walked back to the driver's door, then paused before climbing into the vehicle. "Sorry. We realize it's tricky in an environment like this, but we really have no choice." He paused. "By the way, my name is Bill, in case anyone asks tomorrow morning." Then he disappeared inside the car.

Baier stared after the car as it sped off into the light evening traffic.

Chapter Seventeen

He hardly slept at all. For one thing, the tiny room he had been given held a lingering, nauseating odor like a disinfectant gone bad. And since the windows didn't open, it was not only smelly but incredibly stuffy. The bed was lumpy and hard, which Baier took to be a peculiar achievement of Hungarian Communism.

Mostly, it had been his nerves. It had been weeks since he had seen Sabine, and Baier wondered what sort of condition she was in now after her abduction and incarceration. He didn't know if anyone on the outside had been in contact. Since the Soviets and the Hungarians were almost certainly watching her closely, he assumed that the Station asset on the inside or within the service had been keeping his distance.

He was up and dressed and had even swallowed two cups of bitter black coffee by seven o'clock. At least it had been hot. Baier did not trust himself to eat anything, seeing as how his stomach felt like it was climbing up and down those rolling hills he had observed on the train ride in. He took a seat in the small, Spartan dining room facing the door to check on any and all newcomers. There were two other individuals already seated when he entered, and one more elderly gentleman came in while he waited. At seven thirty, or a few minutes after, a tall, thin individual in a long raincoat entered and approached Baier with hand outstretched.

"Herr Baier," he said in almost flawless German as they shook hands. "Welcome to Budapest. I hope you had a good night's sleep, as you will need it. We have several important appointments today." He remained standing. "I suggest we get started now. I can bring you up to date on today's meetings in the car."

Baier nodded, stood, and followed his new friend to the hotel entrance. Out front, a beige Mercedes sedan waited with the same driver as the night before. Today he was dressed in a neat black serge suit, a white dress shirt, and navy-blue tie. He also had acquired a moustache overnight and managed to look servile and officious all at the same time. Baier was impressed by the transformation. Bill held the back door for Baier, while his other companion got in the backseat on the driver's side.

"I'm glad you were up and ready so early," the new companion said. "They've moved the transport time up to eight thirty, so we can still get to the AHV headquarters in time … but not too early to arouse suspicions." He looked over at Baier. "You can call me Tom, at least for this morning. I arrived from Washington two days ago to help plan and run this thing." He sighed. "As I'm sure you've guessed, this is not ideal, but we've had no real choice."

"Thanks, I appreciate that. And I appreciate everything you guys are doing here."

Tom looked out the window. "How's it lookin', Bill?" The driver gave a thumbs-up. Tom turned back to Baier. "I hope you didn't have anything valuable in your luggage."

Baier shook his head. "No. I figured we wouldn't be going back."

"Good. And you can wait until it's over to thank me."

Baier concentrated on his breathing, trying to settle himself.

"Sure thing. What do you need me to do?"

"Our plan is to follow the wagon with the prisoners, force it over several blocks from the AHV headquarters—we've scouted out what looks like a pretty good spot—and then you and your wife will transfer to another car we have waiting. One of my colleagues from Washington will be in that one, along with another driver from Bill's office to make sure we don't get lost during the getaway."

"How do we know the route?"

Bill spoke up. "Our asset inside was able to get it. Apparently, they take the same route every time." He nodded. "Yeah, I know. Not very good tradecraft. It even gave us some concern since it makes things look a lot easier. But like I said, we don't really have a choice at this point. We've also created a few diversions through some fake construction and roadwork to steer the truck along the route we've chosen."

Tom added, "We're hoping that their reliance on the same path every time they transport people is an indication of overconfidence and carelessness as well. We also hope we're not convincing ourselves of what we want to believe."

"Even with the Soviets involved?" Baier asked.

Tom shrugged. "Again, we hope so. I know I'm starting to sound like a broken record, but we don't have a lot of choices here."

They parked several blocks away with a clear view of the side of the prison, where they expected the transport van to depart for the camp on the outskirts of Budapest. The headquarters formed a huge V at the base of Stalin Avenue, a solid neo-Baroque monstrosity that looked like it could withstand a siege. Baier guessed that its solidity and massiveness had come in handy in the past and might do so again.

"It says something that this same building used to serve as the headquarters for Hungary's fascist rulers during the war, the Arrow Cross," Tom said. "I'm not sure how they explain that one away, if they even try."

"They also use former German and Hungarian concentration camps for prisons," Bill added. He turned to look at Baier. "That's another reason we want to be damn sure we free your wife today."

Baier swallowed what felt like a lump the size of an apple. He found he could not say a word. They moved the car twice to avoid drawing attention to themselves, but each time managed to park with an unobstructed view of the AHV headquarters. Around 8:45, a white van emerged from a garage tunnel and turned onto Andrassy Avenue, but then took the first left onto the streets behind the headquarters.

"Showtime," Bill said.

"Yeah, let's go," Tom confirmed.

They pulled away from the curve slowly, again, Baier assumed, to avoid drawing unwanted attention to themselves. Then they turned down the same street the van had entered.

"No escort?" Baier asked.

Tom shrugged. "They haven't had one on previous trips we've monitored either. Granted, this does look almost too easy. But like I said—"

"Yeah, I know," Baier broke in.

After that it all seemed to move at roughly the speed of light. The van took the second left along Izabella Avenue when Andrassy appeared to be blocked off, and then almost immediately encountered another obstacle and turned right and entered Aradi Street. Two cars pulled out onto the same street, one in front of the van, and one behind it and forced the van to the curb. Four men bolted from the cars and rushed the van. One stopped at the driver's side and rammed a long iron rod through the window and tossed in a grenade, which sent smoke billowing through the cabin. The same individual then reached inside, opened the door, and jerked the driver from the vehicle onto the ground, placing a knee in his neck and holding a pistol to his head. A second officer climbed in, grappled briefly with the other guard, then threw open the passenger-side door. He shoved the guard into the arms of one of the two men waiting at that side of the truck, who began to speak into the Hungarian's ear. His head shook violently, but Baier could still see eyes wide with fear. A third American ran over to the driver and pulled a set of keys from his jacket pocket. Meanwhile, both Hungarians were bound, gagged, and thrown into the trunks of the waiting cars.

The fourth officer trotted over to the car with Baier, Tom, and Bill. Baier could see that the sweat from their exercise was already beginning to wear off some of the makeup Bill had used for his disguise. "They claim there are no more guards in the back, but we'll want to make sure."

He ran back to the van, where his companions were working the lock on the door. One of the men kept yelling something in Hungarian at the truck, presumably an order to stay calm and not cause any more injuries. If so, Baier was sure that those words were directed at any additional guards. But they might also reassure the prisoners.

After about a minute, the doors swung open, but nobody stepped out. Was it empty? Had they all been duped? Then several prisoners descended carefully from the back. Baier strained his neck and tried to focus, leaning around Tom and the driver to get a better view.

Then he saw her. Sabine was the fourth person to emerge into the daylight, her hand across her forehead to shield her eyes from the bright sun. She was wearing clothes Baier recognized as her own, a brown woolen skirt and white blouse that looked wrinkled but none the worse for wear. And Sabine looked even better, at least to his eyes. Still the same porcelain-skinned brunette he had fallen in love with even after all she had been through.

"Go, man go!" Tom shouted as he shoved Baier out the door.

Baier ran to Sabine, swept her up in his arms, and planted the longest kiss he could remember on her startled, trembling lips. "Goddamn, but you look good, Sabine. You really are a sight for eyes that have been sore for weeks." He stroked her face. "I've been so worried and missed you so much."

Sabine just looked at her husband with wide eyes that slowly filled with tears. "Oh, Karl, you've come," she finally blurted out. "I dreamt of this every single night. I've missed you so. That was the hardest thing."

"Hey, you two, save the reunion celebration for later." The words seemed to rush in from somewhere far away. "We need to get the hell out of here."

It was the voice of the man who had subdued the driver. He hustled over and steered the reunited lovers down a side street to another waiting car. Pulling open the door to the backseat, he quickly helped Sabine in, while Baier rushed around to the other side and climbed in.

Baier kissed Sabine again. "Are you all right, Sabine? Have they mistreated you?"

She squeezed Baier's hand. "Not physically, no. The separation and uncertainty have been torture enough." She rested her head on Baier's chest. "My God, it's wonderful to see you." She looked up at Baier. "My parents? Are they all right?"

"Yes, they were all right when I saw them several days ago. I don't think the Soviets or their East German puppets see any use in threatening them anymore. They should be okay." The words seemed to just pour out of his mouth. "I'll have our Berlin office check to make sure. And if necessary, we'll see what we can do to get them to the West."

The driver had not waited to hear the Baiers' conversation but had driven off immediately and was now winding his way through the back streets of Budapest.

"Where to now?" Baier inquired.

"We're going to swing by a safe house to give you two a chance to clean up, catch your breath, and maybe change your clothes," the driver said. "We've also got disguises for you both to try on. Then we'll need to check out the lay of the land, let things cool down a little and map out our escape route." He looked over at his companion. "My name is Dave," he pointed at his passenger in the front, "and this is Charlie."

"Nice to meet you guys. But that won't be necessary," Baier interjected. "I know a way out. I've scouted the border and found a good spot to try to cross."

The officer in the passenger turned to look at Baier. "How confident are you?"

"Pretty confident. I've been there twice and surveyed the border work the Soviets are overseeing. It was not anywhere near finished the last time I was there, and I did not see a whole lot of work going on."

The officer turned back toward the front. "Okay, then. It beats the hell out of anything we've got going. But we'll have to be sure they aren't busy when we get there. And then we don't want to stay in the safe house more than hour or so. It would be best to head for the border as soon as possible so we don't give these guys time to recover and set out any kind of dragnet." He paused, as if to confirm he hadn't overlooked anything, then added, "And to make sure they haven't got a whole lot more work done there in the interim."

"Whatever you say," Baier replied. "Will you be with us for the trip to the border?"

The officer in the passenger seat turned and nodded. "Yep. We're also trying to minimize the number of exchanges to save time."

"What border, Karl?" Sabine asked. "Where are we going?"

"Back to Austria. Hopefully, we should be back in Vienna by tonight, Sabine. Then this will all be over."

The car sped back across the Danube and toward the northwestern part of the city, which Baier noted would be ideal for getting out of the city and on the road to the Austrian border. The safe house was part of a newer apartment block built in the same ubiquitous Warsaw-pact architectural style that was transforming so many of the Eastern European cities into aesthetic monstrosities. Blocks of concrete, metal, and glass siding in a rectangular shape that seemed to start losing its component parts as soon as construction was finished. Baier was struck by the pieces of siding that littered the property in front and the peeling paint already in evidence along the façade. Inside, the apartment was coated in a pale-blue color that Baier immediately despised. It did not help that there was almost no furniture, just a sofa, a pair of chairs, a kitchen table and a bed in one of the back rooms. It was clearly not occupied, and Baier wandered what the neighbors thought. But it would serve their purpose, since they did not plan to stay long.

Sabine showered and changed into the clothes that Sam and Charlie had brought with them from the Embassy that morning, while Baier wolfed down some bread, cheese, and coffee. His stomach had settled some, now that he was with Sabine again, and he knew he would need the energy for the journey ahead. Sabine came out of the bathroom, her hair wet and her pink face looking fresh scrubbed. "My God, but that was a treat. You don't realize how much you miss a hot shower until you've gone without one for a while." She took some bread and cheese, and downed almost an entire cup of coffee in one gulp. "That will help as well." She looked at their companions and then at Baier. "You can't imagine how wonderful that feels. Are you going to change, Karl?"

He shook his head. "No, I'd rather get moving."

WITHIN THE HOUR, they were on the road to the Austrian border. Baier directed the two officers traveling with them to head to the area around Sopron, the border region in a western corner of Hungary that had lost most of its German-speaking inhabitants after the war, when many of the ethnic Germans had been evicted from Eastern Europe. Those that weren't killed, that is. They drove through the same lush green valleys Baier had passed on his way in to Budapest just a day ago. That now seemed like weeks ago—or in some distant past.

After several hours, they approached the border with its rows of barbed wire and regularly spaced guard towers.

"Will you be going over with us?" Sabine asked.

"Hell, yes," the driver responded. "We need to get the hell out of here, too. We don't have any kind of diplomatic cover, so if we get snatched, we'll be living out our days in the same place you just got out of."

"We're still a couple miles north of where we need to be," Baier explained. "Not too much farther."

He directed the driver to catch the dirt country road that swung south and ran parallel to the border. "Let's hope it goes far enough. I remember roads like this on both sides of the border during my previous visits. They served the entire area before the First World War, when this region was shared by Hungary and Austria. Probably for a while afterward as well."

"Well, let's hope it also doesn't get much rougher. I'm not sure how much this piece of shit commie sedan can take."

In the end, the road and car did hold up, although there were two moments when they drove over some ruts and when it sounded like the undercarriage had bounced off the ground and left parts behind. The car plowed on for another half hour, until Baier recognized familiar territory.

"There, there!" he nearly shouted. "That's the area." To his amazement, it looked as though no additional work had been done to secure the border. Rolls of barbed wire sat unattended in the fields, and the guard towers looked unoccupied.

"Any minefields yet?" Sam asked.

Baier shrugged, then shook his head. "I've never seen them placing any in the ground, and the earth here doesn't look like there's been any digging or re-smoothing going on." He pointed to the rolled wire. "Besides, I doubt they'd put those things in before they had the wire unrolled and in place."

"Well, we're here now," Charlie said from the passenger side. He shoved open his door. "So we might as well get on with it."

"Just to be sure, Sabine," Baier instructed, "walk behind me and place your feet exactly where mine have been."

The three of them climbed out of the car, leaving the driver to steer the vehicle off the road, in between a set of trees, and bury it amid the underbrush. Or almost bury it, since the shrubbery only reached about halfway up the body. From the road, it was not readily visible, and the area appeared to be deserted at any rate.

"Whoever finds that thing can have it," the driver said. Then they all set off through the fields, hugging the tree line to avoid detection. Just as they reached the border area and began to inch their way through the open area to approach the crossing, the silence was broken by the muffled roar of a military vehicle and shouting from two men in Soviet uniforms. They were telling them in heavily accented English to halt. Baier was astonished to see that it was an American-looking Jeep. When the Americans continued to move forward, a shot rang out over their heads, and two more hit the ground near Baier's feet.

One of their companions, Charlie, pulled a revolver from the inside of his belt at the small of his back and fired two rounds at the Jeep, one of them hitting the front grill. The Soviet officer in the front passenger seat stood, leveled the automatic rifle at his shoulder, and fired a burst. The American operative with the gun went down, clutching his leg.

"Goddammit, Charlie, put that fucking thing away," Baier yelled. "We're dead meat out here in the open, and more firing will only bring more Soviets." He looked hard at his companions. "I will not endanger my wife this close to home." Baier turned on the driver, who stood about six feet to the front, just about halfway between himself and the wounded Charlie. He felt the blood rush to his face and saw the ground swim at his feet. They were so close. He looked up again. "Where the hell did you get those weapons? Don't tell me you were stupid enough to smuggle them in."

"Damn straight. The chief told us 'under no circumstances

were we to be armed,' but I'll be damned if I'm going into something like this without protection."

"Well, goddammit, now you're going to have to use your wits." Baier turned to Sabine to make sure she was all right. He was stunned by the look of contempt on her face—no hint of the fear and confusion he'd expected to find there. She pointed toward the Soviet officer who had been in the passenger seat. The man handed the automatic rifle back to the driver, leaped down, and walked away from the Jeep. "That fucking Russian," was all she said, more of a hiss than a statement. "I told my parents he was back. And now he's followed us here."

"Herr Baier, what a pleasant surprise to meet you again. It's almost like one of those awful movies Hollywood produces."

Shock erupted and spread throughout Baier's entire body as he recognized the Soviet. The last time he had seen this man was ten years ago, as the Soviet officer had made his way from the coast of Portugal toward a fishing skiff that was supposed to take him and his German companions to South America. Then Sergei Chernov had been a colonel in the Soviet NKVD, stationed in Berlin at the war's end as a counter-intelligence officer. In reality he was a German asset from 1941, when he had bet on a German victory. In all fairness, it had looked like a pretty sure thing at the time. But later on, his path had crossed with Sabine's first husband, the German with the identical name of Karl Baier, after the battle at Budapest. He had encountered Sabine again in war-torn Berlin, where he had worked as part of her black market and human smuggling operation. After that he had fled to South America with some of his German accomplices to enjoy their ill-gotten gains and spend money they had stolen in the Balkans during the German occupation. He'd also gone in search of his siblings, who had fled the Bolshevik Revolution first for Paris, and then for South America.

Baier held his breath and then tried to resume breathing in a slow and measured pace. He was tempted to shout but wanted to cool down and try to gain control of the new situation.

"What happened in Brazil?" he asked. "Didn't you ever find your sister and brother? Or did you just run out of money?"

Sabine said nothing, but he could feel her simmering at his side.

Chernov shrugged and spoke in German. "It seems there was not nearly as much as I had been promised." He laughed. "Crime does not pay, as American actors are fond of saying in the movies. Not always. And sadly, I did not find my brother or my sister. Probably because my brother was dead and my sister had disappeared." He spread his arms wide. "So I came back." He pointed to Baier's companions. "And I suggest we continue in German to avoid revealing too much to your colleagues. Or mine, for that matter. I would hate to have any more harm come to them."

The image of this man dressed in an ill-fitting civilian suit, wading through the surf to reach the skiff returned. He had looked remarkably out of place. Now he seemed to have found his groove again, but how he'd managed to fit back into it and not end up lost somewhere in Siberia after his betrayal of the Soviet system remained a mystery.

"So, how did you get to return? I would have expected your government to put a price on your head, or at least to reserve you a bunk out on the tundra."

Chernov leaned against the Jeep, arms folded. "Oh, there was a reward of sorts, and a suspended death sentence in 1945. But that was easy enough to reverse after Comrade Stalin passed on to that workers' paradise in the sky." His eyes rolled heavenward. "I was able to convince them that I had indeed made a mistake, running off on a rogue operation to recapture Soviet gold stolen by the Wehrmacht, invaders in the tradition of the Teutonic Knights." He pulled out a cigarette and said something in Russian to his Soviet companion, who strolled over to the wounded American with a first-aid kit. "It's fairly easy to convince Russians of whatever you want them to believe when you refer to German invasions and depredations." He touched a match to the end of the cigarette between his lips.

"How convenient," Baier said. "And from your uniform, it looks like you're now in the KGB. In charge of border security, I presume."

Chernov nodded. "Very perceptive, Herr Baier. Those institutional rivalries come in handy at times."

"Yes," Baier agreed, "especially when your intel service has been renamed and reorganized. I was right, wasn't I? Your old club is now called the KGB. Any real difference there?"

"Yes, it is. And no, not much beyond the name and initials. It is sad, though, that so much expertise and memory was erased during Stalin's last surge of paranoia after the war. So many qualified officers eliminated."

"How convenient for you," Baier noted. "That must have removed many of your enemies. But how did you find us? I thought we were more than a step ahead on this operation."

Chernov laughed again. "Oh, come now. Did you really think this would be *that* easy? My colleague in Vienna let me know of your intent to come to Hungary." The smile broadened. "Oh, don't look so surprised, Herr Baier. Granted, Nuchyev is not the brightest star in the sky, but you could not be expected to hide your emotions so effectively in a case like this. And we tracked you from afar. I also guessed that your supposedly tourist-like interest in the border was an ill-disguised ruse. That's why I made sure the work remained suspended." He laughed again. This was starting to get on Baier's nerves. "It was easy to give the border units time off with the signing of the State Treaty today. Had you forgotten? May fifteenth? Remember? Or have you really lost track of time worrying about your wife?"

Indeed he had. "Well, that certainly helped on the timing," Baier said. "But I still don't understand what your game is, Chernov." He motioned toward Sabine, who stared darts at the Russian. "Did you run this entire kidnapping operation from the start?"

Chernov nodded as his fellow officer returned and put the first-aid kit back in the Jeep's glove compartment. The man spoke briefly to Chernov, who looked at the wounded American and then at Baier. "He says your friend needs medical care. The bullet is still in the leg. He was able to stop the bleeding, but he has lost a lot of blood. And of course, there is danger of infection."

Baier glanced over at the wounded American. "Thank you. We'll see to it. That is, if we get the chance." Chernov's smile did not waver. "But why was Sabine snatched?" Baier pressed.

"I convinced my superiors that we needed some leverage to disrupt your plans to work with the Austrians once we had left. We know you're establishing listening posts at the border that will not be very helpful from our point of view. Surely you understand that."

"And surely you understand that I will not be able to change a thing. Nor would I want to. So what was the point of having this leverage?"

"Oh, I'm aware of all that as well." Chernov slid his semi-automatic Makharov from its holster at his hip. "But I needed an excuse to bring us all together again. You see, I have a proposal."

Chernov suddenly wheeled to his left and put a bullet through the brain of his Soviet partner. Sabine shrieked, and Baier's heart seemed to stop, then resumed pumping at a rocket-like speed. "Holy shit," was all Sam could say, while Charlie just moaned.

"You see, it was very unfortunate that your team was able to overpower us and make your escape," Chernov explained, continuing as though he had done no more than blow his nose. "That your comrade there was wounded should help build our story about a firefight at the border where you made your escape."

"How is this *our* story, Chernov?" Sabine said, her first words since Chernov's arrival.

"Do you really think I want you back in Budapest, or anywhere else in the East for that matter?" He shook his head. "No, you will serve a much better purpose back in the West, and hopefully in Austria."

"How so?" Baier asked. Chernov was silent for once and stared at Sabine, as though waiting for her to speak.

"I think I know," Sabine said after a moment. "And if it's what I'm thinking, Karl, we should consider it." She turned to her husband. "Call it payback, and call it an investment in the future of this place."

Baier looked from one to the other, confusion obvious in his creased forehead and open mouth. "What the hell are you talking about, Sabine? Did you two cook something up back there in Budapest?"

Chernov was gazing at Sabine. "No, it's nothing like that. But as always, Herr Baier, your wife is remarkably intelligent and perceptive."

"He'll have to take our word that we'll consider his plan, won't you, you fucking Russian?" Sabine spat. Chernov shrugged, while his smile shrank a little. "If I'm right, it's another money-making operation, as far as he's concerned," Sabine continued. "That's what this man is all about, Karl, money." Sabine shifted her focus to Chernov. "He is not that hard to read."

She turned to Baier. "Remember, I worked with him and his kind before in Berlin. He thinks he detects a coming storm, and he's probably right that those poor bastards over there need a new outlet, a means of escape. Nobody's really happy with the return of Hungary's Stalinist premier Rakosi and his friends, are they, Chernov?"

They both turned to Baier. "Your wife is right again," Chernov said. "And who knows how this new State Treaty with Austria will affect things? As she has already guessed, I need both of you on the other side to assist my plan. And there will be money involved."

"So when did you cook up this new scheme, Chernov? Did

you visit Sabine at the prison you put her in?" He swiveled from the Russian to Sabine and back to Chernov. "And will someone please tell me what it is?"

Chernov laughed lightly, as though he were dismissing the idle daydreams of a child. "No, no, Herr Baier. My first assignment when I returned was at a border post in Mongolia. I believe they were testing me. In any case, the tour there gave me plenty of time to think up something like this. The difficult part was getting the assignment here in Hungary after the fall of Nagy. Apparently, my work on our Western Front during the war and in Berlin convinced them that I had valuable experience."

"Despite your flight and betrayal?"

"As I said, I convinced them it was all an unfortunate misunderstanding, which was a lot easier once Stalin and Beria were gone."

"Well, how fortunate for all of us," Baier replied. "But what about the murders of von Rudenstein and Hardwicke? Those were your doings, weren't they? And it was you pricks who shadowed me in London, wasn't it?"

"Yes, we had you under surveillance in London," Chernov replied. "I saw to that. But that had nothing to do with the deaths of the old Austrian and that retired English spy. I can't give you much help there. Besides, what is it that you are really after, Herr Baier? The shooter or the betrayal?"

Baier's heart seemed to skip a beat. The notion of a betrayal had been at the back of his mind all along, but it had always been little more than a vague suspicion, the faint echo of something from his professional past. "Both. I want to know who is responsible for both."

Chernov considered the ground at his feet before looking up into Baier's eyes. "I can tell you this much. The Austrian was in our custody at the time of his death. I know, because I arranged for him to be smuggled across the border and back into Austria by our people." He smiled again before adding,

"However, his death was not something I engineered. I know little of his crimes, you understand, or who and how justice was delivered. You will have to look elsewhere for that."

"And the betrayal? That's how your side found out about the old Austrian, isn't it?"

The Russian smiled and shrugged. "You have to expect something like that when there are enlightened people on both sides of the fence."

"Cut the bullshit, Chernov. I don't give a shit which of your organizations did the dirty work. And don't speak to me of 'crimes' or 'enlightenment.' Your side killed those men because of the operation they had going in your newly conquered territory. You were afraid they would undermine Soviet rule."

"What operation, Herr Baier?" Chernov asked.

"Figure it out for yourself, Chernov."

"I think I already have. And I'm afraid that if you want those answers, you'll have to raise the subject with your British friends. Ultimately, I believe your answer lies back in London." Chernov smiled again. "But don't worry. We won't have any reason to follow you now."

"I'm so relieved. They were pretty obvious anyway."

"It is so hard to get good help these days," Chernov said. "I'm sure you can appreciate that." His smile broadened. "But are you really sure it was only us involved? These are such uncertain times. There may have been others."

"There usually are. And I plan to find them."

Chernov walked over to Baier and handed him the pistol. "Here, you'll need to take this with you. And don't worry about mines." He swept his arms over the field in front of them. "I was able to hold that part of the work off as well. Now, you'll also need to knock me on the head with it, to make things look authentic." He pointed to an area at the back of his skull. "Or you can shoot me in the shoulder. Which do you prefer?"

Baier grabbed the Makharov. "Right now, I think I'd better shoot you. I might over-swing and break your head open."

Baier took careful aim and pulled the trigger. He was surprised by the flood of satisfaction he felt as he saw the grimace seize Chernov's face when the bullet tore through his uniform and flesh.

"My God, Karl, you haven't killed him, have you?" Sabine cried.

"No, he'll be all right." Baier strolled to the Jeep, grabbed the first-aid kit, and dropped it at Chernov's side.

IT TOOK ALMOST an hour to cross the border. Using a tree branch, they put together a makeshift crutch for the wounded American, and Baier and Sam took turns helping him through the field. After about thirty minutes, they passed the rows of vines that stretched across the rolling curves of earth that marked the von Rudenstein estate. Baier halted to take in the view and gazed at the outline of the estate on the horizon.

"What is it, Karl?' Sabine asked.

"It's just that I know this land and something of the people who lived here. It seems like history has swallowed them whole." Sabine cocked her head, waiting for him to elaborate. "I'll explain it when we get to Vienna. It seems like ages ago now. I guess it is in some ways."

Long after they had negotiated the last of the construction work and were passing the rows of vines, Baier looked up to find the Soviet captain with whom he had spoken several days ago waiting on the road well inside Austrian territory. The captain smiled, stood at attention, and saluted. Then he disappeared back into Hungary.

Chapter Eighteen

"CONGRATULATIONS!" DELGRECCIO SHOUTED. "It's finally over. You must be so relieved."

Baier shook his chief's hand, and the men embraced. Baier felt the tension seep out of his body as he leaned against the wall.

"Thanks, Ralph. I really appreciate that and all the help you and the others have provided." Baier stared at his boss and chewed his lip, then added, "But it's not over."

"Is that because of the shoot-out with the Soviets at the border? If you're worried about our guy, he's fine. Nothing that a quick visit with our medical folks couldn't fix. He'll have to spend a few days in bed, but then he'll be on his way home."

"Well," Baier explained, "that's only one of the complications, which I'll explain later. There are other unresolved issues as well."

"What do you mean?" Delgreccio leaned forward, his hands resting on his desk. "If you're thinking of the von Rudenstein case, hell, let the Austrians figure that one out."

"What about Hardwicke?"

"What do you care? That's the Brits' problem."

Baier shook his head as he pulled away from the wall. "No, it's not, Ralph. That's still mine, in part. So is the von Rudenstein one. Remember, I found the bodies."

"Not quite. The Austrians had to get you out of bed for the first one."

Baier nodded. "And that's what started this whole mess."

Delgreccio frowned. "How so? You still convinced the cases are linked?"

"Yes, I am, Ralph. Maybe it didn't appear so initially, but it's ended up that way. And I still have some things to settle here and in London."

"Well, don't take your sweet time about it, Karl. I've been recalled to Washington to head up a new task force on the Middle East. You'll be acting chief here in a couple weeks. We need you to focus on the business at hand here and in central Europe."

"Oh, I will, Ralph. And getting this settled will help. In fact, I'd say it's absolutely vital that I do so."

THAT EVENING AFTER dinner, Baier watched Sabine as they settled on the sofa in their living room. The plump, off-white piece of furniture was remarkably more comfortable than it looked. He stretched out so that his back rested against the crevice between the seat and back cushions, while his feet rested on the coffee table in front. Sabine watched Baier's evening ritual, then imitated his posture for all of about five seconds before she sat upright.

"I don't see how that can be comfortable, not to mention good for your back," she said.

"Well, I admit, it may not look like much, but it amazes me how these cushions can conform to my body shape and provide just enough comfort and support." He thought for a moment as he surveyed the room. "Maybe you're right, though." He sat up straighter. "This is probably better for now."

Sabine slid over next to her husband. “Is something bothering you?”

Baier sighed. “Well, aside from my anxiety over what you had to put up with inside that prison in Budapest—”

“It wasn’t that bad,” Sabine interrupted him. “I suffered far worse during the war.”

Baier leaned forward. “How can you say that?”

She stroked Baier’s cheek. “Karl, they couldn’t treat me poorly. I knew they had some sort of plan in mind.”

“How could you know that?”

“Because they said as much, first in Germany, and then when they handed me over at the border. This German named Mischka asked if they were serious about taking me to Budapest. He seemed to think it was a silly plan.”

“Did they say at that point what it was?” Baier asked.

“No, I only heard parts of an argument over whether the Americans would agree to such an exchange. When they mentioned Chernov again, I couldn’t believe my ears. That’s when I knew something else was up. Some sort of personal scheme. Did my parents mention his possible involvement when you spoke with them?”

“Yes, they did,” Baier replied. They said something about that ‘fucking Russian.’ ”

Sabine nodded heavily. “Yes, I wasn’t sure if I heard his name correctly that first night. But then I heard it again at the border when the Soviets took me on board and the East German left, although it was in Russian so I couldn’t be sure of the context. In fact, after all that happened in Berlin, I couldn’t believe it was the same man. At first, I thought it must be someone else with the same last name.”

“Did he ever visit you in the prison?” Baier asked.

“Yes, of course. Not very often. Only three times, to be exact. The first time, he came to assure me that I would not be mistreated, and that I would not even have to use this disgusting bucket in the corner to relieve myself. All I had to do, he said, was let the guards know I had to use the toilet.”

"So when did you get the sense of all this discontent there in Hungary? Did you ever leave the prison?"

"Karl, I didn't have to. You could tell from all the dissidents they were bringing in, people from all walks of life. It wasn't just dispossessed landowners and aristocrats or capitalists—"

"Not that there are many of those left, I'll bet," Baier broke in.

Sabine smiled. "You're probably right there. But they were also students, and lots of young people, including from the working class. They seemed to be the unhappiest of all. And they didn't stay for long. They were all getting shipped out on a regular basis. So I got to meet a lot. One time Chernov was there when some left and were soon replaced. He just looked at me and smiled. That's when I thought he might be up to something. I still couldn't believe it when he showed up at the border. I thought we were free of him."

"Do you have a good idea what it is?"

Sabine grabbed Baier's arm. "Of course, Karl. He wants us to run an exfiltration operation—to use us to help with refugee smuggling. That must be why he let us go. He needs someone on the other side, here in Austria, in the West."

"An exfiltration operation? Here, out of Hungary? He thinks we can set one up just like that?"

"Karl, he knows us, and especially me. Remember, we ran this kind of thing in Berlin."

Baier took her hand from his arm and caressed it as he leaned toward her. "But Sabine, that was a different time and a different place. Looking back, those conditions and that time were perfect for that sort of thing. This is no longer an occupied country, and Hungary is an independent country, too, only with hordes of Red Army troops driving around."

"Yes, and with Chernov running things from his end. He's the one taking the risks, which suits me just fine." She was lost in thought for a moment. "And I'd say he already has help in place."

"Can we trust him? Did you get a better sense of what motivates the guy? I mean, aside from greed."

Sabine sighed and waved her hand in a noncommittal gesture. "I'm not sure you can ever figure out what makes a man like him tick. But I get the sense that he's out of his element, a fish out of water."

"How so? What *is* his element?"

"I'm not sure he has one. When he did visit, he spoke several times to me about the loss of his family. You know, he never did find his siblings in South America. I think it's made him perpetually sad. And vengeful."

"So the dictatorship of the proletariat is not giving purpose to his life?" Baier smiled and shook his head.

"Hardly."

"Why all the hinting around and double talk at the border yesterday?" Baier continued. "Why didn't you come right out and discuss it with him then?"

Sabine rolled her eyes. "Karl, I wasn't going to commit to anything there; it would have been on his terms. Let him stew for a while." She shook her head. "What about those two goons of yours who were with us? How do you know they can be trusted? Are you certain they don't speak German?"

"Not exactly."

"Then you can't be sure."

"Those two 'goons,' as you call them, got us out of there. A little more gratitude wouldn't hurt, Sabine."

"They almost got us killed."

"They reacted instinctively," Baier explained. "It's how they're trained." He glanced out the window. "Besides, I can't just plunge forward on something like this on my own. I'll have to discuss it with Ralph and get Headquarters on board."

"Do you think that will be difficult?"

"It depends on how I sell it. I begged off on filling Ralph in on all the details today. As you can imagine, things were pretty hectic on our first day back. But I will have to bring it up tomorrow or the day after. As soon as I figure out a few other things."

"Like the killings?"

"Yes, like the killings."

Sabine lay against her husband's chest. "Whatever else happens, we're here and we're safe. And I've been thinking all day about the best way to pay those bastards back for taking me from you and my parents and using me as a pawn." She seemed to stare hard at some point beyond their walls. "I want to hurt them, Karl. I want to hurt their system and I want to hurt those sons-of-bitches running things behind the Curtain."

"And this is it?"

"It will do for now. I know I can make it work."

"Have you given any thought as to how you're going to make it work?"

"As a matter of fact, yes. That property we passed that you knew so much about and the family .... Tell me about them and their land. It seems to be as good a place as any to start." She glanced around the room. "Didn't you say you had purchased some wine from there? Let's give it a try."

Baier smiled. "Sure. I think there's a bottle or two left."

"A bottle or two? Karl, what have you been doing?"

"It's been a rough week, Sabine."

Baier slid off the couch and walked to the kitchen. He brought back two glasses of Blaufraenkisch and resettled himself on the sofa. Then he began his tale. He told her all about Herr Heinrich Rudolph von Rudenstein, his family, past and present, and the land. He didn't tell her about what he knew of the man's death and his own suspicions. He did promise, though, that once the story was complete he would tell her everything. He figured he owed that much to Sabine and von Rudenstein.

There would be one more trip to London and a few meetings in Vienna before that could happen. And it was not easy convincing Sabine that they would need to be apart again.

"It will only be for the day. I promise I will not stay the night."

"But why, Karl? We've only just gotten back together. I don't want us separated again, not for a long time."

He took her in his arms. "There is just something I have to do. I want to keep my promise to you and others about this murder in Vienna and the other one in St. Andrews. And I need to keep a promise I made to myself to get to the bottom of these cases."

"You can only do that in London?"

"Yes, Sabine. That's where the decisions were made, the ones that started this whole thing. That's where the answer lies." He held her tighter and kissed her forehead. "And when I get back, I'm going to introduce you to someone I believe can help with our exfiltration scheme. If we go forward, that is."

Thinking back, Baier was sure she had known what he had in mind and what he would do. It was why she had gone to sleep that night with a smile on her lips, before and after he kissed her. And she slept through Baier's restlessness when he got up to retrieve the note he had found in his mailbox after they returned home. She must have been truly exhausted.

Chapter Nineteen

BAIER WAITED IN the Belvedere Garden at the hill that ran from the front of Belvedere Palace to the old stables below. A light breeze ran through the trees and caressed the flowers that were blooming in a blend of bright colors. It felt like spring had finally arrived, as though the weather had decided to celebrate the return of Austrian independence and sovereignty.

Baier was sorry von Rudenstein would not be able to enjoy the weather or the freedom. But then again, he could not be sure how much contentment the old aristocrat would have been able to find in this new environment that surrounded his country and his neighbors in Europe.

As soon as he emerged from the walkway that led from the palace, Baier recognized the man. He passed a crop of shrubbery lining the botanical gardens to his left and about fifty yards from Baier's perch on a stone bench to the side of the fountain. It was not the faint resemblance to the shadow that had occasionally crossed his path here in Vienna that gave the man away. Ironically, it was the description Harrison had given after their visit to the opera house. Shorter than Baier but stockier and broad-shouldered, the man was thick-necked as well, although Harrison had left that much out. Perhaps the workman's clothes he had worn that day had hidden that feature. Today, though, the shadow had taken form in the casual attire of a bourgeois Austrian out to enjoy his capital on a fine spring day: loose cotton slacks under an open-necked white shirt and gray sports jacket. Baier stood from his seat on the bench as the man approached.

"So it was you all along," Baier stated. The man nodded. "I take it you are Helmut Meyerhof. I have to congratulate you on your surveillance techniques. You are very hard to spot and even more difficult to pin down."

"Thank you." Helmut Meyerhof smiled. "That's a nice compliment from a fellow professional."

"A colleague?" Baier stepped back. He wanted to appraise this stranger more carefully. "Why haven't our paths crossed before?"

The Austrian signaled for Baier to walk beside him as he began to stroll along the path leading from the bench through the park and away from the main palace. This put them on the route to the smaller outlet, which appeared to have served as a garden house or stables. It had also belonged at one time to Prince Schwarzenberg. There never seemed to be a shortage of palaces in this town.

"Our worlds are not that close, Herr Baier. I'm actually with the metropolitan police in Vienna."

"Well, that explains your surveillance skills. But how did you get my address? And more importantly, why have you been following me? I haven't broken any laws, I hope."

"No, no. Nothing like that." Meyerhof waved his hand in the general direction of the garden before them. "Our mutual friend Huetzing gave it to me. He thought you might like to hear what I know about von Rudenstein. It could have some bearing on your investigation."

"Then why all the mystery? Why all the shadowing? Why not meet me in Huetzing's office?"

Meyerhof stopped to consider Baier with a look of mild puzzlement in his eyes and a tight grin on his lips. "After all this, you still do not realize how complicated this case has become and how it could affect you and your position here? That there are still dangers you face?"

"Dangers?"

"Yes, exactly. Have you gotten your wife to safety yet?"

"As a matter of fact, I have. She's home now. What else is there?"

Meyerhof appeared relieved. "That is truly good news, Herr Baier." He glanced at the blue sky, and then back at Baier. "There are others, of course. But let me get to the real point of my being here today."

"Please do."

"You know that the jacket von Rudenstein was wearing when they found his body was my old one from the war, don't you?"

Baier nodded. "I have learned that, but only recently. How did the old guy come to be wearing your old army jacket?"

Meyerhof resumed walking. "I gave it to him. He had contacted me to arrange a meeting with you Americans. I refused. I told him I was done with that sort of thing, that I had gotten as far away from that world as I could."

"Done with it? How so?"

"Yes, done completely. At least until recently. I worked with your OSS during the war. At the end, mostly."

"How did you know von Rudenstein?"

"We served together in Italy. I even knew the mysterious Mr. Hardwicke." Meyerhof shook his head. "It was a rare thing. We only met because I knew Heinrich so well. For the most part, you and your British allies played two separate games in Italy. I thought at times you made strange allies, that you really didn't trust each other."

Baier nodded. "Yes, there were those of us who distrusted

British plans for the postwar period. But that was mostly in the Pacific."

Meyerhof shrugged. "There was some of that distrust here as well. Then again, we all suffered from illusions."

"Perhaps," Baier said. "But tell me, do you have any idea how Hardwicke died?"

Meyerhof looked over the treetops of the park. "I can't say for certain. I doubt it was the Soviets, which I'm sure you assume was the case. They wouldn't have any reason to kill him once they'd removed his source."

"You mean von Rudenstein, of course."

Meyerhof nodded. "Yes. I'm certain they killed von Rudenstein. It's one reason I'm talking to you now." Meyerhof stopped and considered the path at his feet. "There must be something else there, however. I believe only your British friends know for certain. For Hardwicke, it could be anything. Suicide even." He glanced at the blue sky, dotted with occasional puffs of white. "In fact, I think that's the most likely answer."

"Why?"

"Well, a good professional can make something like that look like suicide, of course. So you can understand why I can't be certain." Meyerhof lit a cigarette and blew out the match. "It's up to you, of course. But I believe if you press a little harder, you will find the cracks in their service that could lead to this sort of thing. Given all that has happened in that service over the last few years, I would be open to any possibility. In particular, you have to consider a betrayal back in London."

"How would that lead to suicide in this case?"

As Meyerhof smoked, he considered the park that lay before them. Finally he said, "A sense of loss that becomes impossible to live with. Loss of loyalty to an organization to which you devoted your life. But mostly loss of a man you had come to trust as a colleague and friend and his betrayal."

"You said earlier that you were out of it now. What do you mean by that?"

Meyerhof started walking again. "I continued working for you Americans after the war. I felt a certain degree of gratitude after your Army pulled me out of a French POW camp in Baden. But I stopped in 1949."

"Why? What happened to all that gratitude?"

"I grew tired of it all and was no longer interested. I decided to devote my energies to solving crimes and making my home a safer place to work and live. Heinrich came to me earlier this year, but I told him I was out of it for good. It's why I gave him my jacket. To show him how I had broken with my past, our mutual past."

Meyerhof quickened his pace, and Baier trotted to catch up. "So how did your old friend take the rejection?"

"Oh, well enough. He was already in touch with you Americans."

Baier halted in his tracks. "Here? In Vienna?" He thought back through all the case files he had reviewed before coming to Vienna. There had been no mention of von Rudenstein.

Meyerhof stamped out his cigarette and turned back to Baier. He stood just inches away, close enough for Baier to spot the patches of stubble on the man's cheeks and chin.

"Based on the look on your face, I'd say no, not here. I couldn't be sure myself," Meyerhof said. "It was why I followed you. To see how much you knew already and whether I should intervene."

Son-of-a-bitch, Baier thought. The pebbles at his feet, the broad outlay of the park, the entire city seemed suddenly out of focus, tilting on a broken Ferris wheel. "How long had this been going on?"

"The relationship goes back to the war."

"I thought you said we and the Brits ran separate operations there."

Meyerhof nodded and smiled. "Yes, you did, for the most part. This was an exception. Heinrich's principal handler was Hardwicke, of course, but for joint operations or joint meetings, an American officer was also involved. It was a man I knew as Cartwright." He shrugged. "I can't say if that was his real name, though."

Baier was speechless. He was surprised, almost in shock. He was also frantically searching his memory for any reference to a man named Cartwright.

After a few minutes Meyerhof turned to go. "Good luck, Herr Baier. I can see you're trying to work your way through this new information. I'm sorry to have confused you, but I thought you should know. Perhaps it will help you find your own way out of the maze."

Baier watched the Austrian amble back toward the botanical garden behind them, where he disappeared. He felt a sudden chill, and he noticed that the sky had turned gray and cool. *Typical*, he thought, *you can never trust the weather here.* He turned and trotted onto Prinz-Eugen-Strasse, where he broke into a run in the direction of the art history museum.

They met in the Museum Square that looked out over the Burgring and the Hofburg below. Baier stood with his back to the Museum of Art History, or the Kunsthistorisches Museum, as the locals knew it. He watched Stein approach from the opposite direction, the Natural History Museum at his back. Baier had chosen the place because it provided a broad, open space, giving him the reassurance and, ironically, the cover he wanted.

Stein approached slowly and cautiously, as though the Austrian wasn't sure what to expect when he circled around the great fountain at the center of the square. His grin suggested a confidence that his step betrayed. The clouds had passed by the time Baier arrived, and his face felt moist with sweat from his jog over. Despite the warm and sunny weather, Stein wore the long beige trench coat that flapped open as he walked, the same one he'd worn during their meetings in the heart of the old city just days ago.

"I was surprised to get your note," Stein began. "I'm impressed you were able to track my office down. To what do I owe the pleasure?"

"Oh, there are still a few loose ends," Baier replied. "I thought you might be able to help me fill in some of the gaps to our story."

"*Our* story? I would think that the real meaning lies with you and your country's role here in Europe. You have a great deal of responsibility now. That lies at the heart of my interest, my motive in approaching you in the first place."

"Let's stick to the particulars of this case before we venture off into more metaphysical matters, Herr Stein."

Stein nodded and smiled. "Fair enough. But this is an odd place to choose for a meeting. Is there something about this place that you find attractive?"

"I like the Bruegel collection," Baier said. "Those paintings remind me of the chaos that has surrounded the many tracks and agendas in this whole case." He glanced up at the towering figure of Maria Theresa at the top of the fountain, surrounded by various lieutenants of her reign. "It seems there's a lot of history here."

Stein stepped in closer, only a few feet in front of Baier. His grin widened. "Well, perhaps we can begin, then. You seem to be interested in the same sort of puzzles that Bruegel introduced to his portraits of village life, which were never very metaphysical as far as I could see. Are you sure you can navigate your way through them?" He spread his arms. "And you are hardly surprised to encounter 'a lot of' history here, as you put it?"

Baier studied the Austrian's face, the thin nose and smooth jaw that appeared freshly shaved, as though he was a late riser. The dark blond hair was meticulously groomed today, not a single strand touching his ears or collar, the part so clean it could have been carved from wax.

"First of all, I was wondering if you're happy now that your wish has been granted?" Baier asked.

The grin disappeared. "What do you mean? What wish?"

"Your State Treaty had been signed, and that troublesome von Rudenstein has been removed. He won't be able to muck things up anymore." Baier paused. "Neither will the British, for that matter."

"So the field should be open for you Americans. Don't fail us now, Herr Baier." Stein took a step back, turning his head at a slight angle, as though to study Baier from a better perspective. "Yes, you're right in that I am happy about the State Treaty. But just what are you getting at on the von Rudenstein matter? Are you accusing me of something?"

"He was in the way. You were afraid he would mess up the plans to win Austria its full-fledged freedom and end the occupation."

Stein nodded eagerly. "Yes, yes, those were important to me. And to many other Austrians as well. But to accuse me of having a hand in the man's murder …."

Baier's lips curved into a tight smile. "Oh, I'm not accusing you of murder. I know you never pulled the trigger. Or even planned on the man's killing. But you may as well have. You could have stopped it all at some point. What I still can't figure out is how you knew so much about their operation and its purpose."

"Don't be preposterous! How would I have stopped it all, and at what point? I only learned of it recently myself. It was your British friends' operation, which they misplayed, not mine. Don't be absurd. Even you can see that now, I hope. You Americans were in a better position to bring a halt to the affair than I ever was, or my compatriots for that matter. In the end, I could only sit by and watch."

"How can you say we could have stopped it? The British didn't ask for our permission."

"Oh, come now, Herr Baier. You Americans were familiar

with von Rudenstein from the war. I knew that much from my own work in the Wehrmacht's intelligence service. And I was certain that you must have maintained some contact."

"Well, I've got a pretty good guess at this point as to how he was betrayed, and by whom. And it wasn't us. I'm also pretty sure you knew more than you let on. Surely someone with your access to the prime minister knew and could have done more. And it really is sad, because the man was nothing but a harmless old romantic. He had a dream about a lost empire that he just didn't want to let go. So someone had him killed. And my guess is that you knew about all that for far longer than you're letting on."

Stein stepped in closer. "Harmless? Is that so?" Spittle was forming along his lips. "Do you think the ridiculous dreams that have led to so much destruction here in Europe have been so harmless? I've had enough of these romantic dreams. We all have."

"Easy, Herr Stein. You're entitled to your view of history and where it may have led, but that doesn't give you a license to allow one of your countrymen to be killed. He had performed a valuable service for your country."

Stein started to walk away then stopped. When he turned back to Baier, his expression was both condescending and incredulous. "He performed a valuable service for you as well, didn't he?" Stein spat at the sidewalk. "I'm sorry you wasted so much effort investigating this story, Herr Baier, especially since you have discovered so little. It was only his death that made me aware something else was going on here. I realized there was something up, but I couldn't be sure how far it went and what the repercussions might be. Why do think I insisted on involving you?"

Baier took a step in Stein's direction. "Because you were looking for a way to stay informed. Since von Rudenstein had been a British asset, you couldn't very well turn to them. And of course, the French and Soviets were out of the question."

"Why is that?"

"Because you knew very well that any interference with the signing of the State Treaty would not come from those two." He paused, as though to catch his breath. "Besides, the Soviets were not to be trusted. They were the ones who saw von Rudenstein as a threat. They killed him. The real question in my mind at this point is why they saw him as a threat. His plans were more of a fantasy that anything actionable."

"Moscow put a lot of work into the State Treaty. They wanted to be certain he couldn't derail the signing. Or its implementation. After he showed up in Moscow, they could not be certain of his influence or role. That's why they killed him and left his body here on the banks of the Danube—a warning, if you will."

"Do you have any proof?"

"Proof? You know how good they are at eliminating anything inconvenient like proof. It's the only explanation that makes sense." Stein's grin returned. "You are correct in asserting that I wanted to stay informed. I was hoping you'd find something tangible for me to use. But as you can see for yourself, you were little help with that." Stein let his gaze wander over the rooftops of the Hofburg and the streets beyond. "More importantly, I wanted to get a better sense of how the Soviets plan to play their game now. What I need to know, and what my government needs to know, is how they will play that game now that we are truly independent again, just what they have in mind for this part of Europe."

"That's something we all want to know. I was undermined in this because I was working blind. That wasn't necessary, Stein. You should have come clean. You should have approached me sooner, as soon as you suspected something."

"And how was I supposed to do that? I told you, it was only after his death that things began to come together. And what makes you think I could trust your country either?"

Baier took a step forward. "Because we were all you had

then. We were your last hope. We still are. It's why you turned to me in the first place. But you should never have tried to play it halfway, Stein. That was wrong."

Stein's grin had a hard set to it. "Perhaps. But I still made sure you were brought in and stayed there. Even then, you were not all that helpful. It took you so long to work through this affair."

"Thanks to people like you, Stein. And you always knew more than you let on. It was probably one reason you kept your distance as much as possible. You never really trusted me. We could have done much more together. You spoke earlier of our responsibility in Europe now. Well, if we're to handle that properly, we'll need more openness and cooperation from your side."

Stein waved at the air between them and frowned. "I tried to help as much as I could. I had other angles I had to play as well, you know."

"Oh, I finally realized that when I followed you that day behind St. Stephens. You also let those other angles get in the way and cloud your judgment."

"How so?"

"For one thing, I wasted a lot of time suspecting it was your people who followed me in London that first day, or that whoever it was did so because of you."

"And why would I do that?"

"To keep track of what I was doing, to see how close I was coming to the truth. You needed something like that because you underestimated your colleague Huetzing. He was too much of a professional and kept his investigation close to his chest. Even then, he was never allowed to get far." Baier stepped in closer. "Which also suited you just fine. You never wanted the truth to go beyond your own desk, did you?"

The two men stared at each other for what seemed like a minute. Baier could hear the drone of traffic along the Ringstrasse just meters away. Swallows danced in the air above them, and a breeze ruffled Stein's hair enough to blur the part.

His hand seemed to reach up of its own accord to straighten it.

"As much as I regret the death of the old Austrian," Baier continued, "what I really find tragic is the death of Hardwicke."

"Who? The *Englander*?"

"Oh, come off it. Yes, the British agent. Von Rudenstein's handler. The man who let his professionalism slip away and allowed himself to be led by the imagination and passion of a man he had known and worked with for years. It can happen in this profession."

"People can become blind to the weaknesses and vulnerabilities of those they work with in our profession as well, Herr Baier."

"Meaning?"

"Meaning a number of things you are still not aware of. But mostly meaning you, my American friend. For one thing, von Rudenstein was a double agent. He was all along."

"Working for you during the war, you mean? I've already figured out that much. Or was there someone else?"

Stein laughed. "Von Rudenstein worked for a number of people. You know of his British connection, and you've guessed that we were able to follow all that. Then, of course, there was your side."

"Oh, of course." Baier hoped the pain from Meyerhof's revelation did not show, at least not to Stein of all people. "But who else, and how far does it all go back?"

"It started during the war, when he was working for the Third Reich as a sort of double agent. You've probably learned that I was involved with his case during my time with what you Americans like to call the 'Gehlen Organization.' I had suspected for some time that he was also feeding information to the Soviets. It was something I hoped you would find out for me. One way or the other."

"Sorry to disappoint you. But von Rudenstein never worked for 'the Bolshies,' as he knew them."

Stein made a derisive sound and waved Baier's false apology

off. "I no longer think that was the case myself. The problem for someone like von Rudenstein was that he could never find a place to settle after the war. He didn't know what to do with his loyalties."

"Yes," Baier said. "At least he kept them from the Soviets."

"The real problem for you," Stein went on, "was that your closeness to the British blinded you to the true cause of his death—something I only recently realized. He may have been killed by the Soviets, but he was betrayed by someone in London. I said as much to your friend Harrison the other day."

"What did he say?" Baier asked. "Who was it?"

"Harrison was not much help. But you Americans have suspected MI6 of being riddled with Soviet agents for years."

"Whom do you suspect?"

"I can't be sure, but we're probably thinking along the same lines," Stein said. "Only two fled to Moscow, and we both know there are more still in place. But whoever it was, it means I had no reason to kill that pathetic Englishman, Hardwicke. He had suffered enough. He probably committed suicide when he found out about von Rudenstein's death and the cause of it."

Baier sighed and glanced over his shoulder toward the museum before turning back to Stein. "I have one other problem, Stein."

"Yes. Only one more?"

"It's a big one that has been pulling at me for a while. Put my mind at ease."

"I'll certainly try," Stein said. He stepped back, and his body seemed to relax inside the drapery of his raincoat.

"I cannot get rid of this nagging suspicion that some of your friends from the 'Gehlen Organization,' people with whom you're probably still in touch, could have decided that it was payback time for all the damage people like Hardwicke did to your side. Not to mention von Rudenstein. You had Hardwicke right where you wanted him—retired and isolated. He was vulnerable and could no longer defend himself."

Stein's narrowed eyes studied Baier's face, his expression incredulous. "What could you possibly mean by that?"

"Surely you've learned how the British played so many of your agents back against you. Well, they did it with von Rudenstein as well. He was fully aware of their game and participated willingly. He helped relay disinformation for Operation Mincemeat to deflect your attention away from Sicily and toward a false invasion plan for Greece, and then he helped with the diversion of your focus to Calais and away from Normandy before the invasion."

Stein appeared nearly apoplectic; his cheeks had grown unnaturally red. "How could you possibly know this?"

"It was in their diaries."

Stein thought for a moment. "I can see why Hardwicke would engage in empty boasting, but von Rudenstein?"

"Insurance," Baier replied. "It's quite simple when you think about it. The old man had given up on the Third Reich after Stalingrad. His goal was to hasten the end of a war that was destroying his beloved homeland, and the Soviets had already seized control of much of the old Empire. Can you blame him?" Baier paused to let this sink in. "So I keep asking myself if some of your old colleagues had a revenge game of their own to play and whether you knew anything about it."

Stein turned to leave, his movements now noticeably tense. "This is all so pointless, Herr Baier. You people need to free yourself of these fantasies of German revenge. No, the real cause lies with you and your friends in the West. You could never prove any of this, regardless."

"Yes, unfortunately we can never take any of this to a court of law, Stein. Regardless of who is guilty."

"We do not work in that sort of environment, do we? But you can always ask that old British spymaster Siscourt to confirm your theories. Have you spoken with him?"

Baier nodded, searching the ground as if for some final piece of the puzzle. "Yes, I've met him. But I haven't been back with my new information. Not yet." He looked up at Stein. "At least I have the final answer on von Rudenstein. The man was definitely not a Soviet asset. That would betray everything he believed in, according to my research. No, you're right, they saw him as a threat. That's why they had him removed. At least I have confirmed that much by speaking with you."

Stein said nothing, only stared out toward the city of Vienna and the hills beyond, as though searching for his own piece of history.

Baier went on, "But that does not excuse your role in this whole affair. You've been duplicitous and dishonest. You tried to use me, Stein. As long as I'm here, I'll always wonder what sort of relationship I'll have with you and your colleagues. You can't be trusted. And since we can't go to court, that is the one thing we need to have. Trust."

Stein laughed out loud, a far from merry sound. His mouth was still open when he looked back at Baier. "Do you really think it will be that easy? Do you have any idea how much I have given your side, especially the American military? And yes, even your own organization, Herr Baier, from our old archives. That is material it would have taken you decades to assemble."

"But it's information we have now. So who's to say how badly we still need your cooperation?"

Stein laughed again. "Well, that might work if our part in the new European drama were over once the files were delivered. There is still the matter of the listening posts we're allowing you to construct on our borders." His eyebrows arched as if he was enjoying their game of one-upmanship. "I assure you that I can make that particular operation troublesome and inconvenient for many in both our governments. And my country will provide a convenient operating environment for your organization, Herr Baier. We are well situated here geographically. It's a new game now. We all have new responsibilities. Or haven't you noticed?" Stein turned and began to stride away from Baier, the Bruegels, and the entire Museum complex. "Think again, Herr Baier. Think again."

Baier knew he would indeed think again. He had learned long ago that there was rarely a final answer in this business. He would do what he could to keep his distance from Stein and nail down just who in London had betrayed von Rudenstein and Hardwicke. And now there was the matter of an American hand. He would have to do without the Austrians or the Germans. Stein was right, the United States had assumed an awesome responsibility for Europe, one that was complicated by the State Treaty and Austria's new position in the middle of the continent. The Germans and the Austrians would be important allies, partners even. But they would have their own agendas in the years ahead, in the new Europe emerging from the ruins of the old.

He could never be certain just how they would play their hands.

Chapter Twenty

BAIER HAD MEANT it when he told Sabine that this was to be no more than a day trip. The flight left Vienna early the next morning at 7:30 a.m. sharp. Since he gained an hour traveling to England, it was still fairly early in the morning when he arrived in London. The trip in from Heathrow seemed to pass in a daze. It was an unusually bright spring day for London, with sunny skies disguising a slight chill in the air that felt like it was getting pushed aside by a wave of humidity. This sort of mugginess could sneak into the city like a silent, slithery reptile. He skipped the Caledonia Club this time around, as there would be no need for a room. It was too bad, because he had enjoyed the comfort and ambiance the last time around.

Baier walked in to find Sir Robert Siscourt standing rigid behind his desk. He wore a different but equally formal-looking suit this time, black with wide white pinstripes. Baier wondered if he was in mourning for some field operation that had gone very sour, like the one with von Rudenstein. The entire affair may have looked sweet when it started, back during the heydays of a world war and the beginnings of a new confrontation between East and West, the kind of conflict that seemed to split Europeans throughout their history and which normally took centuries to resolve. The one seemed to slide right into the other. How long would it take this situation to resolve? Baier took in the grand portraits that hung between the midday shadows that flowed from the thick but fading burgundy curtains, draping the windows and walls in a post-imperial frame.

Siscourt pointed to a chair opposite his desk. Baier noted that he was not being offered a seat on the plush, brown-leather sofa to the side. Apparently, his British host did not intend for this meeting to last long. Baier was fine with that.

"Just how much have you learned?" Siscourt began.

"Enough to know that your side wasted the lives of two men in an ill-conceived operation that smacked more of the war behind us than the confrontation ahead."

Siscourt tilted his head back so that he appeared to be looking down on his guest. "Why do you say that?"

Baier leaned forward in his chair. "Because it was a hopeless quest. You're not going to recreate anything like what existed before in that part of the world."

"Have you informed your Secretary of State? I believe Mr. Dulles is a proponent of rolling the Bolshies back. At least, if one is to believe his speeches." He pointed directly at Baier. "And let's not forget the many failed operations you Americans launched in Eastern Europe after the war."

"So that's what you really thought you could achieve with von Rudenstein?"

"Not quite." Siscourt stood and went to his window, where he looked down upon St. James Square with an expression half contemptuous and half reverential. "If we made one error, it was in mistaking the strength of our position and mistranslating that into a policy."

"How do you mean?"

Siscourt turned back to Baier. "Are you aware of the many

meetings that our Allied leaders held during the course of the war?"

"Of course. Yalta, Potsdam, Tehran, even Ottawa. Why?"

"You fail to mention a very important one that occurred in Moscow in 1944. It may be because your President Roosevelt was not present. It was in October, if memory serves."

"It should. It wasn't that long ago, and especially if it's so damn important," Baier said.

"Yes, of course you're right, Mr. Baier. It was in October, which was not long ago for someone in my position. But in any event, our prime minister sat at a table with that damn Soviet generalissimo from Georgia and drew some figures on the back of an envelope."

"What kind of figures?" Baier sat back and crossed his legs. This was starting to get interesting.

"Small ones. They were associated with the different countries of Eastern and Central Europe. They said things like 'fifty-fifty,' or 'ninety-ten,' and in some cases, 'seventy-thirty.' " Siscourt allowed himself a small smile. Sitting at his desk, he began to rummage in the top drawer. "It was our prime minister dividing the region with Mr. Stalin in terms of the expected influence over the postwar political development of the countries in question."

Baier drummed his fingers on the desk. "This took place as the Red Army was beginning to overrun these countries and where Stalin would have the whip hand?"

"Well, most of them, anyway. We were pretty well placed in Greece, as it turned out." Siscourt raised his hand, which now held an unlit cigar. "I applaud your analogy, Mr. Baier. In any case, it certainly appears foolish now. In his defense, I can only assume—since he did not discuss his thoughts with me—that the prime minister was doing his best to place some kind of restraint on Stalin's power in the region."

"Fat lot of good that did us all."

Baier heard the door open and close behind him. When

he turned, he saw Harrison approach with a document in his hand. It appeared to be several pages long, bound and enclosed within a blue-rimmed cover.

"Have you told him about the Moscow meeting?" Harrison asked Siscourt.

Siscourt nodded. "Yes, just now." He turned his full attention on Baier. "Of course, none of this will ever leave this room. In fact, I would prefer it if no word of this conversation is ever spoken after today. I resisted even agreeing to it, but your colleagues Robert Wainwright and Mr. Harrison," Siscourt nodded in the direction of his MI6 colleague, "assured me it was necessary."

"So, what's in the paper?" Baier gestured toward the document Harrison had delivered, which Siscourt now held in his free hand.

"It's an interesting and well-written document from a young officer at the Foreign Office. Normally, these sorts of things circulate among other young staffers and occasionally make it to the desk of a mid-level superior. If the ideas are truly noteworthy, that official will pass them along as his own, of course. At least, that's what usually happens."

"I take it that was not the case this time around," Baier said.

Siscourt leafed through the document and shook his head. "No, unfortunately not. This one seemed to make it to the prime minister's desk. It advocates a southeastern European Customs Union, with boundaries remarkably similar to those of the old Hapsburg Empire. It would replace the state system that proved so ineffective after the Great War. It might also, the author surmises, create an effective barrier to Soviet influence in the region. The prime minister was enraptured."

"And it inspired the von Rudenstein operation," Baier concluded.

"Yes, I'm afraid so," Siscourt said. "Which wouldn't have been so bad, if it had stopped there. Not that we could have recreated anything resembling the Hapsburg Empire, mind you. We might have been able to undermine Soviet control somewhat and prepare for a better day, as it were. I'm afraid our Herr von Rudenstein moved from asset to handler, as Hardwicke lost control of the man and the operation."

Baier turned to Harrison, who had taken a seat on the edge of the sofa behind him. "And that's when it took a much more serious turn, one that was never intended."

Harrison nodded. "As we discussed in Vienna, Karl."

"But then what happened in Moscow?" Baier thought back to Chernov's warning that the riddle to von Rudenstein's death could be solved in London and Stein's words about the terrible mistake of von Rudenstein going to Moscow, where he had placed himself in the lion's den. "What made the Soviets decide to wrap the operation up?"

"We're not really sure what that was all about," Siscourt said. "He may have thought there was a possibility he could avert the conclusion of the State Treaty. He may even have tried to make contact with an asset of ours there to expand the operation."

"Really," Baier said. "An asset in Moscow?"

"That's my supposition."

Harrison broke in, "We've lost touch with the man. He may have been betrayed by von Rudenstein's presence."

Baier held out his hands, palms up. "But how would the Soviets know about any of this?"

Siscourt replied, "I'm afraid that brings us back to Mr. Hardwicke and his loss of control. In any case, we think von Rudenstein was betrayed while in Moscow, perhaps killed there or more likely someplace closer to home, and then dropped in Vienna on the banks of the Danube as a warning and a statement."

"A warning? Of what?"

"Not to try anything of that sort again," Siscourt said. "That Moscow was not about to let any of its satellites get away, regardless of the cost. Now that that idiot Hitler had let them into Europe, they were not about to permit anyone to push them out."

"So, the Wehrmacht jacket was not a red herring. There was a message in that as well," Baier said.

Harrison bowed his head. "Probably. We can't be sure, of course, but it makes sense."

"And all of von Rudenstein's contacts? Will you be able to work with them or at least get them out?"

Siscourt was silent. He looked over at Harrison.

"There's a problem there as well," Harrison said.

"Such as?" Baier said.

"Well, we seem to have lost contact with them also. Right now, we fear the worst."

Baier thought again of Chernov. How much did the man really know, and was he really as well placed as he claimed? "Jesus, but that hurts." He paused to consider. "So, we're certain that the Soviets killed von Rudenstein. I had figured out that much already. But who killed Hardwicke?"

Siscourt took his seat behind the desk again with a sigh. "We haven't been able to pin that one down as yet. But we believe it was the Soviets as well, perhaps when they pressed him for information on von Rudenstein's purpose in going to Moscow. It's the one explanation that makes sense." The cigar remained unlit, although the left hand now held a box of matches. "For the life of me, I cannot figure out how they were able to get their man or men inside to pull that one off. I was certain we had all their people here under the strictest surveillance."

"And what if von Rudenstein's was betrayed by someone else?"

Siscourt stared at Baier. He sighed, studied the world outside his window, then the top of his desk. When he looked up again, Siscourt glanced first at Harrison, then at his American guest. "Goodbye, Mr. Baier. And good luck."

"Well, in that case, I guess you'll have to keep searching, because that does not sound like the Hardwicke I've heard and read about," Baier said. He studied the British spymaster for a moment to see if there was anything else the man wanted to say. But Siscourt's face grew sad and pale, and the skin at his jowls seemed to sag. His eyes did not move from the cigar he now held in his right hand. Baier saw that the meeting was over, that Siscourt's thoughts had moved to another place, perhaps even another time. He got up to leave.

When he was nearly at the door, Baier stopped and turned back to his host. He smiled, more to himself than to anyone else. "You know, Bob, now that you've mentioned those failed American operations, I recall that a big part of the problem was being betrayed to Moscow. And you know who we suspect was behind that. Maybe you've been looking in the wrong place."

Siscourt did not look up from the matches in his hand. "They would have failed anyway," he mumbled, "and nothing has been proven."

No, Baier thought as he walked into the hallway. *But perhaps you'll see to that. Someday.*

BAIER'S FOOTSTEPS ECHOED off walls lined with history and intrigue as he made his way down the corridor outside Siscourt's office. About thirty yards down, he heard his name called from behind. When he halted and turned, he saw Harrison rushing to catch up in a fast walk, almost a trot.

"Karl, please. Wait."

"I was hoping I'd hear a bit more from you, Tom. Just what is it you're not telling me? I mean, it was pretty obvious your boss was holding back. I almost expected him to break down in tears there at the end. Does he really still suspect the Soviets for the Hardwicke killing?"

Harrison stepped in front of Baier and held up his hands as though to prevent his escape. "Well, that was certainly a nice touch calling him 'Bob' back there."

"What is really going on here, Tom?"

Harrison chewed his lower lip and glanced both ways along

the corridor before continuing, "You remember, I'm sure, me telling you how close Sir Robert and Hardwicke were. Well, this death has hit the old man pretty hard."

"Is he trying to cover something up? Was he the one who ripped those pages from Hardwicke's diary?"

Harrison's face went white, and his eyes grew wide. "How … how did you …?"

Baier blew out a breath of contempt. "Oh, come on, Tom. It was done in such haste that the binding wasn't even cleaned. You could see shreds of paper stuck in the wire rim. The rest of it confirmed what ol' Bob told me today. But there's clearly more."

Harrison glanced sheepishly at the floor before looking up into Baier's eyes. His face had regained its color. Baier hoped his courage had returned with it. "The missing pages contained a suicide note."

"So that settles it. Do you believe it was authentic? Has Siscourt said anything?"

Harrison nodded. "It seems so. I never got to read it, but Sir Robert confided as much. The talk about a Soviet hand is just an effort to protect the man's memory. And he does not want us washing our linen in public, as it were, especially in front of you chaps."

"Does anyone else here know?"

"Yes, and those who are aware seem to agree. But I have no idea what could have caused it. His personal life was pretty clean. No failed romances, family breakups, big debts. Nothing one normally associates with this kind of thing."

"Any further insights or information from Bobby?"

Harrison shook his head. "No, he refuses to discuss it further."

"Have you considered that the man felt betrayed, his life's work ruined by someone back here? That you still haven't cleaned out the rot that infected this place?"

Harrison stared at Baier, then seemed to look beyond him.

"I have. But I'm not going to take it any further. Not right now."

Baier studied his British colleague for a moment, sighed, then reached out to take Harrison's hand. "Thanks, Thomas. This has helped after all."

"Oh, good." Harrison looked as though he had just been relieved of a large weight. His muscles visibly relaxed. "I just hope this makes up for any ill feeling you might harbor after my failure to inform you of the meeting with Stein."

"Oh, don't worry about Stein. We've had a meeting of minds, sort of. But this helps. A lot." Baier smiled and continued down the corridor. Then he stopped again and turned back to Harrison.

"And it's true, Tom. There was a message in the Wehrmacht jacket. It wasn't a red herring. But it didn't come from the Soviets alone."

"Then who ...?"

"I think your people, or some of them, including good ol' Bobby in there," Baier motioned toward Siscourt's office, "already know. As do the people I'm going to visit after this."

As he strolled into the midday sun, past the buildings that lined St. James Square, Baier realized that the final piece to the puzzle was in London after all. It just wasn't where he had expected it to be.

HE STAYED NO more than a few minutes with Wainwright and his deputy, an obsequious twit named Givens who sat quietly for the most part throughout the brief fifteen-minute conversation. Baier remembered the man from their passing each other during the latter's one short assignment at the Headquarters compound down on the Mall in Washington. He had impressed Baier as a real suck-up.

"So, you knew all along, didn't you?" Baier asked.

Wainwright's face displayed no emotion whatsoever. "Knew what, Karl? What are we talking about here?"

"You know very well what I mean, Mr. Cartwright," Baier

said. "About von Rudenstein, the operation, the fuck-up in Moscow. You may not have been involved in the actual running of the operation, but they certainly kept you informed. Perhaps not about every single detail, but most of it."

"How much do you know?" Givens broke in.

"Enough." Baier shifted his gaze to the deputy. "Are you sure you want to discuss this in front of him, Mr. Cartwright?"

"Not really." Wainwright's blank stare stayed in place. "But we're not going into any detail here. I owe you nothing on this. And where did you get that name?"

"As long as we're keeping secrets, I'll hold on to that one. I've figured out that Cartwright was your pseudo during the war, perhaps afterward as well. I've also learned something about your work in Italy during the war."

Wainwright let his mask fall for an instant, flashing a brief smile. "Yeah, I spent time there with the OSS. I've told you that before. It was where I met Angleton. He was already devoted to his Brit friends and still is, as far as I can tell."

"Despite what those clowns have given up?"

"You bet. He refuses to believe they can do any wrong. And the last time I was in Washington, he still outranked you by a whole lot, Karl. As far as he and many others above our pay grade are concerned, the special relationship we've built with these guys here is a lot more important than some drama involving a dead Austrian aristocrat who no longer fit into the Europe we have today. It's the new battleground, Karl. You'll have to make adjustments, like the rest of us. Unfortunately, your Austrian friend couldn't and paid a heavy price."

"How involved were you over the years? Did the Brits hold control throughout? Why didn't you help steer me in the right direction?"

"Orders from Washington, Karl. I was told to let the Brits control the flow of information on this since it was their asset." Wainwright face softened, as though he understood how Baier felt. "I'm sorry, Karl, but that was how I was told to handle it."

"Maybe. But I still think you're a fucking asshole for holding out on me. Don't expect a warm reception if you ever come to Vienna."

"I'm sorry you feel that way. I understand if that's how you think you need to play it."

"It is." Baier stood to go.

Wainwright extended his hand. "Karl, congratulations on Budapest. I'm really glad everything worked out for you and your wife."

Baier nodded. He left without saying anything to either man. And he did not take Wainwright's hand.

Epilogue

As they had agreed, Baier met Sabine the following morning at the café down the street from the apartment of the young von Rudenstein. They shared a pot of Viennese coffee and a piece of marzipan cake, while Baier considered how best to explain his plan.

"How are your parents?" Baier asked as soon as they found a fairly secluded table in the corner by the front window. "You called them this morning, didn't you?"

Sabine nodded. "Yes. As good as can be expected. They are obviously relieved that I am free and back with you, Karl. They can rest in peace now."

"That sounds a little ominous. Do you think we'll have any luck convincing them to move to the West?"

Sabine shrugged as she stirred the cream into her coffee. "We'll see. I told them it will be easy to get them out through Berlin, and that they deserve something better in their late years than that failure the Soviets are creating." She looked up at Baier, her forehead creased with care and sorrow. "They just want to let their lives play out in the home they know, Karl, even if it is no longer the world they knew from before all this madness."

"Well," Baier replied, "we'll just have to keep trying." Then Baier laid out his plan for the exfiltration operation at the border and the von Rudenstein estate.

"How did you get Mr. Delgreccio to agree? Is Washington on board?"

Baier smiled. "They're prepared to let us give it a try. I explained your thoughts on the discontent over in Hungary to Ralph and pointed out we could not very well let those people trying to escape remain vulnerable to capture by the Soviets and their henchmen. Not only would we score a nice public relations coup, but it would be the right thing to do."

"But how do you know the son will agree?" Sabine asked.

"Well, I don't know for sure. But I don't think he has any more interest in the estate or the grounds. And I doubt he cares that much for the business itself, although he might be happy to market the wine. He's probably most happy to take the money and run."

Sabine frowned. "Where will he run? To America?"

"No, dear. It's just an expression. He'll stay right here in Austria, Vienna most likely. Now that the State Treaty has been signed, he'll probably have a lot more in the way of business opportunities, especially in the East."

"How much does he want?"

"I haven't even spoken to him about it. I just have a good feeling about the man. And we can afford it, regardless."

Sabine drained her cup and replaced it on the saucer. "Hurry up then and finish. We can go over there now. This place will be perfect for the plan I have."

"But I have to ask once more: can we trust Chernov?"

Sabine smiled. "Oh, I'm not worried about that. Remember, Karl, I've worked with him in the past. I know his weaknesses and can control him. Besides, he left himself exposed over there." She laughed lightly, as though to herself. "He'll probably need to use it himself at some point."

"Good." Baier emptied his own cup and tilted the pot to make sure they had drunk most of the coffee. "Let's go buy an estate and make ourselves Central European landowners."

"And entrepreneurs in the new and independent Austria," Sabine said.

She stood and strode around the table, following Baier onto the sidewalk outside. Then she took his arm as he proceeded to the apartment of Thomas von Rudenstein. Baier looked down at Sabine and smiled. He felt good about this, more than he had expected he would. They were opening a new chapter in their lives, while closing one in another man's. But they were doing it with all the respect he could muster for the man and his history.

Photo by Didi Rapp

BILL **R**APP RECENTLY retired from the Central Intelligence Agency after thirty-five years as an analyst, diplomat, and senior manager. After receiving his BA from the University of Notre Dame, an MA from the University of Toronto, and a PhD from Vanderbilt University, Bill taught European History at Iowa State University for a year before heading off to Washington, D.C. *The Hapsburg Variation* is the second book in the Cold War Spy series featuring Karl Baier. Bill also has a three-book series of detective fiction set outside Chicago with P.I. Bill Habermann, and a thriller set during the fall of the Berlin Wall. He lives in northern Virginia with his wife, two daughters, two miniature schnauzers, and a cat.

For more information, go to www.BillRappsBooks.com.

84416734R00159

Made in the USA
Columbia, SC
29 December 2017